CLINIC

CLINIC

Christine Johnson

Alexandrian Press
Palo Alto

This novel is a work of fiction. Any
resemblance to actual events or locales or
persons, living or dead, is coincidental.

Published in 1985 by Alexandrian Press
1070 Arastradero Road
Palo Alto, CA 94303
Printed in the United States of America

Library of Congress Cataloging in Publication Data

Johnson, Christine

  Clinic.

  1.Title.PS3560.03737C45   1985   813'.54   85-7331
ISBN 0-916485-03-X
ISBN 0-916485-04-8 (pbk.)

To
Michele Weintraub
and
Trisha Suppes

Acknowledgements

The author wishes to thank Gay Boyer for her several suggestions to improve an earlier draft, and Patrick Suppes for his research into The Warren G. Harding Institute for Normalcy.

CLINIC

Peach Kling

It was a night not unlike most other summer nights in Loma Verde—dry, clear, and cool. I had just thrown Ron Ryders, the director of public affairs at Greenwich University, out of my office. Ryders was a sniveling little wart of a man, the kind of wart Greenwich sent to deal with the *Loma Verde Vindicator*. He had spent nearly two hours twisting my arm to fire Kim Blakely, my flashiest investigative reporter and the gal who uncovered the Kettle daughter suicide attempt. I couldn't have fired Kim if I had wanted to because KUTK-TV had snapped Kim up for their ten o'clock news program just that afternoon. There was a gal with balls. But I digress: the Kettle daughter suicide attempt. This was the first part of what surely became the Loma Verde story of the decade. Susan Kettle was the daughter of Miranda Kettle, the Chancellor of Greenwich. My sources told me she stripped in the main quad of Greenwich, swallowed a bottle of sleeping pills, and ran around the quad screaming, "I want my mommy, I want my mommy!" before collapsing. Her stomach was pumped and she survived. We printed the story that night even though I knew I would have Greenwich on my back.

That wormy P.R. flak, Ryders. What did I owe that son-of-a-bitch anyway? Did Ryders cough up extra Homecoming Game tickets when I cut the on-campus dope death of the Rollo Rum heir from the paper? The bastard couldn't even cough me up Homecoming Game tickets. It's enough to drive a man to drink. Scotch: now there's a man's drink. I'd had enough of this white wine and brie Greenwich party business to feel anemic for the rest of my life. And why, I asked myself again and again, were university settings always crawling with guys who had sissified first names like Duncan and Gardner?

And why in the hell was I trying to have a relationship, as we say in Greenwich Land, with the daughter of one of the big-gun professors, a girl younger than my youngest daughter, who told me she was my main line for Greenwich gossip and who just seemed to have it out for all doctors and university business in general? She had great legs, that's why. High breasts. Tumbling sunlit hair. She ran in marathons. I liked the way she crossed her legs when she lit up a cigarette, smiled that perverse little smile, and hit me with the latest. The following is the blow-by-blow account of the Loma Verde Clinic-Greenwich scandal, as I heard it and as it was reported to me by my two superstar journalists, one of whom was Maria.

"Aren't cigarettes verboten by you marathon runners?" I asked.

"You've been in Loma Verde too long. This place can really get to you after a while. Forty-year-old women running around in Oshkosh overalls, trying to ban cable TV from Loma Verde air waves. For God's sake, Ben, lighten up."

"Any more news about Carpaccio and Miranda Kettle?" I asked.

"They're up in Oregon at the swami's permanent retreat. They were picked up in the swami's personal Rolls Royce. I'm still checking, but it appears that Carpaccio and Miranda Kettle were the two most prominent Bay Area persons to leave with the swami."

Vincent Carpaccio was one of the most prominent internists at the Loma Verde Medical Clinic, Miranda Kettle's husband's doctor, my doctor, actually everyone's doctor, it seemed.
We hadn't broken the story yet but we knew for certain that it
was linked to the Kettle girl's suicide attempt. Maria was looking at all the avenues, and I believe Kim Blakely, our former
flashy reporter, had the link we needed. I wondered how she
could be paid off?

"I paid off Carpaccio's receptionist," said Maria. "God, it
was easier than I would have ever believed. All the twit wanted
was a pair of tickets to 'One Hundred Years of Greenwich University' and an invitation to the preview cocktail party."

"So what did you get on Carpaccio?"

"He only received four personal phone calls at any time:
his wife, his mother, his girl friend—Miranda Kettle I presume,
but she called herself Tamara—and a guy from Italy named
Max."

"A guy from Italy named Max?" I asked.

"Yeah, that's it."

"Any reason why they'd join up with the swami in Oregon?"

"I'll find out before we're finished."

"What about Miranda Kettle? I hear she was quite a prig.
I can't imagine her having an affair with her husband's doctor
and causing a scandal by running away with the doctor to a
swami's retreat."

"She was a prig," said Maria. "But I felt sorry for her. Her
husband spent every free minute he had jogging. He has to, by
the way. Have you seen Pete Kettle recently? When you're as
short as he is you shouldn't be so fat. Almost every night they
have to give dinner parties and when they could have done
something together alone, like I don't know what—have sex in
the morning or something—the guy was always out jogging."

"Maybe he knew what he was missing."

"She *was* a prig. One night Daddy took me to some

bullshit fund-raising dinner. You know, Daddy's really rah-rah about Greenwich, and I sat at a table with Miranda and this obscene little old man, some former director of the V.I.P. Gusset Brain Institute who kept cracking these dirty jokes."

"When was that?" I asked.

"Oh gee. Just a few months ago."

"Go on."

"Well, Miranda almost flipped out. I was laughing so hard I could barely breathe. Miranda leaned over and whispered, 'I'll bet *you're* glad *you're* sitting at this table.' You know, like stop encouraging this old guy with my laughter."

"She doesn't sound like she was a lot of fun."

"She was a bitch, actually. She looked like a school marm, a tight little hair bun and high-necked blouses, always." Maria leaned back, lit another cigarette and crossed her legs. I think it was at that moment that I fell in love with her. "Pete Kettle's coming in to see you," she said.

"Why? Why now?" I asked. The telephone rang. It was Kim Blakely.

"Listen, Ben," began Kim. "You've been like a father to me. You've got some information I'd like and I've got some information you'd like. I've always said television and newspaper should work together, not against each other."

"What's your information?" I asked.

"It's about Miranda and Pete Kettle's personal life. I'll give the information to you in exchange for the suicide note I know Maria has."

"Maria," I said, putting my hand over the receiver, "do you have the Kettle girl's suicide note?"

"I was going to give it to you tonight. I found it lying on the ground in the main quad."

"Why in the hell didn't you give it to me?"

"It just says all the stuff you and I already know. Susan Kettle was upset because her mother was running off to the guru retreat with Carpaccio and she thought her own life had lost further meaning."

"For God's sake, Maria." Back to the phone: "O.K., Kim, it's a deal. What's your item?"

"When do you plan to break the whole story?" asked Kim.

"Tomorrow afternoon. What's your story?"

"Pete Kettle got an undergraduate pregnant and arranged an abortion for her. That's all I know."

"So he wasn't just jogging all the time. Maria here has the suicide note. It mentions that her mother was running off to an Oregon swami's retreat with a prominent Loma Verde professional."

"Who, Ben?" asked Kim.

"You can find that out on your own, now that you've deserted me. Goodbye, Kim." I hung up the phone.

"That's the way to treat her. She's like the rat that deserted the ship," said Maria, prancing around the office.

"Well, I wouldn't put it quite that way. So Pete baby got a little action on the side too."

"I'll find out who the student was, if it's a true story," said Maria. "Anyway I've got to go."

"Why?"

"You want the scoop on Pete Kettle's little abortion story? Plus the scoop on the Miranda-Carpaccio story?"

"We've wrapped it up," I said.

"Oh no we haven't. Carpaccio could be in on the Eele cover-up." Maria smiled. "That's all I'll say for now till I know more. Ciao, baby. I'll be back as soon as I can verify it." She blew out of my office as fast as she had blown in, a breath of fresh air if you discount the cigarette smoke. I laughed to myself and put an old Mills Brothers record onto my ancient stereo. I was singing along to "Glow-Worm" when the phone rang.

"Pete Kettle here. Boyer, I want to talk to you."

"Pete, I know what you're going through and I want you to know that . . ."

"Then why in the hell couldn't you have kept Susan's story out of the paper? After all we at Greenwich have done for your paper!"

"Now wait a minute, Pete. My heart goes out to you and all but just what in the hell do you mean, 'after all Greenwich has done for my paper'?"

"For God's sake, Boyer. There would hardly be a *Loma Verde Vindicator* if there weren't a Greenwich University to feed it news. I take it as a personal affront and as an affront to Greenwich that you took Susan's trauma and made it a seamy public account. It was damned ungentlemanly and I regret to inform you that you will be hearing from my personal attorney."

Before I could say goodbye, Pete Kettle had hung up. Pete Kettle, the medieval-historian-husband of a university chancellor. It was a long way from the early Italian Renaissance to Slaughter House at Greenwich University. Yes, I now had Kettle snapping at my heels, and yet there was another kettle of fish simmering in the background in the name of Duke F. (Fidelio) Eele, a gynecologist at the Loma Verde Medical Clinic. Or perhaps I should say ex-gynecologist because he had been temporarily suspended and was under investigation in a malpractice suit brought by one Peach Kling who said he performed a certain operation on her and sewed her up, leaving one of his tools in her.

"Ben, I hate to bother you when you've got your Mills Brothers music on, but this message came in while you were on the telephone."

Michael Weintraub, my bright-eyed best reporter, walked into my office and sat down.

"Peach Kling phoned here? That's good. Thanks a lot, Mike. Where the hell is the Greenwich Arms Inn?"

"It's the one next to Greenwich that used to be the Mango Hutch Motel. They fancied the joint up and raised the prices."

"I wonder why she's calling from there? Is she having

8

another one of her famous operations?"

"Maybe it's another hot Eele story. I'll be in the office if you need me. Oh, by the way, Eele's into it now at the Clinic up to his eyeballs for being quoted in the *Chronicle* 'Question Man' as saying that some porn film called *Night Shift Nurse* was 'about as tasteless as Gynol-II.' "

"Gynol-II?" I asked, dialing the number of the Greenwich Terrace Inn, but Mike had disappeared. "Miss Peach Kling's room, please. Miss Kling, Ben Boyer at the *Loma Verde Vindicator* here. When? All right. One-half hour. See you then, Miss Kling."

I knew I was on to something hot. Peach Kling had asked her cousin Lester Kling, a private investigator from Los Angeles, to step in and do a little background work on Eele. They said they had something I would be very interested in seeing.

Peach Kling stood in the lobby of the Greenwich Arms Inn. She was a little smidge of a woman, so unattractive it was distressing. Her cousin Lester stood by her side, tall, gawky, bumbling. He looked like a used car salesman from West Covina. "Show him, Lester," said Peach, pushing Lester forward.

"Ben Boyer," I said, extending my hand.

"*Show* him, Lester," she repeated. Lester handed me an envelope. I opened it and found photographs of a couple engaged in sex. It looked kinky.

"What about it?" I asked.

"It's *Eele!*" shrieked Peach.

"Shhhh!" Lester and I whispered together.

"That's Eele with one of his patients. I can prove it," said Peach. I could almost see the hysteria throbbing in her mousy little temples.

"Miss Kling, I run a family newspaper. I don't know what you expect me to do with these photos. Why don't you take them to the *San Francisco Chronicle?*"

"Mr. Boyer, I appeal to you," said Peach, clasping her hands as in prayer. "I don't know where else to turn."

"Miss Kling, the Loma Verde Clinic alone has or at least had a three-doctor committee investigating your case against Eele. He's been temporarily suspended. What do you expect to accomplish with this kind of garbage?" I looked at Peach and Lester. Their eyes had a haunted, hungry look, two Gothic Americans wanting revenge, and right now. "Are you sure the gal in these photos is a patient?"

"I can even provide you with her name and telephone number," said Peach.

"May I take these?"

"Certainly not," said Lester. "I worked damned hard to get them."

"You planning to stay at the Greenwich Arms Inn for awhile?" I asked Lester.

"I plan to stay here until this case is concluded to our satisfaction."

"I'll get back to you, then." I left the two in the lobby. I was hoping I would find Maria back at my office. Naturally she was nowhere in sight, so I decided to call it a day. Back at my place, the phone rang just as I was falling into a hard sleep.

"Don't forget! Carpaccio was a member of that internally appointed committee to investigate Eele."

"Maria? Why in the hell are you calling me so late?"

"It's just midnight. Are you interested in what I have to say or not?"

"Come over and deliver the goods in person."

"I take it that's not a professional request?"

"You get anything on the Kettle abortion?" I asked.

"Eele arranged it."

"That Eele is a wriggler. Just like a real eel. Where'd you get the story?"

"That's a story for another time."

"I've got all night, now that you woke me up."

"Another time, Ben. I have an early morning medical appointment with Joe Kuhl. He's the internist on the Eele investigating committee. The other committee member is Kuhl's wife, Jean. I believe she's a dermatologist."

"Are you going to mention that you're working on a newspaper story?"

"Ben, where's your sense of investigative reporting? I'm just going as a patient. A patient, that is, with a tape recorder in her purse."

"So what seems to be the problem?" asked Joe Kuhl.

"It's this, um, swelling behind my ear."

"Why don't we have a look? Just hop onto the table. Pardon the noise. We'll have bigger examination rooms when they finish enlarging the Clinic."

"Gee, it must feel really good to be a young up and coming doctor in a Clinic like this one."

"Well, let's just say the young doctor is already up. He's done his coming."

"Oh, too bad for the young up doctor."

Kuhl blushed. "I don't feel any swelling in the back of your ears. When did you last feel this swelling yourself?"

"Yesterday afternoon."

"Pierced ears often give that kind of problem. They drain. I think the earring post is the problem."

"It mainly happens after I run."

"So you run?"

"Sixty miles a week."

"That sounds like marathon running."

"It is. But when I run in the rain, my ears swell."

"I think running in the rain is great. It's an old wives' tale that running in the rain will make you sicker."

"Well, I'm not keen on catching pneumonia."

"That's what we're here for if you do." Kuhl flashed a confident smile.

"Isn't that a bit macho?" asked Maria.

"No, it's contemporary."

"What do you think about Eele, that sleazy gynecologist in the Clinic?"

"That Eele is a real wriggler."

"Yeah, a lot of people seem to think so. What do you think?"

"I don't know. When was the last time you had a physical?"

"About a year ago."

"All right then, I'm going to do a physical on you. Then I want you to go to the lab for blood and urine work."

"I don't have the time."

"This is your health. I'd cancel whatever else I had down for this morning if I were you." Joe Kuhl left the examining room and Maria whipped out a notebook.

1. Poster of aborigines on wall.
2. Current issues of *Smithsonian*, *National Geographic*, *Horizon* magazines.
3. Postcard of watercolor painting of an antique store on bulletin board (perhaps to show patients doctor cultivates outside interests, though this is not clear; could be a room shared by another doctor).
4. One tube of English Leather hand cream at basin (again, could belong to another doctor. Strange but perhaps better than pHisoHex).
5. Doctor wears orlon navy blue socks and polyester-cotton navy blue pants.

"Hello again. I thought only the doctor took the notes," said Joe Kuhl, coming back into the room.

"Oh, this is just, ah, well . . . I'm actually gathering material for a daytime serial I want to write and sell. I was thinking of calling it 'Young Up Doctors.' "

"Very funny. So you're a writer?"

"Yeah. But I want to get into TV script writing. And let's face it, people want to hear about doctors."

"I know." Joe Kuhl flashed another confident smile.

"Dr. Kuhl?"

"Yes?"

"I used to see Dr. Carpaccio."

"Why did you stop?"

"He's not here any more."

"What do you mean, he's not here any more?"

"Didn't you read about it in the papers? Carpaccio has disappeared and so has Miranda Kettle. The police are presuming that they're together and on their way to or are at a swami's retreat in Oregon."

"No kidding. Miranda is my patient." Joe Kuhl began walking around the room and grinning.

"You look awfully pleased."

"Let's just say that my style is different from Carpaccio's."

"Like Picasso and Van Gogh or something?"

"Say, you're a feisty number this morning," said Joe Kuhl.

"It's all that energy from running."

"Well, you look like you're in excellent condition. If you like my style I'll see you for another annual exam next year."

"So, did you like Kuhl's style?" I asked Maria when she came back into my ofice late in the afternoon.

"He's a hunk. And damned glad Carpaccio has disappeared."

"Why?"

"Because it's less competition for him. What else?"

"The phones have been ringing off the wall all morning since we broke the Carpaccio-Kettle disappearance. Mostly it's

Greenwich types who either don't believe it or are mad we broke the story. Well, was your trip to see Kuhl worth your while?"

"Not really, but it's a beginning."

"I was down at the Clinic myself. I paid off a little receptionist of Eele's to photocopy Eele's papers on his controversy, and one of the patient papers was about the young woman involved with Pete Kettle and a confidential statement that Kettle had arranged the abortion."

"The one Kim Blakely called you about last night?" asked Maria.

"I'm presuming so. How many abortions can Kettle arrange within a year?"

"Kuhl won't talk about Eele. He did say Eele was a wriggling eel, real original, but that was all. I think I'll have to pay him another visit when I refine my investigative technique. Did you see Peach Kling's cousin today?"

"No. I thought we could see them this evening," I said.

"Oh, I don't want to do that!" groaned Maria.

"You'll never make an investigative reporter if you can't dig into all sides of the story, no matter how trite they may seem at first. Let's face it. Peach Kling is in the center of this Eele case."

"Oh God! How could I have forgotten! Kuhl is Miranda's doctor. God, I wish Kuhl wasn't so closemouthed."

"Someone at the university tipped me off today that Miranda Kettle had heard of the Eele investigation and was secretly gathering information against Eele from Greenwich undergraduates."

"No kidding. Wow, it's a small world. I'm bushed. When do I start getting paid for all my investigative labors around here?"

"When you become more rigorous, more disciplined, in essence, when you become more professional," I said, wondering if I wasn't carrying a good thing too far. "Come on. Let's grab a bite."

"Who tipped you off to Miranda's secret investigation?"

"She wouldn't say. Where do you want to have dinner?"

"Ben, I've just remembered—Miranda Kettle's big buddy on campus is Flora Framingham, the big heart doctor. They live in our neighborhood."

"It's a neighborhood you should have outgrown by now," I said, and I meant it.

"When you start paying me for what I'm worth in information on Greenwich, I'll get my own place." She had a point.

"You can start by accompanying me to the Greenwich Arms Inn," I said. "Tonight. Without complaints."

"Oh God. The Mango Hutch Motel is so tacky. That's where Daddy and his old cronies used to go to order suits from some Indonesian guy." Maria lit a cigarette.

"Was the Indonesian guy a tailor?"

"Well, what else do you think he was? A drug dealer? No, he measured my father for suits, my father gave him some money, and the suits were sent in a month or so. Anyway that's my memory of the Mango Hutch Motel." Maria drew on her cigarette. "You know our neighborhood is called Elderberry Hill. Old Greenwich, that means. The Kettles live there, Flora Framingham lives there. I call all of them the Elderberry over-the-hill gang. Most of the people in our neighborhood are emeriti. Like eighty or over."

"What about Flora Framingham?"

"She's about fifty. She's sort of nice. She has a real drip of a husband. His name is Charles and he's a failed novelist. He just sits on his fat ass all day and Flora supports him."

"Sounds modern enough," I said.

"Always talking about the book he wants to write. God, what a drip."

"Forget the husband. Are you friends with Flora?"

"No. I used to babysit their son. I mean, I know them, but I'm not Flora's friend. Why? Do you want me to talk to her about Miranda?"

"Of course I do."

"Well . . . I guess I could give it a shot. Go over when I know she's home and ask to borrow a cup of sugar or something . . ."

"You're catching on fast, kid. Where do you want to go to dinner?"

"Can't you think about something besides your stomach? Let's just get a Big Mac."

"I was actually thinking of taking you to that nice new Italian restaurant. I hear the pasta's terrific. Homemade."

"Well, I could get into that," she said. I had known she could.

"And then a visit to the Greenwich Arms Inn . . ."

"No!" she groaned again.

"Without complaints. And then I want you to have a little talk with Flora Framingham as soon as possible. I smell a rat at the Clinic."

"What do you mean, you smell a rat at the Clinic? Do you think you're Edward G. Robinson or someone? What do you mean anyway?"

"I'm not sure yet. I have a hunch, but I need to see a few more connections. Come on, let's eat," I said. Maria uncrossed her long runner's legs and I found my eyes fixed on her face.

"Stop staring like that. You look peculiar."

"I'm just your friendly prospective employer. You get me the connections I need to tap a real Clinic scandal and you're on the payroll."

"You're just looking for trouble." Maria brushed her honey hair with her fingers this way and that.

"I'm just bored. I thought your impression of the Mango Hutch Motel would be more of a Motel No-tell."

"The Elderberry over-the-hill gang is just lucky to make it up the hill. The Mango Hutch is only a boring appendage to the Faculty Club. Too bad they had to go and change the name. Mango Hutch had such a funny, sleazy ring to it. I suppose they took down the statue of the naked Hawaiian lady in the front."

"Well, you can see that for yourself," I said, asserting my authority for all it was worth. "Tonight."

"Oh God!" Maria began looking for an ashtray.

"No complaints."

Following a frustrating dinner at which Maria had decided to play up her youth (she was twenty-two), we drove to the Greenwich Arms Inn, née the Mango Hutch Motel. "Listen, kid," I told her, "I don't like your college sophomore act. If you want to work as a newspaper reporter you have to grow up. If you don't want to grow up, then re-enroll at Greenwich, but for God's sake, stop talking about daddy and giggling every five seconds. If you want to work for me you've got to be more professional. Look at this story as a marathon. You're going to finish it as strong and as fast as you can." Maria began to light a cigarette. "And smoking won't help the race."

"Is that a Loma Verde-style request for me not to smoke in your car?"

I didn't answer her. We were at the Greenwich Arms Motel and I was reconstructing the various details of the story aloud in the parking lot. "All right. Peach Kling filed a malpractice suit last month against Eele. A three-doctor internal committee was appointed by the Clinic to investigate Eele, as other charges have been made against him in recent months. One of the members of the investigating committee has run off to a swami's retreat in Oregon with the Chancellor of Greenwich. The daughter of the Chancellor of Greenwich tried to commit suicide in the main quad yesterday, leaving a note which blamed her mother. Miranda Kettle was doing some private investigating on her own about Eele up until the time of her disappearance. Pete Kettle had earlier arranged this year an abortion for a Greenwich undergraduate which Eele performed. Say, I'll bet Miranda, during the course of her talking to Greenwich undergraduates about Eele, learned about Pete's little arrangement, don't you?" Maria sat quietly, and a curious kind of radiance lit up her face. This was her kind of story. The girl was a born newshound. "Time to meet the cousins Kling," I said. "Got your notebook and tape recorder? Good girl."

When we entered Lester's room, the two were watching "The Wild, Wild World of Animals" on PBS. It seemed a little uptown for the Klings, but one thing I've learned in this business is that anything is possible.

"It's on sharks," said Peach, barely looking up from the television. "Oooh, look at those jaws. So scary!"

"And now we come to the eel, a sharp-toothed and short-tempered creature," said the narrator, and with that Peach's head riveted up from the screen.

"He is sharp-toothed and short-tempered!" she cried.

"How did your day go, Lester?" I asked, as discreetly as I could.

"I'm on the trail," he replied cryptically.

"Well, that's good. Lester, Peach, meet my assistant, Maria Forsythe."

"Like *The Forsythe Saga*?" asked Peach.

"Not exactly. So you watch a lot of PBS TV?"

"It's my only friend and companion sometimes." Peach broke into tears.

"There there, Peach," said Lester, patting her back in his bumbling fashion. "We're going to make sure that rat Eele pays for what he's done to you."

"He's a slimy eel," sniveled Peach. "Sharp-toothed and short-tempered."

"Miss Kling, is there anything you can think of which was improper or unusual about Eele in the course of your visits to him for consultation prior to the surgery?" I asked.

"What do you mean?" Peach looked like a pin in a bowling alley.

"I mean, was he ever at any point unprofessional with you? I'm thinking of those photographs that Lester obtained, of course."

"Mr. Boyer, what are you intimating?"

"Did Eele ever come on to you?" I asked, less delicately, thinking that Eele must have been pretty desperate if he had.

"Never. I did detect alcohol on his breath on more than one occasion."

"Really? A drinking problem then? That's the first I've heard of anything like that regarding Eele."

"He was never on time, always running late. It was quite usual for him to be behind an hour at least. And how he liked to brag about all the abortions he had performed!" Peach stood up and pounded her fist into her hand, an act which almost certainly indicated a strong desire for vindication.

"Don't worry, Miss Kling. We're possibly on to something of far more rotten and far larger proportions than we can even imagine. As far as I'm concerned, we're just sitting at the tip of the iceberg."

"I'm coming to that conclusion myself," said Lester, patting the envelope of pornographic photographs he had taken out of his pocket.

"Well, let's all keep in close contact. Remember, Maria and I are working every avenue we've got and we're going to dig as deep as we can. I think we'll flush that Clinic out before we're through."

"A real medical Watergate, huh?" asked Lester.

"Maybe so," I said. Maria was shifting from one foot to another and yawning. "So let's stay in touch." I was anxious to wind things up so as to concentrate on Maria. "Remember, Miss Kling, we're working with you on this. We won't let that Eele get away. He'll never practice medicine again after we've finished with him."

"A real medical Watergate?" asked Maria as we returned to the car.

"Why not?"

"It sounds corny, that's why not. Peach is a real drip. Lester's a jerk, too."

"What we reporters must endure! Let's have a nightcap at my place."

"Just drop me off at home, please. I'll show you where Flora Framingham lives."

"So that will be your assignment for tomorrow," I said, hoping to conceal my disappointment. "Have a little chat with Flora. Get her impressions on Miranda's disappearance, Eele, whatever you can."

"When do I get paid?" She pulled her skirt over her beautiful knees.

"When you make the connections we need for the Loma Verde scandal story of the century."

"You're a cheapskate." The little vixen stuck out her tongue and shut her father's front door in my face.

In an effort to learn what exactly a hunk was, I scheduled an appointment with Joe Kuhl. Because of a cancelation (as the receptionist told me at least a half dozen times) I was able to see him that *very* afternoon. I wondered if Kuhl was the kind of guy who wore those mirror-type sunglasses? My sweet Maria had talked me into getting a pair only a month ago, only to announce at a Greenwich party how much she hated them. I wondered if Joe Kuhl drove a Mercedes. One of Maria's great lines was that doctors shouldn't be allowed to drive Mercedes because they had enough to live down in their chosen professions and should drive something more humble.

I parked my humble Chevy Vega in the Clinic parking lot and as I was walking toward the building I noticed a Porsche with the California license plate HOT EELE. There was one guy who didn't know when to quit. Maybe Eele was in really bad shape. Booze can do strange things to you.

"Hello, Mr. Boyer," said the young man. I wondered if this guy was a male nurse (I heard the Clinic was beginning to hire male nurses). This kid was far too young to be a doctor. "I'm Joe Kuhl." I was surprised, for he seemed a mere boy, a little scrawny to be a hunk though Maria had mentioned he was a runner. I doubted that he either wore mirror glasses or drove a Mercedes. "So it's time you had an annual exam. I need to know your date and place of birth."

The usual questions were asked: did I drink, smoke, exercise? Kuhl examined me and pronounced me physiologically ten years younger than my age. My opinion of him was slowly improving. We chatted about the newspaper life being hard on one and the ongoing construction of the Clinic. Then I began my interrogation. "Must have come as quite a shock to you internists that Carpaccio struck out to join some guru setup."

"Well," said Kuhl a bit self-righteously, "it doesn't come as a surprise to some of us."

"Oh?"

"Well, let's just say Carpaccio has a record of experimenting with self-help organizations." The kid knew he was with a newspaperman. He clearly wanted to talk.

"Like est, Esalen, those kinds of things?"

"Exactly. He was a little naive."

"It wasn't exactly naiveté which drove him to run off with Miranda Kettle."

"Well, you know this guru in Oregon preaches sexual abstinence," said Kuhl, with a grin.

"I thought I knew Carpaccio better than that. He's been my doctor for ten years."

"I always said he looked like an acolyte to me."

21

"I tell you, it's a real scandal at Greenwich. They've come screaming at me for the past week about the way the *Vindicator* has covered the events."

"Miranda Kettle was a very nice lady. She was my patient." Kuhl looked away as he spoke, in order, I believe, to show a kind of stagey deference.

"So I guess you knew her pretty well."

"I would never have guessed that she would run off with Carpaccio to a guru retreat. But," he said, and he paused a moment or two, "she did seem to gravitate toward medical circles. You remember that when the Dalai Lama came to Greenwich she invited almost all medical people to the formal dinner."

"I certainly do remember that. The *Vindicator* printed the guest list."

"Well, there you go." His tendency toward generalizations annoyed me.

"Then of course there's Eele. Now there's a catch. I believe I saw his car in the Clinic parking lot. I thought he'd been tossed from practicing until the Kling case had been investigated," I said.

"He's not practicing. That much I can tell you." He emphasized the "*I can tell you.*"

"I heard through the grapevine that you, your wife and Carpaccio are, or were anyway, the internal investigating committee."

"I must say you've got a healthy grapevine."

"I suppose you'll be looking for a new committee member."

"Yes, I suppose we will," he said, rising quickly. "It's been a pleasure meeting you, Mr. Boyer. You're healthy and in good shape. Keep playing tennis. You might try to take up a little jogging here and there."

"That's one scrawny hunk," I said to Maria when we met in my office later that afternoon. "An obnoxious tendency to overgeneralize also, but that's typical for a doctor."

"Also for a newsman," she replied. "That's what Daddy says anyway."

"I suppose you still want this job?" If I were less sophisticated I might think she had a Daddy complex. She sat, lit a cigarette, and put her feet up on my desk.

"I saw Flora. Oh God, let me just tell you this story. Don't interrupt me. It's just a weird story, it probably has nothing to do with anything. But, oh, did Joe Kuhl have anything new to say?"

"Yes, he said that Carpaccio often became involved in self-help type groups and that Miranda had a tendency to gravitate toward doctors."

"Big help. Isn't that already apparent?"

"Kuhl seemed fairly willing to criticize Carpaccio."

"What about Eele?"

"Claims Eele is out of the Clinic, but I saw Eele's Porsche in the parking lot. Bright red with a personalized plate reading HOT EELE."

"Any mention of who would replace Carpaccio on the investigation committee?"

"Not a word to me. I think he's a competent doctor. He thinks I'm physiologically ten years younger than my age, by the way. That would make me forty-one. Physiologically, that is."

"Joe Kuhl dishes out the bullshit." This was the bitchiest thing she had said to me to date. "He told me that *I* was in excellent condition."

"You are."

"But you know, I lied, said I didn't smoke. I don't think he's scrawny."

"Oh really? Well I do." I pulled in my stomach, my one worst feature and the result of a life of too many greasy hamburgers at the office.

"Well, turning to Flora Framingham," said Maria between puffs, "by some curious stroke of fate, Flora was home this morning. That's a medical school doctor for you. I tried the old I-need-to-borrow-sugar trick. Her jerk husband Charles answered the door. He prattled on and on about how time flies. I mean I don't think I've seen either of them in a couple of years. They asked me what I was doing. I said 'getting a job on the *Vindicator* soon I hope.' " Maria paused dramatically and gave me what is known as a meaningful look.

"Go on."

"Well, they thought that was great. I asked them what they'd been doing and they said they just took a trip to Death Valley."

"Does this story have a point?"

"I'm just trying to give you the flavor of the Framinghams. Charles is the biggest jerk in the world. He told me he wanted to write a novel, as usual, and that he had attended a creative writing workshop last weekend. He said he met a woman who had seven kids and had published four novels. I said, 'Well, I guess that proves that anyone can write a novel if they really want to,' and he said, 'Yes, but this woman didn't have a twelve-room house to take care of.' "

"So Charles takes care of things for Flora?"

"Yes. It's a pretty unusual story, even for the Elderberry over-the-hill gang. I suggested in an obviously joking manner that maybe Charles could write a novel about all the latest stuff around Greenwich. He didn't seem to think it was a very good idea. Flora and he seem pretty upset by the whole thing. I ingratiated myself a bit and the next thing I knew we were all sitting down eating Danish pastries and drinking coffee and Flora was off and running. The weird thing about the Framinghams is that they serve Danish pastries and coffee even though Flora goes on TV from time to time to tell people to change their diets and all."

"So what was Flora off and running about?" I could see that keeping Maria on the topic was no easy matter.

"Well, I admit I threw a dagger into the conversation when I said, 'I think Pete Kettle is a rat of a husband.' "

"You mean there's other evidence that he was a rat of a husband?"

"Not really. But I sure got a response out of Flora. She agreed completely. I figured she'd learned, probably from Miranda herself, the outcome of Miranda's little investigation, so I said I'd heard about Miranda's secret activities. Flora said that Miranda had admitted she was doing the investigation because of Eele's reputation for botching abortions and she was worried about the undergraduate girls at Greenwich. Flora said there were surprisingly few reported abortions but that Eele took care of most of them, and that's what alarmed Miranda. Then Charles had to get in his two cents about how bad abortion is but Flora shut him up pretty quickly."

"What's a dynamic woman like Flora doing with a guy like that?" I asked.

"Well, her first husband was some high-powered doctor but it's commonly thought that Flora didn't like the competition so she went from overcompetence to undercompetence."

"So what are Charles's goals in life, outside of talking about novels he'd like to write?"

"I don't know. Flora told me a couple years ago that his dream is for their house to be photographed for *Architectural Digest*, which isn't too likely because it's not very elegant, and for the two of them to be photographed for *Town and Country* magazine."

"*Town and Country* magazine? Why ever for?" I asked.

"Hey, I don't know why people want the things they want.

Why do I want to work for the wimpy *Loma Verde Vindicator*?"

"You're treading on thin ice."

"Well, Charles finally flaked off to go buy some groceries and Flora seemed to want to talk. She thinks Eele is about the worst thing that has ever happened to medicine in Loma Verde. She told me Eele performed an abortion on a girl after it was way too late to do it safely, and it had nearly cost the girl her life."

"That's good, Maria. Those are the kinds of details we need. Flora wouldn't be willing to talk to me, would she?"

"I don't know, Ben. She'd have to know you'd protect her. She's got her reputation and all. I don't think a doctor who's as hot for media attraction as Flora wants any questionable P.R."

"How'd she get started as a media doctor, anyway? Is she a good-looking woman?"

"Fairly good-looking. She's got a great figure for her age. She did a show for PBS on exercise which was extremely successful because everyone loved her waistline. Now she's going all over the world talking up exercise. In fact, I think one of the main reasons she was so open and friendly with me was because I run."

"So she travels all over the world touting the virtues of exercise and healthy habits for long life and Charles stays home and takes care of the house and their kid?"

"That's about it. Oh, I'd mentioned I'd seen Joe Kuhl since Carpaccio disappeared and she said Kuhl is the cream of the crop."

"That's one crappy crop." I hated hunks as well. "Did she say anything about Carpaccio?"

"No. You know these doctors are closemouthed about each other in general."

"I guess Eele's the one exception to the closemouthed rule," I said.

"And I don't think they really even like to badmouth Eele. I wouldn't be surprised if Kuhl and his wife are praying that this whole Peach Kling thing blows over so they don't have to present the results of their investigation before the authorities."

"I'm sure you're right there. So you did get a feeling from Flora that Miranda might have known about the abortion Pete Kettle arranged for the student?"

"I'll tell you this. I got a feeling that if Miranda found out about it at all she'd have told Flora. Oh by the way, do you want to hear a really hot new media story? Joe Kuhl is doing a twenty-two-part weekly series called 'Your Health.' Flora suggested Kuhl to PBS because she thinks he's so great."

"When does it air?"

"Soon, I think. Like in a couple of weeks. It'll just be five-minute segments. You know, Joe Kuhl talks about vegetables, Joe Kuhl talks about exercise, Joe Kuhl talks about the latest in laser surgery . . ."

"These doctors are too much. Who in the hell do they think they are? Joe Kuhl.has a nonscrawny ego problem to make up for his scrawny physique."

"I don't think Joe Kuhl is scrawny in the least. I think he's cute and so does PBS or they wouldn't have chosen him to do their little series." Maria crushed her cigarette.

"Joe Kuhl wouldn't like to see you smoking."

"Blow off," she answered. "Want to see the new Woody Allen film tonight? I don't think we have anything conclusive, as we say both in the media and in medicine. You know, Joe and Flora could work with us. They're media medical personalities. They might even understand what we're doing if we 'fess up to them that we're trying to uncover a scandal."

"Maria, doctors are thicker than thieves. And I have no doubt that as much as they love being media doctors they'd both resent the classification."

"I'll tell you this. I'd resent being in a profession with HOT EELE. What about Peach and Lester?"

"Not tonight. I'd rather see Woody Allen."

"Where's that investigative spirit, Ben?" The girl was a

real quick study.

"We'll let old Lester gather the data for a while."

"You think he's a good investigator?" she asked.

"I don't know. He got those sex photos pretty quickly, but I don't think he has a sense of what is most important in this case."

"Well, do we?"

"Yes, damn it," I said. She was beginning to make me mad. "We're going to put these egotistical, insensitive doctors in their places."

"I hope you like your popcorn without butter, Ben. I can never go to a movie without buying popcorn. But forget the butter."

"Well, I suppose butter isn't on Flora's list of health foods."

"It's not that," she said, lighting yet another cigarette. "I just can't stand to get my hands all greasy in the theater."

Woody Allen's humor has a way of making me open up, especially with women. After the film, at Maria's suggestion we went to the Granite Planet, a punk-style health food restaurant in downtown Loma Verde, for coffee. I decided to get down to business with her, that is, find out if she had any interest in me outside of getting a job on the *Vindicator*.

"I really like you, Ben. I really like men of your generation. But you see, I'm in a period now of inner expansion. Also, there *is* this guy Ted. He's a dancer."

"What kind of dancer? A dancer like Gene Kelly? Nureyev? A tap dancer?"

"He's a classical dancer."

"Well, does that mean you're serious about each other?" I should have known she'd go for a ballet dancer.

"No. He's got his things to do and I've got my things to do. In fact I haven't seen him in over a week. I have to be honest with you, Ben. It's more fun being with you than with Ted. You know more, you enrich me. With Ted it's just—I don't know—it's just my appreciating Ted's dancing, his art. I mean, all we do is talk about Ted's career."

"How's his career going?"

Maria shrugged. "It's really tough for dancers, you know. He's twenty-six but he has to lie and say he's twenty-two or companies won't even look at him. He has a good shot at dancing with the San Francisco Ballet. He's got such a beautiful style, and such a beautiful body . . ." Her voice trailed off.

I sucked in my stomach. "Well, I'm glad he's got a shot with the San Francisco Ballet. I hear they're pretty good."

"They're one of the best companies in the country right now. Anyway, I never know what end is up with Ted. He says he'll come over at eight and it's ten or later when I see him. . ."

"So he's a little unreliable?"

"I guess you could say that," she sighed. "Anyway, lately I've got my heart set on helping to break a Loma Verde scandal. You know I really hate doctors and I suspect a lot of other people hate them too."

"Doctors make too much and know too little, not to speak of having the biggest egos in town, especially this town. This coffee is horrendous . . ." I put my cup down and gestured for the check.

"What can you expect from a health food restaurant? I told you, we should have had a tisane."

"A what?" I asked.

"Herb tea."

"It's too late in life for me to change from coffee to herb tea. But it's not too late for me to give a young person a shot at something. Michael Weintraub is a young pro. I mean a real pro. Tomorrow morning he's interviewing a famous gay

novelist in San Francisco. I believe she's staying at the
Hopkins. I want you to go up with him and watch how
s the questions, watch how the questions are formulated
and especially watch how he plays with the answers. Weintraub
is a very funny kid. I have no doubt he'll be a syndicated columnist before he's thirty."

"Well, if you think I'll learn something . . ."

"Hell yes, you'll learn something. Call the paper before
nine and get Weintraub's schedule. I'll leave a message in his
box that you'll be going up with him."

"Who is this famous gay woman novelist?"

"I can't remember her name offhand, but she's making
news at the moment with a book, lightly veiled fiction about her
ex-girlfriend who is some well-known actress. I can't think of
the details right now. Go up with Michael and find out for
yourself. Listen to Michael's questions. He's really great."

"If Michael is so great, how come he's not working on the
Clinic scandal?"

"I can't have everyone working on the Clinic scandal. Besides, you're doing an A-number-one job, kid."

"Really?" She was growing unbearably radiant.

"First class. I'll make you a reporter if you can dig up
more dirt than we can handle."

"I thought Lester was doing that for you."

"Oh yes, old Lester. I suppose I should be having a chat
with Lester tomorrow. And why don't you make another appointment to see Kuhl?"

"But Kuhl said I was in excellent condition."

"Tell him you like his style and you need to talk to someone about your future. Say you feel anxiety. All young people
feel anxiety about their futures." I stopped and looked at her.
She showed no signs of anxiety. "But this time get him to talk
about Eele, Carpaccio, Miranda, anyone. You understand?"

"I'll do my best. But it's almost impossible to get an appointment within a week."

"Bull shit," I said. I liked to emphasize the *bull*. "You're a faculty kid. They make allowances for people like you. Say you're very distressed and only Kuhl will do. I want you to see him by Friday. And remember, keep your mouth shut tomorrow morning at the interview. Just listen to Weintraub's questions and the woman's responses. Listen and learn."

"I have no interest in a big conversation with a lesbian."

"Never say you have no interest in talking to someone. You never know what you can learn." Maria sat back in her chair, appearing to absorb this information in a way which made me feel grateful to have lived fifty-one years.

"Ben's got the hots for you, hasn't he?" asked Michael Weintraub the next morning, speeding into San Francisco behind the wheel of his '69 Pontiac Firebird.

"I don't know," answered Maria casually.

"Take my word for it, he has. Whenever he plays the Mills Brothers I know he has the hots for a new lady."

"How many new ladies has he had lately?"

"He doesn't do too badly for a guy his age."

"What's the story on his ex-wife?"

"I'm not sure. They've been divorced for years. His wife left him for a psych professor."

"Yes, I know. Bill Zhivago. Almost sounds romantic! Slow down! They're putting more cops on 280. Where do they live anyway? Siberia? They're not on campus."

"I think Ben mentioned they live in the city. He once told me his wife shanghaied him out here sort of against his will. He was a big guy in Miami."

"Have you ever been to Miami?"

"Yeah. It ain't Loma Verde, that's for damned sure."

"Sometimes Ben sounds like it's only boredom that drives

him to want to uncover a gigantic Loma Verde Clinic and Greenwich scandal. Do you mind if I smoke in your car?"

"Must you?"

"No. I think I hear the reproving voice of Loma Verde at the wheel."

"It just stinks up my car. That's why I don't like it."

"So who's the famous gay lady?"

"Dyke Upjohn. Her new novel is *Betch: A Butch*. I'm going to have to ask her if her real name is Dyke. This might be a case of built-in lesbianism."

"Good God. Do these kinds of interviews interest you?"

"I *make* them interesting."

"I knew a girl in high school named Dyke."

"I'll bet she took a lot of harassment. What kind of kid were you? Did you smoke grass, snort cocaine, drink?"

"Not really," said Maria.

"No vices, huh?"

"Nothing like that."

"They say a girl who's got no vices like that is good in bed."

"I don't believe this. I haven't heard that line since I was about fourteen on Waikiki Beach!"

"Yeah, it's an oldie all right. Who's the lucky guy in your life? It ain't old Ben, that I know."

"I see a guy named Ted."

"Let's see. There once was a guy named Ted . . . You want to help me with this limerick?" asked Michael. "What rhymes with Ted? I know. There once was a guy named Ted, whom Maria preferred instead, of cocaine, grass and hash, or a tequila bash. They preferred to stay home in bed."

"I'm unimpressed, considering Ben considers you his whiz kid and all."

"Don't judge me on the merit of one lousy limerick. Listen to this one: There once was a Dyke named Upjohn . . ."

"Listen, can you drop me off at the KQED studios on

Eighth and Brannon after the interview? I'm meeting someone there."

"Ted?"

"No. Flora Framingham. She's doing one of her little TV numbers and has invited me to watch."

"Well, the girl's on the trail! Good for you. Keep your nose to the grindstone. You'll get your story sooner or later."

"Why aren't *you* interested in this story?"

"My father's head of orthopedic surgery at Greenwich. I've just decided to let someone else do the investigating."

"But Michael, you might be sitting on some vital information!"

"I doubt it. The day I told my dad I wasn't going to medical school he cut me off emotionally, and now I don't give a damn what happens at Greenwich or at the Loma Verde Clinic. I'll let you uncover all the putrid little scandals vich abound in such vast and secret numbers."

"Great Transylvanian accent, Michael."

"I'm a 'Sesame Street' junkie. I got this accent off the Count, ha ha ha."

"What's the biggest Loma Verde Clinic scandal that you know of?"

"You don't seem too interested in the Muppets," said Michael. "I'm looking forward to meeting Dyke Upjohn, by the way . . ."

"Michael, come on! I'm sure you know something. You grew up in a medical family."

"And you grew up in a Greenwich family. So what? Do you follow the Greenwich scandals?"

"No, not exactly . . ."

"So what's the big deal about the Loma Verde Clinic? Eele is a heel, Carpaccio and Miranda Kettle are an item . . ."

"That's what people want to read about! Medical scandals!"

"Why don't you elevate your mind? Muppet Power!"

"Get serious, Michael. Elevate my mind with people like Dyke Upjohn? Forget it. For one, I don't care about Dyke Upjohn. I'd much rather read about a Loma Verde medical scandal. What is Dyke Upjohn's book about anyway?"

"It's about her two-year relationship with Lou-Lou Rodin, some French actress. Some crazy French trip."

"My father told me that my mother used to say that every woman should have at least one Frenchman."

"In this case it's not clear who's the man and who's the woman."

"Come on, Michael, with an attitude like that, you're not going to get very far in your interview. Dyke Upjohn will smell a macho man a mile away and that'll be the end of your visit."

"Don't worry about me. I love these kinds of interviews. I love ingratiating myself . . . and then going for the big kill."

"Why the big kill?"

"It's eat or be eaten. You'd better get your Loma Verde scandal, but believe me, you'd better keep at least one doctor on your side. You might need medical attention one day."

"Who should I keep on my side?"

"Who are you seeing now?"

"I *was* seeing Carpaccio till he got enlightened or whatever and ran off with Miranda. Joe Kuhl told Ben that the swami preaches sexual abstinence. Perfect for Miranda!"

"Do you know Joe Kuhl?"

"Yeah. I had a physical with him just a few days ago."

"Keep Joe Kuhl on your side. He's a good doctor. Kind of an ego problem there but it's nothing unusual for a doctor."

"Did you know that Joe Kuhl is going to be a television personality soon?"

"No kidding. Ms. Dyke Upjohn's room, please. On PBS?"

"Yes. A weekly series of five-minute segments. I think it's called 'Your Health' or something like that."

"I guess that's what happens to you when you're a good-looking guy with an ego that needs stroking. What do you think Dyke will look like?" whispered Michael.

"Miss Upjohn will meet you in the lobby," said the woman at the desk.

"Probably like a dyke."

"Hello." A tall beautiful brunette woman held out her hand.

"Miss, um, Ms. Upjohn?" stammered Michael.

"You're with the *Loma Verde Vindicator?*"

"Yes," replied Michael, who took several moments to pull himself together.

"I went to Greenwich myself ten years ago."

"I'm Michael Weintraub and this is Maria Forsythe. I loved your book, by the way. I really did."

"Really?" Dyke's smile mocked Michael's schoolboy nervousness. "Most men don't like my book at all."

"Oh well, they're all just crazy!" said Michael, and his voice cracked. "Say, let's have a drink. I think there's a bar straight through the lobby."

"You a journalist, too, Maria?" asked Dyke.

"Let's just say I'm learning. Michael's teaching me how to interview."

"I'll have a bloody Mary," said Dyke.

"I'll take a, ah, Virgin Mary," said Michael, after an embarrassing deliberation.

"Does that describe your state of mind?" asked Dyke playfully.

"I really like your sweater, Dyke," said Maria. "I love white mohair. It looks great with that skirt."

"Thank you. Michael, I must say, you look a bit nonplussed. What were you expecting? Me to come roaring in on a motorcycle?"

"Oh, no, Ms. Upjohn! You're just, ah, much more, you know . . ."

"Ladylike than you expected? Thank you. I'll take it as a compliment, for the moment anyway."

"So. Well, that's a great book you wrote. Someone was just telling me that everyone deserves one affair with a French, ah, person. Do French persons make the best lovers?"

"I think that if you really read my book you'd know I have a very clear answer to that question."

"I suppose that is sort of general. In fact, I'll bet men are always surprised to see how, um, well, how beautiful you look."

"Well, Maria, what's bringing you to journalism?" asked Dyke, turning her back on Michael.

"I think we should probably keep on the topic of your book," said Maria.

"I'm really very interested in what drives people into journalism. What are you working on now?"

"Well, it's kind of a long story. But briefly, there's a couple of scandalous doings right now at the Loma Verde Clinic. There's a really sleazy gynecologist who really botched up an operation on a woman and he left a tool in her and . . ."

"Who is it?"

"Well, his name is Duke Eele."

"Eele! I should have known. I thought that worm would have been banned from the Clinic years ago. I can't even believe he's still practicing!"

"So you know Eele?" asked Maria.

"Only too well."

"Well, actually he's not practicing. He's been temporarily suspended from the Clinic and he's under investigation on this woman's charge," said Michael.

"Who is this woman?"

"Oh, you know, she's just a woman," said Michael.

"A typical response from a male! Who's the woman, Maria?"

"Well, her name is Peach Kling and from her appearance you'd think she'd be too intimidated to file malpractice charges against a doctor, but it's the only thing on her mind. She wants to make certain he never practices medicine again."

"Well, right on for Peach Kling! I want to meet her. Do you think I could get together with her in the next few days? Oh, by the way, I have no intention of taking your big story away from you. I know how hard it is to break into journalism. But for my personal satisfaction I'd like to relay to her face-to-face my hopes for her success in ridding Loma Verde of Duke Eele."

"Gee. O.K. Why not? I could tell her you want to meet her."

"Listen. Why don't you come too, Maria? You might be interested in what I have to tell Peach, especially for your story. But call me tomorrow morning at my hotel. I'll leave the afternoon open. I'm scheduled in the morning for interviews and a book signing at Macy's. But I think it's worth the trip to Loma Verde to meet this woman. It's been great to meet you, Maria. I'll see you tomorrow. Now, Michael, is it? I'll tell you why I wrote this book . . ."

Maria, sensing she had been excused from the interview, left the bar. Forty-five minutes later Michael reappeared in the lobby. "Get a good interview?" asked Maria.

"I think so. Sorry she shoved you off like that. Ben'll probably be mad."

"No, he won't, and you know why?"

"Yes, I know why. You now have a new possible link in the Eele case."

"Did she say how she came to know Eele? I mean, she talks like she was a patient."

"Oh, no. We only spoke about her book. I suppose that all in all it was more profitable for you than for me. God, she's a fox. What a waste of womanhood."

"You were pretty obvious about being shocked."

"I still can't get over a good-looking woman who's gay."

"I'm just glad she's willing to meet Peach tomorrow. Dyke might be just the zest this story needs. Now, we need to go to Eighth and Brannan. I shouldn't be too long."

"Women are running my life!" moaned Michael.

"That's between you and your mother."

"We're looking for Dr. Flora Framingham. She's supposed to be here shooting a segment today," said Maria to a receptionist in the television studio lobby.

"Listen. Let's make this fast. I've got to get back to the paper to type up my interview," said Michael.

"Listen, Michael. I hung around by myself in the lobby of the Mark Hopkins while you chewed the cud with Dyke Upjohn. I've *invited* you to participate in what might be an interesting new angle to the Loma Verde Clinic story."

"I assure you, Maria, I'm not interested in anything about the Clinic or Loma Verde doctors. All you're going to learn is that some doctors are so damned egotistical that they're dying to be on TV. Big deal!"

"What about your dad? Do you think he'd do a TV segment on orthopedic surgery?"

"My dad's too old looking. He's past wanting to be on TV. He's the kind of old-fashioned pre-TV doctor who just wanted his kids to be what he thought was the best thing to be in the world, a doctor."

"Sally will show you into Studio C," said the receptionist.

"Well, Sally, I've noticed that Public Broadcasting will be doing a lot of doctor-medical series in the next few months," said Michael to the young woman who led then through the maze of halls, rooms, and studios.

"Yes. We've got Flora, who's a doll, and next week we'll begin Joe Kuhl's series. That one will really be a winner. I haven't met him personally but everyone says he's handsome and really a nice guy."

"He's my doctor," said Maria, more than a little impressed

with herself for being able to convey this information.

Michael rolled his eyes. "I guess you're not on the 'I hate doctors' bandwagon, Sally."

"I'm not crazy about the profession, but I think it's great that PBS can bring medical information into our viewers' homes."

"Excuse me," said a man with a microphone standing beside a woman holding a camera. "Do the two of you watch Public Broadcasting programs, and would you mind having your answers televised?"

"Why, no!" said Michael. "I love PBS."

The woman began to film. "What's your favorite program on PBS?"

"Well, I love 'Sesame Street.' And I loved the Masterpiece Theatre production of Disraeli. Except it should have been eight segments instead of four. Did you know that the guy who played Disraeli was the tour director in *If It's Tuesday, This Must Be Belgium*? You know, with Suzanne Pleshette? You know, kind of a cult film for the 'Love Boat' crowd?"

"What's the catch?" whispered Maria.

"What's the catch?" laughed the man, and the camera was turned onto Maria. "The catch is, are you two members of this public broadcasting station?"

"Well, um, I think I used to be," stammered Michael.

"Well then, I think it's time for you to renew your membership," said the man as the camera continued to roll. "How about you?" he asked Maria.

"I think my family has an annual membership."

"Well, good. O.K. Cut the camera. I appreciate your candidness. May I have your names and the towns where you live? We'll probably be using this on TV for our fund-raising drive. We're trying to show that there are decent intelligent people like you," he pointed at Michael, "who watch public television and don't support it."

"I come to a place I don't even want to come to and end

39

up being made to feel a schmuck," said Michael to Maria between his teeth.

"Well, wasn't that fun?" said Sally cheerfully. "You just never know what's going to happen when you come to this TV station. I think Flora's ready to see you now."

"Hello there, Maria," said Flora, whose face was painted orange.

"I guess that's TV makeup?" asked Maria.

"Oh, yes! Sometimes I forget to wash it off until I'm halfway out the door. I must look like a pumpkin but they assure me here that if I didn't wear it I'd look dead. *And* since this is a program about health I suppose I should look as alive as possible. Say, I know you," she said, looking at Michael. "You're Winston Weintraub's son. Gosh, I haven't seen you in years."

"This is Michael Weintraub, a reporter at the *Loma Verde Vindicator* and the personal favorite of the editor's," said Maria.

"Well, I don't know about that," mumbled Michael.

"Sure you do. Ben Boyer thinks that Mike here has a not too distant future as a syndicated columnist. Sort of a male Erma Bombeck."

"Give me a break. I just got bullied on camera about not having a PBS membership and now you're comparing me to Erma Bombeck."

"Well, Flora, what was your segment about today?" Maria asked as she groped around in her purse for a cigarette.

"It was an anti-smoking segment." Maria quickly took her hand out of her purse. "And you know that smoking a pack of cigarettes a day is as bad or worse on a person than carrying around excess baggage of one hundred and fifty pounds?"

"What?" exclaimed Maria.

"That's right. Well—you certainly don't have anything to worry about, you, the marathon runner."

"Well, since we're being so candid . . . " began Michael, giving Maria a snide look.

"All right, Flora. We're ready to roll," said a voice over a loudspeaker.

"Excuse me. This shouldn't take more than a few minutes."

"How long do we have to stay here?" Michael asked Maria.

"Till I get a sense of Flora's TV persona. What are you complaining about, anyway? You get to be on TV! Michael Weintraub expounding his views on Masterpiece Theatre to the entire Bay Area!"

"I get to be on PBS to say I don't support it."

"Shhh! Let's listen to Flora . . ."

"In short," began Flora, "cigarettes are one of every man's most common enemies. So, instead of seeing a cigarette as a friend, get up and take a deep breath. Come to see deep breathing as friendly. And remember, the person who coined the phrase 'kissing a smoker is like licking a dirty ashtray' knew what he or she was saying. Quitting cigarette smoking will probably improve marital relations. There is every reason to quit smoking, and a long and healthy life is the main one."

"Marital relations?" whispered Michael. "Say, that doesn't mean sex life, does it?"

"All right. Cut. Thanks, Flora," said a voice over the loudspeaker.

"Well, that's how we produce my segments," said Flora cheerily as she walked back to where the two stood.

"Gee, Flora, you're really becoming the jet-set doctor of preventive medicine," said Maria.

"Oh, I hope that's not how people see me!"

"So, you're off to Germany next week, Flora?" asked a man walking toward the trio.

"Berlin. A conference on heart disease. Bob Sayers, I want you to meet Maria Forsythe and Michael Weintraub, two reporters from the *Loma Verde Vindicator*. Bob is my producer."

"You've got a real winner with Flora Framingham," said Michael.

"Michael's dad is Greenwich's chairman of orthopedic surgery," said Flora.

"I knew an orthopedic surgeon who gave up his practice to endorse some special mattress on TV," said Bob.

"The lure of television is tremendous, but I don't think my father's about to follow the trend at this point."

"Listen, Flora, can we give you a ride home or do you have a car?" asked Maria.

"Oh, I drove up, but thanks. Actually I was thinking of going to Magnin's to look for a pair of shoes."

"Oh, gosh. I would love to go to Magnin's," said Maria.

"Well, would you like to come with me? I'm assuming that Michael drove you up, or am I assuming too much?"

"I've got to get back to type up my story anyway, so I'll be pushing off. Oh yes. Don't stink up Flora's car with your crummy cigarettes, Maria." Michael waved and walked away.

"Nice young man," said Flora. "But he seems to have a chip on his shoulder. What did he mean about your stinking up my car with cigarettes?"

"Oh, Michael . . ." sighed Maria convincingly. "He confessed to me that when he refused to go to medical school his dad cut him off emotionally. He may be screwed up for life."

Flora shook her head. "What a pity. I just can't stand these egotistical doctors who expect their kids to follow in their footsteps. Well, shall we go? I must say, having company is a delightful surprise. You're always so chic, Maria. Maybe you can help me find an attractive pair of shoes. I want to look good in Berlin because I'm giving the keynote speech at this conference."

"You really do get around. I was actually thinking I needed a new pair of shoes too."

"Well, let's go then. I rarely have the time to shop any

more it seems."

"I can imagine. I suppose Joe Kuhl will begin to feel pretty busy after a while on TV."

"Oh, he's busy enough now. He's a first-class doctor. Does a lot of second opinions, that sort of thing."

"Do you think Joe Kuhl would be a good person to talk to about stress?"

"Are you feeling stress, Maria?"

"Well . . . sometimes . . ."

"It's partly your age, if you'll forgive a generalization. But you know, most of *my* stress occurred in my thirties. Yes, I think Joe might be just the doctor to see. He might even want to run some tests on you. Who knows? You might have a small heart problem which contributes to your stress and which a simple medication could treat. Do you ever feel dizzy? Out of breath? Anxious in a crowd?"

"Well, um . . . well, sometimes. Actually, not too often. But my dad's pressing me to apply to graduate school. He's almost as bad as Michael's father."

"I think that at your age you should be making your own plans," said Flora, driving out of the parking lot.

"Well, I plan to move from home just as soon as I get hired by the *Vindicator*. And Flora . . . " Maria paused and debated a moment before confessing. "Ben says he won't hire me until I help him crack either the Carpaccio case or the Eele case. He even thinks there's a possible connection between the two stories." Flora shook her head and remained silent. "Well, I mean, Carpaccio *was* on the Eele investigating committee until he vanished with Miranda Kettle."

"I really don't think there's any connection there. Journalists have such big imaginations. I personally think that many of these so-called investigative reporters are like flooding dams since Watergate was sprung open."

"Well, I think it's really unprofessional of Carpaccio to take off like that. He was my doctor, a lot of people's doctor, and he had a commitment not only to his patients but to the investigation."

"Maria, doctors are only human."

"Well, let me put it this way," said Maria. "I know that Miranda Kettle is one of your best friends. Do you think that running off with Carpaccio to a swami retreat in Oregon is what you'd want for your friend?"

Flora paused at a stoplight, and took a white bag out of her purse. "Have some Gummi Bears."

"Are Gummi Bears on your diet program?"

"Between you and me, no. Gummi Bears are not on my diet program, but I'm hopelessly addicted to them. And between you and me, I think that Carpaccio would run away to a swami retreat rather than report his findings on Eele. He knows Eele better than Joe and his wife do, and he's also spineless. I've *always* thought Carpaccio was spineless. He's always aspired to being a society doctor. He loved to brag about being one of two doctors invited up to Bosnian Woods to take care of those old rich codgers every summer. I was actually surprised when he turned down the Dalai Lama's invitation to become the Dalai Lama's personal physician. You'd think that taking care of the Dalai Lama and his aging, impotent old monks would be like being the doctor at Bosnian Woods."

"The Dalai Lama asked Carpaccio to become his personal physician?"

"Oh yes. At Miranda and Pete Kettle's dinner for the Dalai Lama a few months ago. I suppose I'm telling tales out of school, but that's the story. Carpaccio is so hungry for publicity and shoulder-rubbing with celebrities that I was surprised he turned the Dalai Lama down. I always had the feeling that he wanted to be in the center of a scandal, and dragging dear sweet Miranda off like that certainly puts him smack dab at the center of *quite* a scandal."

"What kind of guy would want to be in the center of a scandal?"

"Someone who's bored," replied Flora.

"But what about Miranda?"

"Well, between you and me, Miranda was really bitter about Pete's heavy jogging schedule. She felt he never spent any time with her."

"I heard a rumor that Pete Kettle arranged an abortion for a Greenwich undergraduate which Eele performed."

Flora hit the car brake. "I haven't heard that, nor would I believe a story like that for a second. Pete might give too much of his time to jogging, but he would never become involved with an undergraduate."

"Why not?"

"Maria, do you think Ferragamo shoes are as good as everyone says they are?"

Maria, not wishing to push a possible source too far, sat back in her seat and ate a few Gummi Bears. "Well, Flora, you're too pretty to wear Ferragamo shoes. You need something with more pizzazz. Blue suede high heels or something."

"You really think so?" asked Flora with a self-conscious little laugh.

"Oh yes, I really do! I hear Berlin is an extremely funky place."

I was on the phone with Lester Kling when Maria strolled into my office late in the afternoon. Lester had been calling me on the hour since our noon meeting to give me the blow-by-blow account of his surveillance of Duke Eele. I must say, Lester was nothing if not thorough, and wanted me to know as much as he could learn from tailing Eele. "Well, Maria, Weintraub told me about your morning. So, Dyke Upjohn wants to have a meeting with you and Peach Kling? I must say, this is even more than we could have wished for. Weintraub says that

Dyke is beautiful."

"Incredibly beautiful. A Greenwich graduate. *And* boiling over with hatred for Eele. She clearly didn't want to get into it with Michael sitting there, and she clearly wanted to do the interview more than talk to me. But she told me to call her early tomorrow morning at her hotel. She said she'd like to drive down to Loma Verde to have this meeting with Peach."

"Well, make certain you call her. How about Flora? I heard about your little shopping expedition. Are those shoes you're wearing new?"

"Yes. We went shopping for shoes. Do you like them?"

"Well," I said, not quite sure. "They're different. Blue and red suede. Is that the new look or something?"

"Yes. Italian. Flora tried to get a pair but they didn't have her size. She's kind of hard to fit. She wears an eleven. But then she's over six feet tall."

"I can't imagine the big, so to speak, heart doctor wearing blue and red suede shoes with high heels."

"Oh, Flora was ready for a different look. She's going to give a conference on preventive medicine in Berlin next week. She wants to look good."

"So what did she end up with?"

"Oh, she ended up with carnelian kid pumps. In her size the selection is limited."

"Well, I see you helped Flora by giving her some fashion advice. How did she help you?"

"You mean, what did I learn?"

"I wasn't just whistling 'Dixie.' "

"Well . . . Flora thinks it's possible that Carpaccio might have left Loma Verde rather than squeal on Eele, who was a buddy of his."

"Eele was a buddy of Carpaccio's?"

"Well, Flora didn't exactly say *buddy*. She said he knew Eele better than Kuhl and his wife. She said Carpaccio was spineless, always trying to rub shoulders with celebrities, one of two doctors always invited to take care of the codgers up at Bosnian Woods each summer. Say, Ben, have you ever been invited to become a member of the Bosnian Club?"

"No. I guess they don't think I'm important enough." There was a time when this question would have nagged me; there was a time when I would have given my eyeteeth to become a member of the Bosnian Club. But like a lot of youthful aspirations, the dream vanished in the wind. Now just to look at Maria when she smiled at me was my pleasure and my aspiration. She lit a cigarette. "Must you?" I asked.

"For God's sake, Ben. I haven't had a cigarette in hours. Do you think I would smoke around Flora Framingham? Just think of the things I'm sacrificing to get this story. Where were we? Oh yes! Carpaccio. Flora said something very weird. She said she thought Carpaccio was the type of guy who would relish being at the center of a scandal. I asked her to elaborate and she said he was probably bored. I said I'd heard a rumor about Pete Kettle arranging an abortion for an undergraduate and she almost went through the windshield. Come to think of it, I almost went through the windshield, too, she hit the car brakes so hard. My guess is that she knows all about the abortion. She knows all kinds of things, I'm sure of that. But she immediately changed the subject after I mentioned Pete Kettle. She *did* acknowledge that Miranda and Pete had a lousy marriage due to Pete's heavy jogging schedule. Oh yes! Did you know that when the Dalai Lama came to Greenwich he invited Carpaccio to become his personal physician?"

"No."

"Well, Flora said it was a pretty hush-hush thing and that she was shocked Carpaccio turned down the Dalai Lama's offer, considering how much he loved publicity and celebrities."

"So the most interesting angle is that Carpaccio might know something about Eele that he'd rather not admit knowing."

"That's right. That's Flora's view anyway. You know, I like Flora. She's sort of goody-goody and all but she's really nice. Michael is a pain in the ass. Why do you think he's so great, anyway?"

"Because he is," I answered. "He's the best reporter I have. And the youngest, next to you, when you're hired."

"I think if you were really serious about hiring me, you'd hire me now."

"You uncover a good juicy scandal and you'll be hired, don't worry."

"Did Michael tell you that he and I will be on PBS TV?"

"Oh yes, he told me the whole thing. He feels he really got tricked."

"He did! It was funny! Did you know his dad won't talk to him because he refuses to apply to med school?"

"These egotistical doctors! I simply can't believe it! Well, would you like to hear about my day?" I looked at my watch. "Good. It's five o'clock. Time for a drink. You ought to drink Scotch, Maria. You really don't know what you're missing."

"I think I do. So, how was your day?"

"You know," I said, taking a sip (Glenfiddich, my drink for as long as I can remember), "old Lester is more of a dynamo than I would ever have given him credit for. Do you know that he's done a lot of work for Garvin Mitchell, the famous L.A. divorce lawyer? He had some great stories about trailing Arabs around all the Hollywood bordellos, that kind of thing, but the main thing is that he's been trailing Eele. He overheard Eele in conversation with Eele's attorney during a lunch at La Folie yesterday. The lawyer told Eele that there was probably no way he was going to escape the Kling charges and his best bet would be to leave the country."

"Leave the country!"

"That's right. Leave the country. I heard Lester's tape of the conversation. We're going to see Lester tonight and you're going to hear it for yourself."

48

Michael Weintraub appeared at my door. "You still mad about your little TV appearance?" asked Maria.

"He's already sent his membership check in, haven't you, Mike?" I asked.

"Like hell I have. They won't get a penny from me till hell freezes over. I think their programming's been shitty for a long time. And the air time they give to Loma Verde doctors is highly questionable."

"Come on now," said Maria, "Flora's not so bad."

"Just boring, which is worse. The Upjohn story is ready now. Listen, Maria, after you have your little chat with Upjohn and Peach what's her name, I'd like to see Upjohn again for a follow-up."

"Follow-up of what? Are you trying to convert her to heterosexuality?"

"Oh yes! Just what I want in my life! A famous lesbian who's ten years older than I am!"

"Calm down, Mike," I said. "Sometimes you act like you're twelve."

"Maybe a lesbian who's ten years older than you has something to teach you," said Maria.

"Maybe she doesn't want to teach me and maybe I don't want to learn."

"It's clear you don't want to learn." Maria blew smoke in his face in so inappropriate a manner that I felt twinges of jealousy.

"Knock it off, you two," I said. "Maria, ask Upjohn if she has time for Mike tomorrow after your little chat with Peach. And I think we'd better get going now, Maria. I want you to hear Lester's tape of Eele's conversation with his attorney."

"I can't imagine *that* would be anything but sleazy. I think you're both wasting your time."

"Mike, here's a bit of advice from the old to the young. You're a talented guy, but don't let your feelings about Loma

Verde doctors eat you up." Michael shrugged my comment off and walked away.

Maria and I headed for the Greenwich Arms Inn, where Lester and Peach were waiting for us.

"I had quite a day. *Quite* a day," said Lester, producing a small cassette player. "Just listen to this." He turned it on and sat back in his chair like the cat that swallowed the canary or, in this case, the eel.

"As your attorney, I don't think our case looks very good. There's a good chance you'll be suspended."

"What if I decided to leave the country?"

"You know, Duke, that's the best thing you could do. Of course if you wanted to spend a lot of money, we could dig up some dirt on Peach to weaken her case."

(Pause)

"What do you think of the food here, Tom?"

"Not bad, not bad at all."

(Pause)

"I think I could really relish digging up some dirt on Peach Kling. What's money for?"

"Well, Duke, that's what I always say. You know, I shot an 86 on the Greenwich course last Sunday. I was thinking what's money for if not to enjoy?"

"I could enjoy slicing that Peach Kling till she was permanently canned and stored on the shelf . . ."

"Play any golf, Duke?"

"Yes, but I like fast cars even more. Yes, I do believe I'd be willing to spend a little money to dig up some dirt on Kling . . ."

"Just say the word, Duke, and I'll have the best P.I. in the business here within forty-eight hours."

"All right, Tom. You have a deal."

"It'll cost you."

"I'm prepared to pay. Yes, I think I could relish this kind of activity."

"What's money for, Duke, anyway? Right?"

"Right!"

"What's the best car on the road right now, Duke?"

"Porsche. Purrs like a little pussy . . ."

Lester turned off the cassette player. "They don't say anything substantial after that, but you get the drift."

"What are you going to do to protect Peach?" asked Maria.

"I don't need to be protected!" exclaimed Peach. "I've never done anything I'm ashamed of! Well . . . I did cheat on an eighth-grade U.S. Government test. But surely that's not material for the likes of Eele and his attorney!"

"Would they try to invent something false?" I asked.

"That's more than likely," said Lester. "It happens all the time in this business. But no P.I. worth his salt will handle the case. Eele has a slimy reputation. He'd have to pay a P.I. a lot of dough to touch it, probably more than he's willing to pay. I'd have to agree that the best bet for him would be to leave the country."

"But I don't want him to leave the country. I want to get him and get him good!"

"Now, now, Peach. He'll never practice again. We'll make sure of *that*," said Lester.

"May I use your telephone?" asked Maria. "I have to telephone my doctor. Hello. Yes, I'd like to see Dr. Kuhl tomorrow morning. No, I can't wait four weeks! I'm under extreme duress and I need to see the doctor and only Joe Kuhl will do! You just tell Dr. Kuhl that I must see him no later than tomorrow. After that might be too late! Yes, please call me back at this number—321-6275, room fifteen. I'll be waiting for your call." Maria put the receiver down. "How'd I do, Ben?"

"First class. You see, Lester, Maria has it on fairly high authority that Carpaccio was in on an Eele cover-up. She's trying to see what Kuhl might know. You remember that Kuhl and his wife are on the same investigating committee."

"There's the phone!" exclaimed Maria.

"I'll get it," said Lester. "It might be one of my sources. Hello? Oh, just a minute please. It's for you." He handed the telephone to Maria.

"Yes, I can be in at eight-thirty tomorrow morning. Yes, I realize Dr. Kuhl is doing me a really big favor. Tell him thanks a bunch. Goodbye." Maria hung up the telephone and shot a dazzling blonde smile in my direction.

"What did I tell you?" I asked. "These doctors always make allowances for faculty members and their families. If your name were Maria Doe from elsewhere you'd wait a month!"

"I intend to rely on chiropractors from now on!" said Peach.

"Don't worry, Miss Kling," I said, "there's no way Eele's attorney or any of his equally sleazy associates can harm you. We'll all see to that. Remember, we're all working to catch the eel."

"Peach," said Maria, "tomorrow, if you're free, there's a woman who'd like to talk to you. I met her this morning during an interview she had with a *Loma Verde Vindicator* reporter—oh, she's a novelist—and in the course of conversation she mentioned she had attended Greenwich *and* knew Eele."

"She knew Eele?" exclaimed Peach.

"She didn't tell me how, but she's very sympathetic to delicensing him and all she wants to do is meet you and tell you her own personal experience with Eele."

"This wouldn't be in a novel or anything?"

"That I can't say. Who knows what goes on in these novelists' minds? But as I said, she's really sympathetic to your cause and she might have something to contribute to your case."

"When would she like to meet me?"

"I'm calling her tomorrow morning. We'll set up a time, say, two o'clock for now, but I'll get back to you to confirm it. How does that sound?"

"It sounds good. I need all the support I can get." Peach began to tremble.

"These may interest you, Miss Kling," I said. "They're the results of a poll taken by the *San Francisco Chronicle*. They asked their readers what they thought of doctors in general and eighty-nine percent replied that they disliked them and thought they were overpaid." I handed Peach the article from the morning paper.

"How could I have missed this?" asked Peach. "May I have it?"

"Of course."

Peach ran to a table where she carefully taped the article into some sort of scrapbook. "This is my record on people's reactions to doctors," she said, showing me the book. I must say, Peach would be great in the *Vindicator* morgue, for she was thorough. Pages and pages of clippings about malpractice suits and other questionable medical stories were carefully captioned with dates and sources. It was an impressive piece of recording. "Feel free to make use of the *Vindicator* files if you need any articles," I said, always appreciative of someone's interest in newspaper stories.

"Oh I have, and I think the *Loma Verde Vindicator* staff I've encountered are the most considerate, helpful, and educated of any paper I've asked for clippings. And I've asked all the newspapers statewide. One thing you can easily see," she said, flipping through the pages, "is that most people hate doctors."

"Well, you're fortunate to have Lester to look after things." I was beginning to think about taking Maria out for a drink and maybe dinner. "We'll keep in touch."

"I'll call you as soon as I set up a time with Dyke Upjohn. Where can you be reached in the morning?" asked Maria.

"Well, I'm so nervous that I've taken a room at this motel.

At least Lester is licensed to carry a gun." Lester pulled up his trouser leg to reveal a handgun strapped to him.

"Gosh, I must say, Lester, that's impressive," said Maria. "You're sort of like . . . well, you're not exactly like any of the TV detectives. You're an original."

"Anyway, I'm in room twenty, and I'll be ready to see this writer whenever she can come by."

"So, you two ladies will talk tomorrow. And Lester, do keep in touch on my private line."

"Will do," said Lester, rolling his pant leg back down.

"Oh God," said Maria in the car. "Seeing Lester and Peach is the worst part about getting this story. Why do they have to be such jerks?"

"Lester is *no* jerk. He's been able to get any information he's wanted so far. And he'll hang in till the case is solved. Want a drink?"

"Sure. Why not?"

"How about dinner?"

"Ted's meeting me at eight. Thanks, but I can't."

"He might not show up till ten. You said so yourself."

"He will this time. I owe him some money and he's coming for it." I glanced over at her in the car, shocked by what I had just heard. How could such a beautiful girl care about a guy who obviously didn't care about her? "Say, what's a smart cookie like you doing with a guy who will only show up on time to get paid back?"

"When you talk like that you alienate me, Ben."

"You mean 'smart cookie'? Is that what alienates you? All right then, intelligent woman. Is that better? What's an intelligent woman like you doing with a guy who isn't that involved with you?"

"I'm not that involved with him."

"Do you sleep with each other? Make love? Have sex? Whatever you call it these days? Or is he just one of these fairy ballet dancers?"

"Ben, I honestly do not respect you when you talk like that. If you'll just drive me back to my car, I'd really appreciate it."

I drove her to the *Vindicator* parking lot, feeling like the ass of the century. I was comforted only a little when Maria said she'd stop by my office the next morning after her appointment with Joe Kuhl. In my day, a girl like Maria Forsythe would never have waited around for some fairy dancer to show up. She would have been standing men off, one by one, and falling at her feet would have been every red-blooded male's pleasure. I was feeling out of touch and out of tune. I walked into my office, poured some Scotch, and put on an Ella Fitzgerald record.

"Well, Miss Forsythe, you're back soon. How's everything going?" asked Joe Kuhl.

"I don't know. I'm hyperventilating or something. Yesterday when I was driving I felt like I was going to faint."

"Dizziness? Nausea?"

"No, just light-headedness. I felt numb, but I thought I was dying."

"How long did this sensation last?"

"Oh gee. About an hour."

"Any recurring sensations?"

"Yes, I felt it again a few hours later."

"At what time?"

"Three p.m."

"And how long did it last?"

"About an hour."

"Any other sensations?"

"No, none at all. I just feel so tense and stressed."

"Sounds like you had a P.A.T."

"A what?"

"Paroxysmal Atrial Tachycardia. It's just a minor little heart attack. You probably have a mitral valve prolapse or a murmur."

"What?"

"I'm sending you to cardiology right now for an echogram." He reached for the telephone.

"Now, hold on! I came here to talk to someone professionally about my stress, not to have a bunch of tests."

"Of course," said Kuhl, smiling and putting down the receiver. "Let's talk about what got you into this state."

"Well . . ." Maria hesitated. "I'm really intensely involved in a newspaper story which will, if I get the story, get me hired."

"In other words, if you break a story then you get hired. In other words, you've given up TV script writing?" He grinned at her, which made her nervous.

"Well, everyone has to make a living. Anyway, I've been working hard and I don't even know if it's going to pay off. It's giving me a heart attack, obviously!"

"Miss Forsythe, a P.A.T. is not a heart attack. What kind of story is it that will or will not give you employment?"

Maria paused, stared at the aborigine poster on the wall, and decided against telling the truth. "Are these guys your colleagues?"

"So I see we're feisty again this morning. Let me guess. You're working on either the Carpaccio-Miranda story or the Eele story and you've come here to see what I know." Kuhl picked up a pencil and smiled a little too victoriously for Maria's taste.

"You're pretty smart for a doctor."

"We do our best."

"I hope you're aware that isn't an opinion shared by most people."

"Are we bantering? Or is there a communication problem here?"

"Classically, it's referred to as repartee." Kuhl stared at his pencil. "Well, what do you know? Has Carpaccio covered for Eele? Is that why Carpaccio split to a swami retreat?"

"How would I know?"

"Because you're on the Eele investigating committee! Play dumb for the other patients, but not for me!"

"Miss Forsythe, I think you should see another doctor. I don't think I can help you."

"But Dr. Kuhl," said Maria sweetly, "you're the only doctor I *want* to see. You have such an excellent reputation, you're young, you're handsome . . ." Maria looked at Kuhl and smiled, "You're about fifty pounds lighter than Carpaccio. God! Every time I saw him he looked like he had gained another ten pounds. It was revolting!"

"That's why he'll be so happy at Baba Rhum's swami retreat. I hear all they do is eat."

"Baba what?"

"Baba Rhum. That's the name of the swami. The rumor is that he gets such rich and prominent people because they employ only former chefs from three-star French restaurants in the retreat's restaurant."

"Oh my God! Where did you hear that? Or are you just making it up?"

"I assure you I'm not making it up. But back to you. Did you really have these two episodes of light-headedness?"

"Yes."

"Then I'll see if cardiology can take you now for the echo," said Kuhl, picking up the telephone.

"No!"

"No what?"

"I have a morbid fear of cardiologists."

"You know, I think you've made these two episodes up just to see if you could get information out of me."

"I came to see you," said Maria, smiling as radiantly as she could. "Look, my pulse was 60 ten minutes ago and it's 90 now."

"Well," said Kuhl, disarmed. "I don't think that means a thing. You're simply excited to get the story."

" 'The eye of the experienced physician spellbinds the lunatic.' "

"What?" Kuhl was obviously at a loss for words.

"From *Agony Point* by Pycroft, 1862."

"Where did you learn that?"

"I was a literature major."

"Perhaps you ought to go back to school, get out of the newspaper business."

"Actually, I'd love to write for someone like PBS."

"Oh really? I'm making my first tape of my health series this afternoon," said Kuhl.

"Oh, Michael and I would love to see it!" exclaimed Maria.

"Who's Michael?"

"Michael Weintraub, my partner. He adores PBS. Could we drive up to watch?"

"Well, we're filming it in Golden Gate Park. I suppose if you and your, um, partner really want to see me . . ."

"Oh, we do! But why Golden Gate Park?"

"Because it's a special on running, that's why."

"Of course. I should have thought of that. When and where?"

"Well, why don't you meet us at the studios on Eighth and Brannan at four and you can follow us."

"Oh, I'll be your biggest fan! And at least you won't be wearing those tacky blue polyester blend pants if it's a running show."

"What?"

"So long, and try to think of our encounter as a million times more interesting than the rest of your day." Maria strode out of the office and into a telephone booth as fast as she could.

"Ben! I've found out the swami's name!" said Maria.

"You found out too late. Kim Blakely broke the swami's name and the whole food bit on a televised news break early this morning. That's probably how Kuhl found out!"

"Well, it's not a wasted trip. Can you spare Michael Weintraub? He and I have been invited to watch Kuhl tape his first segment this afternoon."

"I doubt Weintraub will agree to another PBS visit. But if you think he'd be helpful, I'll agree to it. These goddamned egocentric doctors . . . inviting you to see him tape his segment indeed!"

It was a bitch to learn that Kim Blakely had scooped us on the swami story. I knew that I was going to have to send Maria up to the swami center to get a first-person account. I needed a young pro like Weintraub to go with her and knew convincing Weintraub to accompany Maria wasn't going to be easy. The two didn't seem to be hitting it off and Weintraub wanted no part of the Carpaccio-Eele story anyway. At least the ashram practiced sexual abstinence. I could see Weintraub trying to fool around with Maria at the swami camp just for the sake of a little old-fashioned journalistic iconoclasm. The little bastard kept books by Mencken on his office desk and wasn't above seeing whatever he could get away with in the name of his idol. Weintraub was my promising star, a fair-haired boy after my own heart, except my heart had mellowed into adoration for Maria while Weintraub, quoting Mencken, claimed no blonde was worth losing one's head over. Poor Mike! He was a doctrinaire kid, but sometimes that's what it takes to make it big in the newspaper business. A dying breed looks to its icons, and Mencken is laughing in his grave. Yes, I decided to send Weintraub and Maria up to the swami camp and give Weintraub strict orders to obey the rules.

Within an hour I got hold of a Baba Rhum ex-convert who lived in Loma Verde and she was in my office by noon, ready to tell me everything she knew. Why I hadn't thought of this sooner galled me, but it didn't stop me. I made Weintraub sit in on the meeting. The sight of an anorexic isn't a pretty thing, and Michael blanched and avoided shaking the poor girl's hand. Janet Davidson, a Greenwich computer programming type now living with some famous professor of computer science, was about as skinny as a woman could get and still stand. Mike began to stare at his watch and say he had to see Upjohn that afternoon, but I shot him a look which shut him up. He and Janet sat down and she began to talk.

"As a child I was fat. I don't mean just plump. I weighed one hundred and fifty pounds by the time I was eleven." Michael started biting his nails. "I only lived for food. It was my whole life. By the time I was sixteen I weighed two twenty. You get the picture. When I was twenty-two I heard a new swami, formerly a Greenwich philosophy graduate student, was espousing sexual abstinence in favor of the metaphysics of input and output . . ."

"The metaphysics of input and output?" I asked.

"Yes," she answered somewhat hesitantly. "Food. You know, the input and the output . . ." Michael began to laugh.

"Shut up, Weintraub," I said. "Go on, Janet."

"Well, Baba Rhum has a very involved theory of input and output. You know, after he studied at Greenwich, which he called his 'wilderness period,' he went to Paris to train as a chef. You know, he is the only Californian ever to be a chef at a three-star French restaurant."

"Which restaurant was this?" asked Michael, bright boy that he was.

"Taillevent. Baba Rhum actually credited one of his philosophy professors who is a gourmet and quite knowledgeable about Paris's three-star restaurants for turning him on to Taillevent."

"What professor was this?" I asked.

"Oh, I can't remember offhand. You could find out who the gourmet philosopher of Greenwich is by a quick call to the Philosophy Department. Anyway, Baba Rhum, who was Peter Schwartz at the time he became a chef at Taillevent, said he first heard a voice calling to him as he was preparing a marquise au chocolat and pistachio sauce. He said the voice was calling him to return to California and preach the beauty of input and output to those who understood that great food was a holy sacrament. You know, Baba Rhum and his disciples see Paris as their homeland and make regular pilgrimages each year to eat at the restaurants Baba Rhum considers worthy of holy sacrament."

"I suppose output is . . ." started Michael.

"That's right," said Janet quickly.

"But why sexual abstinence?" I asked.

"Oh, Baba Rhum believes that sex takes away the drive for the higher input. Anyway, he got a bunch of us together, mainly fat Greenwich misfits, I might as well add, and he bought an Oregon ranch with some money his grandmother had left him. At first he did all the cooking but as the news of his retreat spread and he began to attract rich or famous people, he employed other former three-star French chefs. Oh God!" Janet buried her head in her hands. "The rest is like a nightmare. I'll leave this book with you. It's Baba Rhum's *Metaphysics of Input and Output* and arguments for the importance of one over the other."

"It looks like you haven't been eating a lot of three-star food lately," said Michael. I gave him a look which iced any other insensitive or stupid thing he might have had in mind to say.

"Food makes me sick," said Janet solemnly. "I live now for computer programming."

"I like software too—but of a different species," said Michael.

Weintraub's crack had zoomed right past her.

"I've got to get back to work. Read Baba Rhum's book and call me if you have any questions. Remember," she said, rising, "I don't resent Baba Rhum or his followers. I just realized I was slowly killing myself."

"A little food wouldn't kill you now," said Michael. I wanted to slug Michael for that imbecilic remark.

"I know what's best for me." She smiled wanly and left my office.

"If Baba Rhum attracted fuckups like her, how did he manage to later attract famous or successful people?" asked Michael.

"The food, Weintraub, the food. You and Maria Forsythe are going to study up on Baba Rhum's theories and present yourself this weekend as converts."

"Nothing doing, Ben!"

"Or you're fired."

"Fine, God damn it. Kim Blakely told me to come up to KUTK any time I need a . . ."

"Bullshit, Weintraub. What are you scared of? Here's a real opportunity for you to get a story. I want you to do it, Michael. You're the only reporter I have who could pull this off."

"What about Forsythe? Personally, I don't think she's serious enough."

"She's good, Michael. Give her a chance."

Michael heaved a sigh. "All right. Just this once. For a joke, that's all."

Michael Weintraub waited on the editorial floor of the *Loma Verde Vindicator* for Maria, who in turn was to await the arrival of Dyke Upjohn from San Francisco. "Do I have a game plan for you, kid," said Michael to Maria.

"You're turning gay to get a better response from Dyke Upjohn."

"I'm turning asexual so I can accompany you to the swami joint up in Oregon. Believe me, asexual is fine for me as far as you're concerned. I might, however, find some fox I can convert to sexual pleasure. You know, explain what my idea of a three-star final course is all about . . ."

"Michael, what are you talking about?"

"Sex, you jerk."

"No, I mean *what* are you talking about, us going up to the swami joint?"

"Our big boss Ben Boyer, who prefers to think of himself as Ben Bradlee, has given us the delicious assignment of checking out the Baba Rhum swami joint up in Oregon. We met an ex-convert today, the ugliest, skinniest, what do you call it— anorexic?—I have ever seen in my life. She said she weighed five hundred pounds when she was five and shit like that. She went to Greenwich and met Baba Rhum, who was Peter Schwartz at the time, and he collected all of these fat fuckups and they went up to the ranch his granny bought him so they could live for food. The story's more complicated, of course, and here's Upjohn now so I'll tell you the rest later. Get packing for tonight."

"I have an assignment from Ben Bradlee Boyer for you too, Michael. You're accompanying me today to see Joe Kuhl tape a 'Your Health' segment," said Maria.

"No way!"

63

"Hi, Dyke. Did you have a pleasant ride down? Did you take 280 or 101?" asked Maria.

"280. I'd almost forgotten how beautiful it is down here. Oh, hello, Michael. If you don't mind, I'd rather not have you join us to meet this woman."

"Of course, Ms. Upjohn. I understand completely."

"I rather doubt that," replied Dyke.

"I'd really just like to get a few more minutes of your time to ask you your opinions on other gay writers such as Jean Genet, Oscar Wilde, Willa Cather . . ."

"Michael, I'm a writer. Put your little tag onto someone else. I'd like to see your interview with me before it's printed. I told you that's my rule."

"Here it is, Ms. Upjohn." Michael handed her the typed pages.

Dyke scanned the pages briefly and looked up at Michael. "Better than I might have expected. That'll do."

"Well, that's just fine, Ms. Upjohn. I'm glad it suits you, because as far as I'm concerned you're a leader in the higher output." Michael sneered and walked away.

"What did that little jerk-ass mean?" Dyke asked Maria.

"Beats me. It's probably another one of those male reverse compliments."

"Get off it and grow up! He's just a little jerk-ass nothing. He's a worm. Do you have a car or shall we take my rental car?"

"I'll drive us. It's just the Greenwich Arms Inn . . ."

"That must be a new place."

"Oh, it's not! It's just the old Mango Hutch Motel with a different name and higher prices."

"Oh God. The Mango Hutch Motel," said Dyke as the two walked to the car. "I once talked an idiotic sociology professor of mine into meeting me at the Mango Hutch Motel. When he showed he had clammy hands and bad breath. He couldn't get it up so I told him I was gay and he seemed so relieved."

"So why did you ask him to meet you at the Mango Hutch?"

"Material for my work! I *knew* he couldn't get it up. I could just *tell*. He's been my role model for the impotent male in most of my writing. By the way, he's dead now. The poor old wilted penie got knocked off in an airplane crash."

"Oh, I remember that one! That was Bruce Robertson," said Maria. "I guess you heard about his problem with the graduate student who sued him for sexual misconduct . . ."

"I can't imagine what he did to her. Maybe he just breathed heavily into her ear. Well, here we are, I see. The name has changed but the place remains the same. What's this woman's name?"

"Peach Kling. Her cousin Lester, who's a private investigator, might also be around. He's collecting information on Eele."

"What's he got?"

"Some photos of Eele and a patient having sex."

"Good! What else?"

"A tape of Eele and his sleazy attorney talking about trying to dig up dirt on Peach or else Eele leaving the country."

"You mean this guy, Lester, has actually been trailing Eele?"

"Yes. You know, private investigation. He looks like a real drip but he seems to know how to collect incriminating evidence. Oh, maybe I shouldn't say this, but Peach is pretty timid. She looks like she could go into shock over profanity."

"You mean to say she's naive?"

"Well, she acts like she's been living under a rock or something and that this thing with Eele has been like a bombshell to her. She's collected news articles from all over about malpractice suits and she has them in this nice, neat notebook."

"So I'll go easy on her," said Dyke with a smile. "Remember, I'm only here to give her my support and to share a story. I'll share it with you too, Maria, but only on the condition that you don't reveal my name if you use my experience with Eele for your story."

"Don't worry. I protect my sources. That is what I'm supposed to say in the newspaper world, isn't it?" Maria called Peach Kling's room from the lobby. The two met Peach in her room. Peach, equipped with a pen, a notebook, a copy of Dyke's latest book, and Lester's tape recorder, had mustered a calm, resolute look.

"Peach, this is Dyke Upjohn," began Maria.

"Yes. I read your book thoroughly. I suppose I should ask you if Duke Eele had anything to do with your . . . your abnormality?"

Dyke burst into laughter, but appeared more amused than hostile, much to Maria's relief. "Peach honey, I was gay before I ever met Duke Eele. Anyway, no man has anything to do with my sexual preference, which, by the way, *is* preference and not abnormality. But ten years ago when I was a student at Greenwich I had a lover who unfortunately became pregnant." Peach looked momentarily confused, and then she shuddered. Dyke paused and waited for Peach to absorb this information. "Turn off the tape recorder, honey." Peach turned off the machine. Dyke lit a cigarette and Peach ran around the room looking for an ashtray. "My lover was given a recommendation by the Greenwich health service doctor to see Eele. To his credit, or so we thought at the time, Eele was one of a handful in the Bay Area who would perform an abortion without the patient having to go through the whole under twenty-one rigmarole, you know, signed statements from three shrinks saying that you're too mentally unstable to be a mother and other such garbage. Anyway, having an abortion was a very big deal back then."

"Excuse me," interjected Maria, "but if a few politicians have it their way it will be a very big deal again."

"Right you are, Maria. But let's keep to the story. We can get into that other topic later. My friend, to make a long story short, had waited more than three months. Eele told her not to worry, that he would make it safe and that she wasn't more than ten weeks along in his estimation. Well, my friend was five months along. She lost a lot of blood during the procedure and almost didn't make it. She was hooked into an I.V. for days. When she was finally released from the hospital, Eele callously told her not to worry, that she could get pregnant tomorrow if she wanted."

"What happened to your friend?" asked Peach softly.

"She's O.K. She's a star on the pro tennis circuit but believe me I thought she might have died in the hands of Eele."

"That's a slimy eel," whispered Peach. "But your friend is alive and I am alive and what matters now is that we convict Eele. I want to be the one who puts that stinking Eele out of business!"

"Well," said Dyke, puffing away at her cigarette, "that's a noble aspiration. I hear your cousin is keeping track of Eele."

"Oh, Lester doesn't think I should spend too much time talking with you, Ms. Upjohn. You see, Eele has threatened to dig up dirt on me and, well, you're so outspoken about your own life . . ."

"Say no more, Peach, my dear. I just wanted you to know that I support you in your efforts to get Eele. I always knew he'd get his one day. You do all women a service. Well, Maria? I'm ready to go when you are."

"Listen, Peach," said Maria. "I might not see you for a few days. I'm leaving tomorrow evening to check out the swami retreat where Carpaccio and Miranda Kettle have fled. You see, Dyke, we think Miranda has a lot of information on Eele. She was concerned about the undergraduate girls who saw Eele, and had decided to conduct her own investigation. We have some theories as to why Miranda left Greenwich with Carpaccio, and if they're correct, we might have an even bigger scandal than now meets the eye."

"I just hope we get that Eele, and soon!" said Peach,

dabbing at her eyes.

"It sounds like there's a good team working right now to prosecute that bastard Eele," said Dyke. "Thanks for allowing me to tell you my story. It makes me feel very, very good. And don't worry, Peach. I understand your cousin's concerns and they don't bother me in the least. Men's concerns never have."

The two walked back to the car, and Dyke began to open her door when she was nearly hit by a bright red sports car. "Hey, get your low-slung penis off the road!" she screamed, but in vain, for HOT EELE had vanished from sight.

"My God! That's Eele!" cried Maria.

"Eele! That slimy no-good . . ."

"Dyke! I think he's been tailing us! Or Peach."

"That fucking, no-good nothing!" hissed Dyke.

"Dyke, do you think he's going to . . . going to . . ."

"Claim that Peach Kling has a lesbian friend? Who knows? Anything's possible. The only thing to do is to confront him! Is that son-of-a-bitch listed in the phone book?"

"Dyke, hold on! Maybe he *wasn't* tailing us or Peach."

"Don't be a fool. He thinks he can smear Peach Kling by insinuating she's gay because she's met me, and he's not going to get away with it. I'm going to get him before he gets any further."

"Dyke, I think we'd better think this out."

"Listen, Maria. Now is the time to act. If you wait, God knows what will happen! I know that man! If he's planning to smear Peach Kling, he will. But that goddamned bastard's not going to smear her, and especially he's not going to use me or my name to smear her. *I'll* see to that. We need to find a telephone book, and fast."

Dyke grabbed at Maria's sleeve and pulled her into the

manager's office. "Eele, Duke. He lives in Forestbridge. That figures. Out there with the horsey set. Well, God damn him. Drive us to Forestbridge! If Eele can tail us then we can tail him."

"Drive to Forestbridge?"

"Maria, frankly I find your hesitation appalling."

"But Dyke, we don't even know if he was following us or not."

"Maria, you will never make the grade. The way you're going I think you'd better go back to whatever else you were doing before you decided to play investigative reporter."

"All right, let's go. You're right. I need to make a telephone call at some point within the hour. I have a late afternoon appointment in the city."

"Can this appointment wait? Are you out to get Eele, or aren't you?"

"I am. I'm out to get all doctors like Eele. But I'm not just out to get doctors. I'm out to uncover a scandal."

"Well then, please get in the car and get driving to Bourbon Boulevard in Forestbridge. It just figures that old boozer Eele would live on a road called Bourbon Boulevard! God damn him!"

"All right. We're off to Forestbridge. What's the chance that we'll find him?"

"Where in the hell else will he be? He's been temporarily kicked out of the Clinic. What else does he have to do but booze it up or play golf on the Greenwich course?"

"The Greenwich course! Why don't we look there first? It's closer at least."

"That might be a good idea," said Dyke, lighting a cigarette.

"May I have a cigarette? I'm out. A little Valium might help at this point also."

"Listen, Maria. I want to get an answer out of you. Are you anxious because a knife-happy, woman-hating gynecologist is on the loose and doing something very dangerous and it makes you mad, so mad that you're shaking? Or are you shaking simply because you're scared?" Dyke lit Maria's cigarette. It was the first Cartier cigarette Maria had ever smoked.

"I'm mad, I'm scared, and I'm getting sick of having you shove me around. You're over thirty and famous. Big deal. Does that give you the right to push me around?"

"You're young, Maria. You don't know what a worm like Eele might have up his asshole."

"You mean 'sleeve'?" asked Maria sweetly.

"Yes, sweetheart, I mean sleeve." Dyke looked at her watch. "I'm sure that flatworm is headed for the golf course for a round with one of his fellow flatworms. We can be there in five minutes."

Maria started her car. "What will we say to him if we see him?"

"We'll confront him with the facts. We'll tell him we know of his plans to smear Peach's reputation, and that we've seen him following us."

"But," said Maria, hesitating somewhat, "don't you think we ought to tell Lester what we're doing first?"

"Fuck Lester! Who in the hell is he, anyway? Some jerk-ass private eye? Who cares about Lester?"

"Well . . . O.K. It's funny. I've lived at Greenwich for twenty-two years and I've never been on the golf course."

"Here's your big chance."

"I've never smoked a Cartier cigarette. I'll bet they cost a lot."

"I wouldn't know. A friend buys them for me. Who's that woman waving at us?"

Maria looked to the left and saw Flora Framingham, dressed in jogging gear, waving to her. "Oh shit, it's Flora Framingham!"

"Who's that?"

"The big heart doctor."

"The doctor with the big heart or what?"

"Hello!" said Flora running breathlessly to where Maria had stopped at a light. "My goodness, Maria! I would never have guessed you were a smoker! There's enough smoke in that car to choke an elephant."

"Flora, this is Dyke Upjohn, the novelist," said Maria, trying discreetly to put out her cigarette.

"Oh yes! *Betch: A Butch*. I must confess I haven't read it. Well, where are you two off to?"

"The golf course," replied Maria.

"Not a lot of aerobic exercise in golf. Oh, there's your green light. By the way, Maria, can you stop by this evening? Charles and I want to have a little chat with you about Brazil. Didn't you go there last fall?"

"Yes, but I don't think I'll make it tonight. I've got a hectic schedule. But I'll call you. See you!"

"So *that's* Flora Framingham. At first the name didn't register. She's a hot item in medical circles."

"She sure is. She's our neighbor."

"Still live at home?"

"With my dad. My mom died when I was seven."

"So you've been to Brazil?"

"Yes. A graduation present from my father. I went to Rio with a friend."

"Pretty nice graduation present. Did you like it in Rio?"

"Loved it. I could live there in a minute. Everyone does the samba. It's just dancing, beach, sun, and . . . there's his car!"

"The HOT EELE. The hot shit Eele. Come on!" Dyke and Maria jumped out of Maria's car and walked toward the golf house.

"What are we going to say?" whispered Maria.

"Leave it to me. There he is. Dr. Eele," began Dyke in a cheerful voice.

Duke Eele, who was buying golf balls, turned around. "Do I know you?" he asked, looking confused.

"Sure you do. You helped a friend of mine out of a real problem about ten years ago. Anyway, as you were following my associate and me, I doubt there's any need for an introduction."

"Following you? Young lady, I don't understand what you're saying. I've never seen you in my life." Duke Eele turned his back on Dyke and examined a golf ball.

"Listen, Eele, for your own good, I think we'd better have a little talk," whispered Dyke, taking Eele by the shoulder.

"I assure you, my dear woman, that I've never laid eyes on you, don't know your friend, and certainly have never followed you anywhere." He jerked away from Dyke's grasp.

"I suggest you come outside with me or I'll make a scene."

Eele, looking more confused than ever, put the golf ball on the counter and walked outside with Dyke and Maria. "I assure you, I've never laid eyes on you. I can't imagine what you want. I don't know who you are. It's possible that I may have treated a patient you say is a friend ten years ago but I've treated thousands of patients." Maria looked at Dyke. "Now may I resume what I was doing before you came here?"

Dyke looked at Maria. "All right. Excuse us. It must be a mistake." Eele walked back into the golf house.

"I'm sure he has no idea of what you're talking about," said Maria to Dyke.

"I think you're right. Loma Verde is such a small town. I suppose it's just a coincidence after all. Very strange, however. I'm not wholly convinced. Drive me back to the newspaper. I've got to get back up to the city."

Back at the *Vindicator* offices, Dyke waved goodbye to Maria and was walking to her car when a receptionist ran up to Maria and said, "Ben wants to see you and Dyke at once!"

"Dyke! Ben wants to see us!" called Maria.

"Who's Ben?"

"The editor. He's in on the Eele story."

I had to hand it to Maria. She had really gotten up to her ears in the Loma Verde Clinic story. I was impressed when she told me that she and Dyke Upjohn had trailed Eele from the Greenwich Arms Inn to the golf course. I was almost sad to shoot her down with Lester's account of Eele's visit to the motel. "Old Lester saw Eele meet a prostitute at the motel," I said. "Eele had no idea that Peach was there, of course. Oh yes, Lester got some incriminating photos of Eele and his afternoon friend."

I watched Maria's face fall. "Sorry for the goose chase, Maria," said Dyke. "I really thought that Eele might try to hurt Peach's reputation by using me. I should have known he's too stupid to know how to make any real attempt to do anything as difficult as blackmail."

"Well, girls, it was a good try." I realized at once that Dyke might think I was being too patronizing. "By the way, Ms. Upjohn, I've begun your new book and I must say I'm really enjoying it."

Dyke gave me a blank look, shook Maria's hand, and began to walk out of the building. "Oh, Maria," she called. "Keep me informed of the latest developments in the story. I'm listed in the Manhattan book." Dyke waved and disappeared.

"These things happen when you're on the heels of a good story," I said, putting my arm around Maria. "Win some, lose some. It's the name of the game." Maria shrugged. "Listen, I've talked Weintraub into accompanying you to this Joe Kuhl television deal. He's been boning up on the swami joint. He'll fill you in on the fine details this afternoon. We've booked the two of you on an eight o'clock flight to Portland this evening."

"But Ben! I don't want to go to a swami joint for a weekend with Michael Weintraub!"

"You'll probably never see each other once you're there. I think the women and the men are segregated for the most part. You'd better run home and pack a few things. Weintraub will be waiting for you at the office at three-fifteen. Good luck, kid. I know you're going to have a ball."

I watched Maria walk away, and wished it were I who was accompanying her to the swami joint. There's nothing I'd love more than to break a few of the swami's rules, beginning with the one on abstinence. I had to trust that Weintraub wouldn't have the same idea, and pride prevented me from asking him to play fair ball and to keep his nose clean.

"I'm only doing this Joe Kuhl deal at PBS to further my own career," said Michael Weintraub, tossing Maria's suitcase into the trunk. "I wouldn't spend two seconds on it otherwise. I don't mind telling you, Forsythe, that I don't think you're really a serious journalist."

"Watch my suitcase, Michael! You can at least be civilized, can't you?"

"I'm looking forward to a lot of good food. Other than that I don't give a goddamn about this story. But I intend to find out as much as I can. I'm going to fill you in on the details of how we're getting in right now."

"To the swami joint?"

"That's right. Baba Rhum has a pay weekend program called 'Gourmet Weekend.' A person can sign up for the weekend like we have, and if we find it to our liking which we won't, we could stay on for some pre-initiation work program." Michael looked at Maria. "Are you taking all of this in? Good. I just hope to God that Kim Blakely doesn't show up. She's been getting too many scoops on this wretched story. Her scooping us is the only reason I've decided to get involved.

We're going to clean this story up now, and fast."

"Are you saying, Michael, that because you've decided to become involved, the true story will be broken?"

"I am," said Michael, turning onto the freeway.

"Well, I just want you to know that I've worked damned hard to uncover all the little connections!"

"But not hard enough, Forsythe. But enough of that for now."

"No! Not enough of that! I spent the early part of this afternoon trailing Eele . . ."

"Yeah, and I heard you trailed him under the wrong impression."

"So what? Everyone makes mistakes. Do you know how he spent the early part of the afternoon?"

"Yes, I do, and if you'll forgive me, Forsythe, it has nothing to do with making your connections." Maria leaned back in her seat and lit a cigarette. "Oh, by the way, no smoking at the swami joint. I think I'd better fill you in on the swami's beliefs. Basically the swami goes in for metaphysical dualism. The main concept is input and output. The food you eat and . . ."

"I get it."

"Right. Well, you have mental input and physical input and then you have mental output and physical output. You get it?"

"Oh no."

"Yep, oh no. That's about it. It's a total involvement with input and output and it revolves around gourmet food. The main argument, as Baba Rhum likes to keep a certain philosophical level to his talk, revolves around the question of what is more important, input or output."

"Oh my God."

"Now you're probably wondering why Baba Rhum has a sexual abstinence rule. He says sex takes away the drive for the higher input."

"Are we going to be around a bunch of fat, horny people?"

"That's doubtful. Look at Miranda. You said so yourself, she's a frigid number."

"But still . . . well, I suppose that when she found out that Pete baby arranged an abortion for an undergraduate she flipped out."

"Now, since you're going to have an opportunity to see Miranda more than I, your job is to get her to talk about Greenwich, about what she knows about the Loma Verde Clinic, all of that. She's probably seething with resentment, and who knows?—maybe she *wants* to talk. Meanwhile I'll be trying to smoke Carpaccio out on his involvement with Eele. It's possible that he really might have split up to the swami joint rather than report his findings on Eele."

"But what about Joe Kuhl and his wife? The big question is what do they know?" asked Maria.

"The big answer is that you're supposed to find out. I heard that Kuhl's wife Jean will be on part of his segment tonight so maybe you can meet her. But you'd better get some information out of her fast. Oh yes. We're supposed to call Ben before we leave for Portland this evening. He's getting sick of having Kim Blakely break stories that *you*, Forsythe, should have been on top of. You're getting ashes all over my car, by the way."

"Sorry, Michael. If you don't mind, I'll just sit back and think about the various things I should be asking Jean Kuhl and Miranda Kettle."

"Silence is O.K. with me. I'll just be your chauffeur."

"I'll drive us back down to the airport if you'd like."

"Nothing doing, Forsythe. I wouldn't trust your driving. I have a feeling you wouldn't be a very good driver."

"Well, that's a stupid feeling to have. It makes you look like an idiot."

"Say, Forsythe, when you and Upjohn were driving around tailing Eele, she really *was* in the driver's seat, wasn't she? You know what I mean. Wasn't she *quite* aggressive, sort of the 'take charge' type? Sort of the male role?"

Maria sighed. "Don't be a jerk. She's as anxious as Peach
and I am to stop Eele. You know it wasn't just a stupid decision
to trail Eele. Lester taped Eele and Eele's lawyer discussing how
to ruin Peach's credibility. I mean, look what Eele could have
done with a meeting at the Mango Hutch Motel between Dyke
Upjohn, me, and Peach if he had wanted to really ruin Peach
instead of just messing around with a prostitute."

Michael laughed. "I've got to hand it to you, Forsythe.
Like a good reporter, you at least don't give a shit what people
think about you."

"What do you mean?" asked Maria.

"Well, I mean *you* were there with Dyke and Peach. Eele
could have implicated you in his smear campaign had he been
more on the ball in the first place."

"Well, no one would think I'm gay!"

"Don't worry, Forsythe. Eele's not bright enough to pull
off a smear campaign. Sit back and listen to the music."

Joe Kuhl, dressed in a navy cotton warm-up suit and running shoes for his television filming, was looking for his wife.
"Where's Jean?" he asked the man who was loading the cables
into the truck. "She was supposed to be here by now."

"Hi, Joe," said Michael.

"Oh, hello. Michael Weintraub?"

"Sure am."

"Hey, I just saw your dad yesterday. Asked about you and
he said you were in the . . ." Joe stopped and looked at Maria.
"So you're *both* in the news business. Partners, huh?"

"Well," said Michael quickly.

"That's right," said Maria.

"Out to uncover a big Clinic scandal," said Joe dryly.

"That's right," said Maria smiling brightly.

"You won't find one here."

"I've already told her we *wouldn't.*"

"But Miss Forsythe persists. Well, Mike, you remember Jean, don't you? Have you seen her around? She's supposed to be taping this first segment with me."

"Dr. Kuhl, we have the music you requested," called a woman's voice to Joe.

"Here's the rainmaker machine you requested," announced a man to Joe. "It cost a fortune to rent."

"It will be money well spent, I assure you," replied Joe.

"Sounds like quite a production," said Michael.

"Yes, but Jean is supposed to be in it and she *knows* she's supposed to be here right now. I'm beginning to get worried."

"Listen, Dr. Kuhl. Would you like Michael and me to stay here and wait for your wife?"

"That might not be a bad idea."

"We'll do that, Joe," said Michael. "Just give us an idea where in Golden Gate Park you're filming and we'll bring her with us if you'd like."

"I'd really appreciate that, Mike. Do you know Golden Gate Park very well?"

"Like the back of my hand."

"Well, we're filming right in front of that beautiful big old white conservatory. Not exactly in front but, you know, the closest running space near the building."

"We'll find you," said Michael. "Don't worry."

"We've really got to get going," said Bob Sayers, walking back and forth with a clipboard like a man who was about to have an anxiety attack.

"Bob, this is Mike Weintraub and, um, Miss Forsythe. Bob Sayers, my producer."

"We met just yesterday," said Maria. "You're Flora's producer too. Really into medicine, aren't you?"

"It's the coming thing for television in the eighties," said Bob brightly.

"Mike and Miss Forsythe are kind enough to wait for Jean. Mike knows approximately where we'll be filming and will bring her as soon as she gets here."

As the truck pulled away, Maria said, "Smart thinking, Michael. We can quiz Jean for information on the Carpaccio investigating committee."

"Just like a woman to be late for her husband's first television segment!"

"Knock it off, Michael. I'll be right back. I'm calling Ben." Maria walked into the lobby and was recognized by the receptionist who had greeted her and Michael the previous day.

"You just can't keep away, can you?" laughed the receptionist.

"We're working on a story," mumbled Maria. "May I use your telephone? Dr. Kuhl's wife hasn't shown up yet and we're waiting to take her to the shooting location. May I speak with Ben Boyer?"

"I'm glad you called," I said. "Susan Kettle came into my office not even an hour ago with the most extraordinary story. You can't believe it! 'My Life with a Swami Mommy'! We've scooped that goddamned Kim Blakely this time, and we've scooped her good! Normally I'd have Weintraub write the story but since he's up there with you, I'm writing it myself! And I'm having a ball! I haven't had this much fun with a story in years. Pete Kettle will sue us for libel now for certain. Let him do it! He can't win a damned thing!"

"Swami Mommy?"

"That's right. Susan Kettle claims that Miranda's conversion wasn't simply overnight, so to speak. Apparently she'd been seeing Baba Rhum during his monthly visits to the Bay Area, and for at least a year. Don't forget, she has a real interest in mystical things. Recall her fancy dinner for the Dalai Lama. Susan claims that the Dalai Lama sat at Miranda's right side that night and Vincent Carpaccio sat at her left side."

"How cozy."

"Yes indeed. Susan said her mother had been moving into a more mystical state for a long time. She said Miranda found out about Baba Rhum from Gerry Fitzgerald, the big-shot philosophy professor who had Baba Rhum as an undergraduate."

"The Peter Schwartz days?"

"That's right. I tried to get in touch with Fitzgerald, who's supposed to be some kind of gourmet himself, but I was told he was off in the south of France with his new young wife."

"Good old Greenwich gossip. Well, did Susan Kettle say anything of real interest?"

"What do you mean 'of real interest'? For God's sake, the girl has labeled her mother a 'Swami Mommy' after attempting suicide. How much more interesting do you want? What are you doing anyway?"

"We're waiting for Jean Kuhl to show up for her husband's TV segment. Kuhl has already left for the filming and Mike and I are supposed to take Jean to the location when she shows. I think she's here now. I should probably get going. We're going to ask her some questions about the Eele investigating committee."

"Be discreet. Call me before you leave for Portland. And remember, if Weintraub tries anything funny at the swami joint, put him in his place. You know what I mean."

"I doubt Michael's going to try anything funny. He's already told me that he can't stand me and that he's only going to further his career, for the food, and to seduce a woman at the retreat."

"Seducing a woman at the retreat will probably land him on his ass outside the entrance. You tell him to watch himself. He knows the swami's rules. It's only for the weekend, for

God's sake. Can't that horny little bastard cool it for two nights?"

"Ben, you're beginning to sound angry. I'll tell him to behave himself. But you know Michael. I've got to go now. They're waving at me and Michael looks like he's about to have a conniption fit. Talk to you later."

Maria handed the phone to the receptionist and was startled when the receptionist said, "Must be more interesting in the good old newspaper business than I thought! And to think people assume that newspapers are a thing of the past!"

"Come on, Maria, we're an hour late!" called Michael.

"Thanks for the phone," said Maria.

"We don't have all day for you to sit and chat with someone," said Michael. "I thought you were about to send out for coffee and crullers and make it a real klatsch. Maria, this is Jean Kuhl. Jean, this is Maria Forsythe."

"I like your jogging suit," Maria said to Jean.

"Oh, that's why I'm late! I didn't know we were supposed to meet at four. I thought it was at five, and there I was at Macy's looking for a cute jogging outfit."

"Well, you sure found a cute jogging suit," said Michael solicitously.

"It looks great. Your husband's my doctor, you know," said Maria.

"Oh really?"

"Yes. He's treating me for, um . . . stress."

"It seems half his patients under the age of seventy are stress patients. I'm glad I'm a dermatologist."

"The patients who don't get under your skin, right, Jean?" asked Michael. Jean laughed and Maria rolled her eyes. "You get in the back seat, Forsythe."

"Oh, I'll get in the back seat. Maria's legs are longer," said Jean, speaking what was obviously the truth.

"No, Jean, I'll get in the back seat and give you the privilege of sitting next to Michael."

"So, you're both reporters with the *Loma Verde Vindicator*. You know, I almost became a reporter after I graduated from college, but I thought, why not apply to medical school? So I did, and to my surprise I got in!"

"Aren't you being a bit modest?" asked Michael as he surveyed Jean's not so subtle curves.

"Michael's dad wants him to go to medical school," said Maria.

"Wishful thinking," mumbled Michael.

"Isn't your father the chairman of orthopedic surgery at Greenwich?"

"That's right."

"Let's see now, Michael. Do you know where we're going?" asked Jean.

"Like the back of my hand."

"You have driven around this block a couple of times now," said Maria.

"I'm just trying to find the entrance to the park!"

"But I thought you knew the park like the back of your hand," said Maria.

"I *do*. But I sometimes forget how to get *into* the park."

"Gee. I'm beginning to get a bit nervous. I realize it's my fault because I was late, but I'm supposed to be *in* this segment. Joe's counting on it!"

"Don't worry, Jean. I'll get you there," said Michael. "Don't you have some questions you'd like to ask Jean, Maria?"

"Oh, yes. Jean, everyone knows that Dr. Eele is a disreputable character. I know you're on the Eele investigating committee with your husband. Didn't it surprise you when Carpaccio, the third member of the committee, took off to a swami joint with Miranda Kettle?"

"I suppose it surprised me about as much as it surprised anyone."

"Were Carpaccio and Miranda having an affair?" asked Michael.

"I really don't know. I can't imagine two less likely persons to have affairs. Vince was a very stable, almost boring sort of guy. And Miranda, well, she had a reputation for being quite buttoned down."

"A prude," interjected Michael. "Frigid, probably."

"Sex is always on Michael's brain," said Maria.

"She was a frigid bitchy prude. Right, Jean? Right, Maria?"

"Well," said Jean, "I really didn't know her that well. It seems a little unfair. But I did know Vince Carpaccio and I must say I was shocked when he took off to a swami retreat, abandoning his responsibilities to his family, his patients, and his colleagues."

"Who's taken his place on the Eele investigating committee?" asked Maria.

"We haven't found a third party, actually. It's most disturbing because Vince knew more about the Kling case than either Joe or I . . . Oh! Watch out! You just missed that little dog. There! Turn there! There's the park entrance!"

"Knew more about the Kling case?" asked Maria quickly.

"I can't say any more about it. I'm sorry. Oh! There they are! There's Joe! Isn't he gorgeous? Isn't he handsome?"

The three parked and quickly jumped out of the car. Jean ran over to Joe.

"Where have you been?" asked Joe. "You're over an hour late!"

"I'm sorry, Joe. I had no idea it was a four o'clock shooting. I thought it was for five. But do you like this new jogging outfit?"

"Let's roll!" bellowed Bob Sayers. An audio man put "Singin' in the Rain" over a loudspeaker and the rainmaker began to spew water before the camera.

"Yes, we're in the rain, singing and running," said Joe Kuhl, smiling like a golden boy before the camera. "I'm Joe Kuhl and this is my wife Jean, and we're runnin' in the rain for

'Your Health,' a new weekly program dedicated to fitness and health in the eighties. Some of you out there may be fair-weather runners. Well, I say a fair-weather runner is like a fair-weather friend. What are you going to do when the skies are threatening to storm? You're going to run in the rain! Running in the rain is great! It's an old wives' tale that running in the rain will make you sicker. But if some of the weaker among you out there get pneumonia, that's what we doctors are here for!"

"That jerk," whispered Michael.

"I think this is funny," Maria whispered back.

"Well, then you've got a perverse sense of humor, Forsythe, and it's not to your credit because perversity only looks good when the perverse one can back it up with some intelligence."

"Shut up, Michael."

"What did Ben have to say?"

"Oh, you won't believe it! Susan Kettle came by the *Vindicator* offices with the story of the week. 'My Life With a Swami Mommy'!"

" 'My Life With a Swami Mommy'! Why am I up here? I should be down there! Goddamn it! That would have been *my* story if I weren't stuck up here at this bullshit ego TV trip! Who's writing the story? Did he give the story to Tom Branduzzi? Who's doing the 'Swami Mommy' story, Forsythe?"

"Ben's doing it and he says it's lots of fun."

"Oh shit. Why am I here? Susan Kettle comes in with a gigantic confessional and I have to be stuck up here watching Joe Kuhl act like an asshole. I'm telling you, Forsythe, there'd better be a good story up at the swami joint or I'll make sure you don't get hired."

"Quiet on the set, for God's sake!" called a voice over a loudspeaker. "All right now. I want a couple of shots of typical Golden Gate joggers. That gentleman over there, for instance. Sir! Sir!" An elderly man in a warm-up suit stopped running and walked over to the film location. Within a few minutes he was in front of the cameras with Joe Kuhl.

"Would you mind telling us, sir, how old you are and how long you've been jogging?" asked Joe.

"Not at all. I'm eighty-nine and I've been jogging for thirty-five years. I'm a real fixture around these parts."

"I understand you're the famous Larry Levin and that you've been a waiter at Sam's Grill for the past fifty-three years," said Joe.

"That's right. Fifty-four years next June," said Larry Levin.

"Well, you certainly look in great shape, Larry. Besides the obvious benefits of fitness, are there any other reasons you jog?"

"Yes. I like to meet other joggers, especially pretty young women. But I won't go out with any woman over the age of thirty-five."

"Well," said Joe, laughing, "you heard that, folks. Larry here won't go out with a woman over thirty-five. Yes, it's true, you can meet some fine people when you go to Golden Gate Park to jog."

"Help! Help!" called a woman's voice. "Someone's snatched my handbag!"

"Cut the cameras!" called a voice over the loudspeaker.

"Which way did they go?" called Joe.

The distraught woman looked at Joe a moment and said, "I wouldn't tell *you*! The guy who snatched my purse was jogging!"

"Well, I assure you, not all joggers are purse snatchers!" replied Joe hotly.

"Let's go get the son-of-a-bitch!" exclaimed Larry Levin.

"Listen, grandpa. You're not up to it! The guy who snatched my purse was about six four, two twenty, and under twenty-one!"

"Let's get going," whispered Michael.

"Why? I think this is a riot! Maybe the old guy can catch

the jogging purse thief!"

"Come on, Forsythe. It's getting late and we have a plane to catch. I also want to call Ben. I'm really mad about missing the 'Swami Mommy' story. What did he get out of the Kettle girl, anyway?"

"I don't think he got much. When I asked the same question he acted like 'what a thing to ask.' Like wasn't it enough that Susan Kettle called her mother a 'Swami Mommy'?"

"At least she gave the story to us and not to a TV station. She probably has a fondness for the old *Vindicator*. Sort of sees us like a part of her happy childhood years."

"Michael, *I* don't see why Susan Kettle would give the *Vindicator* her big 'Swami Mommy' story. After all, the *Vindicator* covered her suicide attempt in all its glory on the front page just a few days ago!"

"And so the old *Vindicator* lives up to its name. Vindication on all sides! Ben told me he was just getting back at Greenwich for not cooperating on a few other stories when he printed the Susan Kettle suicide attempt."

"He told *me* it was because Ron Ryders from Greenwich P.R. wouldn't cough up Homecoming Game tickets after Ben agreed to coverup the Rollo Rum heir on-campus dope death."

"Same thing, Forsythe. Listen, I think we really ought to get going. Let's just say good-bye to someone here and leave."

"Jean!" called Maria. Jean Kuhl, looking down at the mouth, walked over to Maria and Michael.

"Well, it looks like the filming's been momentarily disturbed. And all because of one purse-snatching jogger! If this were one of the big networks, the cameras would keep rolling so we could finish our segment. I told Joe to hold out for ABC or NBC, but no. Joe just had to go with PBS. He's always been so civic-minded."

"Well, I'm sure one of the biggies will pick him up before you know it. He looks like a real winner," said Michael in an ingratiating manner.

"You're darned right he's a winner! I'd only marry a winner and I'll tell you this. Joe is worth a lot more than this lousy PBS is paying him!"

"Well, I'm sure he'll get what he deserves someday," said Michael.

"He might even get what he deserves sooner than you think," said Maria. "Oh, by the way, Jean, Flora Framingham painted a picture of Vincent Carpaccio as a celebrity-seeking publicity-hungry sort of guy. It doesn't quite go with your view of him as boring and stable."

"Can this conversation wait?" asked Jean impatiently. "I think my husband has run off to find the purse snatcher and frankly I'm very concerned. God! That's Joe for you. Always worried about the other guy!"

"Did you ever see Carpaccio as celebrity-seeking?" persisted Maria.

"Well, the Dalai Lama thing and what is that? Bosnian Woods? He was always the doctor at Bosnian Woods."

"Well, listen, Jean. It's been a real pleasure watching you and Joe film. I'm sure you'll have a big success with 'Your Health.' Come on, Maria, we have a plane to catch." They began to walk away and Michael whispered, "Did you *have* to say that Joe might get what he deserves sooner than she thinks? God, Forsythe! You are so stupid."

"I don't care, Michael. Joe was acting like a jerk."

"Yes, Joe was acting like a jerk but you should keep at least one jerk on *your* side for that random ruptured appendix."

Baba Rhum

"'You are grieved over the food that is not eaten, but you speak the words of the wise. The wise do not grieve over the food that is not eaten or the food that is not made.' Namaste, and welcome to Baba Rhum's ashram. Did you have a comfortable flight to Portland?" The young woman in a scarlet sari who stood at the front of the old farmhouse had a Moon-shaped face and a loony, caved-in grin.

"It was fine," replied Michael.

"'Namaste' means 'I salute the god within you.' Please come in. I'm glad the taxi could find us. Sometimes the drivers spend hours looking for us. You have had a long evening and as it is our custom to rise at four o'clock in the morning, I will show you to your rooms."

"Four o'clock in the morning?" gasped Michael.

"It is said that if ignorance is bliss, that is the reason we like to sleep so much. We are all here to learn, Gentle One." The young woman smiled and bowed her head. "So then, here are the women's quarters. Your room is very simple but I trust you will find it comfortable. Namaste and goodnight, my friend." The young woman bowed again. Maria barely had the chance to exchange glances with Michael before her door was shut. Maria sighed, put her suitcase on the floor, and sat on her cot. She took a notebook from her purse and began to write.

1. You are grieved over the food that is not eaten but you speak the words of the wise.
2. Dumb-looking woman in red sari let us in (not fat).
3. Room is rustic but not bad. Nice quilt on bed.
4. Four Godiva chocolates (shell, tennis racket, walnut, flower) at nightstand.
5. A bound book of Baba Rhum's philosophy, beginning with the phrase the woman quoted to me.
6. Must rise at 4 a.m.! Glad I'm used to early morning running but I feel sorry for Michael.

Maria tore off a sheet from the notebook and wrote "Must find telephone!" and underneath "Ask about Miranda." She lay down on the cot, drew the quilt over her, and fell asleep.

Michael, on the other hand, was having a more difficult first night. He was put into a room with a man who snored so violently that the cot rattled. Michael sat on his cot, took his notebook out of his pocket, and wrote the following: "For my entire life I have been a pushover. My mother always had the last word until I graduated from high school. Then my father had the last word until I graduated from college. I thought I had broken away at last when I joined the *Vindicator*, and now I'm stuck in this godawful swami joint with a guy who's snoring so loudly that his cot is shaking and I know I'll never get to sleep and they wake you up in this joint at four in the morning. I'm going to get a confession out of Vincent Carpaccio before I leave this place. The best part about this joint so far is the woman who let us in. Maybe I'll get a confession out of her before I leave." Michael put down his notebook, tried a piece of chocolate, and opened *The Teachings of Baba Rhum*.

"Namaste. Good morning! Did you sleep well?" A Chinese woman in a turquoise sari bowed before Maria.

"I haven't quite got the pronunciation of the greeting. Amaste?"

"Namaste," said the woman, laughing. "I salute the god within you. Because this is your first morning at the ashram, perhaps you would like to meditate privately in your room. This morning until six o'clock we are meditating upon the following teaching of Baba Rhum: 'O Swami of Swamis, regarding one who knows that which is uneatable, changeless, beyond destruction and beyond time, how can such a person eat or cause to be eaten?' I am certain that you will come closer to the truth by sunrise, at which time we would like you to join us for breakfast in the main dining room. And after breakfast you may choose the discussion group in which you wish to participate. Today we are pondering two very difficult gastronomic questions: number one, what is the more delicious, the brioche or the croissant, and number two, who makes the best strawberry preserves, the English or the French? You will find Baba Rhum's teaching for this morning on page eighty-seven of the book on your nightstand."

"May I ask one question? Is it possible to meet with the swami's followers after the discussion group?"

"I am sorry, Gentle One, but each of the ashram members must go on to his or her labor following the discussion group. Private conversation will be impossible."

"An old acquaintance of mine—two, in fact—are ashram members. I would just like to say hello to them."

"You will have an opportunity to greet them at breakfast, Gentle One."

"Miranda Kettle and Vincent Carpaccio."

"You are speaking of Tamara Partha Truffle and Gupta Gateau. They are here."

"That's good. And do you have a telephone I might use?"

"We at the ashram rarely have use for a telephone but we keep a public phone for the use of our weekend guests in the main dining room. It may be used from one until three in the afternoon. Namaste. I will see you at breakfast." The woman bowed and quietly shut the door. Maria lay down on her cot and fell asleep.

"Namaste! Greetings to both of you!"

"Vincent Carpaccio?" asked Michael.

"In the past," replied the rotund man in a chartreuse robe. "I am now Gupta Gateau. And you are Michael Weintraub. I knew your father in my past life. Namaste! Namaste!" The former Carpaccio shook Michael's sleeping roommate.

"What is it? What is it?" shouted the man.

"It is morning! Namaste to you both. We will meditate for two hours on the teaching of Baba Rhum which you will find on page eighty-seven of your books by your bedside. Then please join us for breakfast and an after-breakfast discussion group. Namaste! We will see you after six."

Carpaccio shut the door and Michael's roommate groaned. "I can't believe I'm here," said the middle-aged man.

"Why are you here then?"

"Listen, kid. Are you into this swami stuff?"

"Why?"

"Are you into it?"

"No."

"Why are you here then?"

"Why are *you* here?"

"You answer me first, kid."

"Well . . . I'm here for the food. I heard this joint has swell food and I'm a restaurant critic."

The man eyed Michael suspiciously. "Oh yeah? What publication?"

"*Loma Verde Vindicator*, Loma Verde, California."

"I know where Loma Verde is, kid! What do you think I

am, anyway? Well, I'll tell you why I'm here. I'm here to look for my daughter. I have every reason to believe that she was kidnapped by this sect last month."

"That's horrible!"

"Damned right it is! My name's Sam Whitt. I'm from Seattle."

"Michael Weintraub. How do you do?"

"Not well, I don't mind telling you."

"I can imagine."

"No you can't. Not until you've had your own son or daughter. What a godawful place to wake up in. I slept horribly!" Sam Whitt sat up in his cot and stretched.

"*I* was awake until at least two. You seemed to be sleeping fairly well till then, anyway."

"Well, not after then. I'm getting up. I'll be damned if I'll sit in this room for two hours!"

"What are you going to do?"

"I'm going to take a look around this place. I plan to find my daughter today. I'll be damned if I spend another night here." He rose and Michael said, "Hold on. I'll come with you. I'd like to check this place out too. Do you think your daughter knows you're here?"

"It's highly unlikely. She's changed her name two or three times anyway. First she called herself Jennifer, then Wind Spirit or something like that. Now she's got some Indian name. I'd never remember it in a million years. Who was that guy who woke me up? Is he the swami or whatever they call it?"

"No. He's just a disciple. I know him, actually. He used to be a colleague of my father's in Loma Verde."

"That so? What does your father do?"

"He's a doctor."

"You mean that fellow who woke me, that big guy in the greenish robe, is a *doctor*?" asked Sam.

"Well, he was. In his former life, as he put it."

"That's the goddamned disturbing thing about this outfit!

The way they go about, attracting professional people! Do you know that William F. Bockley and William Crockley are here? They're disciples! All my life I've tried to show my daughter— her real name is Ann—that a man or woman could get real gratification in life with a chosen profession. I'm a tax account- ant and I like my work. My wife's and my friends are all pro- fessionals. My wife teaches high school English. Ann has always bucked the tide, wanting to strike out on her own with some vague idea, first about being some kind of artist and then this spiritual stuff. How can I ever persuade here to return when this place is crawling with doctors, lawyers, and celebrities?"

"How old is Ann?"

"She's twenty-five. I suppose that's a little old for me to think I can help her . . ."

"Well, I keep hearing that all these people come up here because the food's so good."

"Ann never cared two cents for food! She's as thin as a rail! I just can't see what attracts her to this place." Sam began to pull on his pants. "I'll tell you this. It's creepy here. It's very weird. I'm at least going to try and talk to Ann and then I'm getting out. Nothing's going to keep *me* here another night."

"You'd better hold off until you've tasted the food."

"Listen, I know your generation is tolerant. Young people are always tolerant. But this is a creepy business. Let me tell you, *very* creepy. Did you see the look on the fellow who woke us? It was very creepy. I don't care if he *was* once your father's colleague."

"But he was, until just last week."

"This country's going to go down the tube."

"You can't base that generalization on one swami joint."

"Listen. When William F. Bockley joins a swami retreat I *know* this country's going down the tube."

"Well, I guess I've just never given William F. Bockley that much credence for anything."

"I don't know anything about the guy, personally. He

could be a fairy for all I know. But he used to stand for old-fashioned American virtues."

"Yeah. Like being rich and having a sailboat."

"That's right! Being rich, having a sailboat—the good life. Now what do you suppose he's doing? He's here worshipping a fat young self-declared swami. That beats all!"

"But what about Crockley? A famous biochemist, a Nobel Prize laureate—what's he doing up here? Personally I think his being here is stranger than Bockley's being here."

"Well, I don't know. Do you want to come have a look around this place with me? Lord, it's dark. I only have a pocket flashlight."

"I'm ready when you are."

"I've got to admit, something smells pretty good," whispered Sam as he opened the door and stepped into the hall.

"Smells like bread baking or something. I've lost my bearings. My colleague spent the night in the women's quarters and I don't think I remember where they are."

"Over there," whispered Sam, pointing to the left. "That's another creepy aspect of this place. Separating the men and the women! Good God, I hear they even separate married weekend guests!"

"Yes, it's weird all right. And do you know the part about input and output?"

"Oh God. The most prurient part of all! And my daughter getting hooked up in a deal like this! My wife and I have asked ourselves over and over where we went wrong."

"You're not responsible for your twenty-five-year-old daughter, Sam."

"I just can't figure it out. I mean if she really loved food, well maybe there might even be a shred of reason for why this place attracts her. But you should see her. Five four and about ninety-five pounds. I mean really tiny. Never had an appetite. Never. My wife and I used to worry so much when she was a baby. She never seemed especially interested in food. Then when she was growing up we used to tell her that if she didn't eat we'd send her to a hospital and they'd hook her up to an I.V. for feeding. She only liked chocolate-flavored milk. I'd have to run out late at night for Nestlé's Quik . . ." Sam's voice trailed off and he looked away. "I just don't understand it. You're probably about the same age as Ann and you seem so much more sensible."

"Ann's probably just looking for a group of friends with something in common."

"Some group of friends! Why can't Ann just look for some normal friends? Jesus, it's dark. I suppose you'd probably like to see what the kitchen looks like since you're writing a story on the food. Why don't we have a look?"

"Why not?"

"What about your colleague? She a writer too?"

"Yeah, I guess you could say that. Actually, the paper sent her up here with me to learn how to, um . . . review a restaurant. Of course, this restaurant, as it were, is unusual. We really don't know what to expect."

"What does your dad think about all of this business, a local doctor joining up and all?"

"Oh, I don't know. I'm sure he thinks it's weird."

"Know anything about that Baba Rhum?"

"He went to Greenwich. His name was Peter Schwartz and he studied philosophy."

"That figures!" snorted Sam. "Philosophy, my foot. What in the hell is philosophy good for?"

"Well, I guess it can be useful when the right questions are discussed."

"And what in the hell are the 'right questions'?"

"Namaste." A young woman bowed before Sam and Michael.

"Young lady, do you know my daughter Ann Whitt? She's twenty-five, about five four, very thin. I'm her dad and I'd just like to say hello to her."

"You will be able to greet Baba Rhum's disciples at breakfast. In the meantime, as both of you are not meditating, I will ask you to join us in the kitchen. We have many mouths to feed."

"I'm not much help in a kitchen," said Sam.

"Me neither!" agreed Michael.

"Gentle Ones, you are here to become one with food. You must fuse yourself with food, bond yourself to it, meditate upon it during preparation to bring out the spiritual vibrations. Come with me, please."

The three walked down a stairway and into a large kitchen. Five men and five women, all dressed in white robes and turbans, stood at counters, chopping vegetables, kneading bread dough, and stirring pots on the two large electric ranges. All of the kitchen helpers were chanting.

"My God!" whispered Michael to Sam. "There he is! William F. Bockley!" Michael walked over to where Bockley stood, stirring at a pan on the electric range.

"Wahee hollandaise sauce, wahee hollandaise sauce, wahee hollandaise sauce," chanted Bockley.

"William Bockley?"

"I am now Raj Béarnaise."

"What are you doing here?"

"I am nurturing the hollandaise sauce while I cook it. I am keeping my vibes and its vibes in a positive mode."

"But what about your writing?"

"I have just finished a book. It is called *God and Output* and it is dedicated to Baba Rhum."

"But what about your family, Mr. Bockley? What about your sailboat? What about your strong stand on escalating nuclear warheads?"

"You are speaking of my past life, Gentle One. I have no further need of it. The vibe life is all-important, ergo, my presence in this kitchen."

Michael looked closely at the former Bockley, who in his

white robes seemed to be rotting in place. The same television face was there, but decay appeared to have crept around its edges. The former Bockley looked like a southern mansion gone to ruin. "May I just ask you this one question, Mr. Bockley?"

"Raj Béarnaise, Gentle One."

"Raj, what happened to that accent you used to have, that sort of hammed-up English accent?"

"I have no need for artifice. I have found spiritual fulfillment. Here are some tomatoes. Please quarter them."

"Mr. Bockley," began Sam, "what about your sailboat? What about the regatta? What about the good life?"

"Yes, I saw myself as a bon vivant and as a sophisticated man of the world. But I realize now that my times on the sailboat were a way of escaping artifice and a prelude to the higher spiritual life via input and output. My next book in fact will be called *Input Ergo Output*. Here are tomatoes for both of you to chop. Please chant 'wahee tomato' as you chop. You will find yourselves developing a spiritual rhythm to the chopping and a closer association to the tomato."

"I just can't bring myself to say that," sputtered Sam as he began to chop a tomato.

"Humility is difficult to achieve. But if I can achieve humility, anyone can. Come now. Wahee tomato, wahee tomato, wahee tomato . . ."

"Wahee tomato, wahee tomato, wahee tomato," chanted Michael.

"Gentle One, forgive me, but I do not hear a spiritual quality to your chant. You sound as though you are the chorus to a rock and roll song."

"I don't feel it at all. I want to leave," said Sam.

"Sit down and have a freshly baked croissant and a cup of Italian roast coffee," said a young woman, who took Sam by the arm and led him to the table. "Raj Béarnaise has simply forgotten the difficulty he himself experienced before he gave himself over to Baba Rhum." The young woman pushed Sam into a chair. "The coffee is delicious, as you will soon find out. Our beans are from Graffeo in San Francisco."

"Oh, wahee wahee tomato, baby! Wahee wahee Wyoming!" chanted Michael.

"Gentle One, again I do not feel a spiritual quality to your chant," admonished the former Bockley.

"Perhaps you would rather help us fertilize our vegetable garden?" asked an older woman sternly.

"Oh no. I'd rather chop tomatoes. Wahee tomato, wahee tomato, wahee tomato . . ."

"That's better," said the former Bockley, and he returned to his stirring and chanting.

"Listen, do you know my daughter, Ann Whitt?" Sam asked the young woman who was pouring coffee.

"We will speak later. We must now meditate on the food, Gentle One." She put her hand on Sam's shoulder, closed her eyes, and whispered "O Swami of Swamis, regarding one who knows that which is uneatable, changeless, beyond destruction and beyond time, how can such a person eat or cause to be eaten? Please meditate upon this, Gentle One."

Sam meditated, or appeared to meditate: he was staring into his coffee cup. The former Bockley, having taken Michael in hand, was chanting "Wahee tomato" in unison with his new spiritual protégé. Michael appeared to enjoy chanting and was swaying from side to side as he chopped the tomatoes. The former Bockley, however, remained motionless as he chopped. At one point he leaned over and whispered to Michael, "We could make this chant into a fugue but I can't persuade the others that a fugue has spiritual value."

At dawn, one of the kitchen workers proclaimed, "The sun is rising. Let us give thanks for another day of food. O Swami of Swamis, when one gives up all the stomach's longings, being happy with the stomach abiding in the self, then he or she is called wise. Let us bring forth the morning feast."

Michael was given a large tray of brioches and Sam a

large tray of croissants to carry into the dining room, where fifty persons seated at two long tables awaited breakfast. "At least they don't separate the men from the women during mealtime," whispered Michael to Sam. "Do you see your daughter?"

"No. Not yet. Well, my God, there she is. Over there." Sam pointed to a woman in a blue sari who was laughing and pouring coffee at her table. "It looks like she's gained five or so pounds. I must say, it's an improvement."

"She looks like a real nice girl, Sam."

"Put the breads on the table," instructed the former Bockley.

"Is Baba Rhum here?" asked Michael.

"The swami only appears in the evening," replied a woman carrying a tray with plates of eggs Benedict.

"I've got to talk to my daughter. Ann! Ann!"

Sam's daughter looked up. "Namaste, Gentle One," she said calmly. "I am Chitra Marzipan. Welcome. Did you have a pleasant sleep?"

"Of course not!" One hundred eyes looked at Sam. "We'll be able to talk privately, I assume."

"Yes, Gentle One. We will talk after breakfast if you wish."

"Well, I wish it, Ann. I haven't made this trip down here for my health."

"I assume you have come for your spiritual health." Everyone at the table laughed. Maria walked into the dining room and the former Ann said, "Namaste, Gentle One. Please sit down." Maria looked at Michael and sat down next to Miranda Kettle.

"Namaste!" said Miranda. "How wonderful it is to see you here! You are Professor Forsythe's daughter, aren't you?"

"Yes. Hello, Dr. Kettle."

"Please call me Tamara Partha Truffle."

"Why?"

"Because it is the name which Baba Rhum has given to

me. If you should decide to stay, Baba Rhum will give you a name as well. Namaste, Michael Weintraub. I used to know your father."

"Hello, Dr. Kettle."

"I would like you to call me Tamara Partha Truffle."

"What's wrong with Miranda?" asked Michael.

"It is a part of my past. I am here now."

"But what about Pete and Susan? What about your friends like Flora? How could you just leave everyone like that?"

"Gentle One," said the former Miranda, more calmly than Maria had expected, "many things have happened which have brought me closer to the god within myself."

"But what about Dr. Carpaccio?" asked Maria.

"Gupta Gateau? What do you want to know about him?"

"I want to know why he just took off and left his family and his practice all behind!" whispered Maria loudly.

"I suggest you direct your question to Gupta Gateau," replied the former Miranda serenely.

"Let us pray," said a man's voice at the head of the table. "O Swami of Swamis, who knows that the wise rejoice and give thanks each morning for another day of feasting, shed the light of your deeper knowledge upon us that we may learn to recognize the god within us through input and output. Namaste, Gentle Ones. I especially would like to welcome our weekend guests. Would our weekend guests please stand?" Michael rose first, then Maria, and finally, after some hesitation, Sam. "Welcome, Gentle Ones. Welcome to our ashram and our glorious food. Let us all welcome our weekend guests!"

"Namaste!" exclaimed everyone in the room.

"Please be seated, Gentle Ones. We will all have the opportunity to talk with our guests following breakfast. Enjoy!"

Michael, at the other table, had seated himself next to the former Carpaccio and across the table from the former biochemist William Crockley. "I must say," began Michael, "this breakfast is really good, but is it so good that you guys would leave your careers behind to live here?"

"My past life no longer interests me," said the former Carpaccio.

"But why? You were a prominent internist. I don't get it. What about you, Professor Crockley?"

"My name is Partha Paté," replied the former Crockley. "I am here to purify my sperm."

"Your sperm? But what about biochemistry? Maybe you could do some work up here."

"I have thought about researching the effect of semiconductors on food."

"But what about your family? What about the woman who was artificially inseminated by your sperm? What about the baby? Hey, and what about the sperm bank? Are you still donating to the sperm bank?"

"I have made many mistakes in my past life."

"What about your views that blacks are smarter than whites? What about Asians? You never said anything about Asians." The Chinese woman in the turquoise sari stared at the former Crockley.

"I made many mistakes until I accepted Baba Rhum as my master. I know now that we are all One with nature, and that we must balance our energies with that of the seasons and the moon's cycles. Raj Béarnaise, the hollandaise sauce is excellent! Raj is becoming a swami saucier, you know."

"Is that so? I always thought you sauced things up a bit, Mr. Bockley."

"Raj," corrected the former Bockley. "Yes, I seem to have been given a gift, a divine gift for sauces. I praise the god within me for this gift, because sauces are such an integral part of our cuisine. You are not eating, Gentle One."

Michael took a bite and said, "But, Dr. Carpaccio . . ."

"Gupta Gateau," corrected the former Carpaccio.

"Gupta. What about the Eele investigating committee?

What about that poor woman who was left with a tool sewn inside her by a callous and ruthless, not to mention lousy, doctor? Doesn't she deserve to have you present your findings before the Loma Verde Clinic board of directors, Gupta Gateau or no Gupta Gateau?"

"Gentle One," replied the former Carpaccio, smiling, "the vibe life is an alternative to a tool in the body."

"Hold on! You haven't been here one week and you were a doctor for almost twenty years. You're not going to tell me that you've changed overnight and that you no longer give a damn about people who are sick or need help, or about the state of medicine!"

"Silence, Gentle Ones. Baba Rhum is here to announce an important event," said a woman, rushing into the dining room. Within seconds, Baba Rhum walked into the room. "My God!" exclaimed Sam, who was seated at Maria's table. "He's got Henry Warringer with him!"

Baba Rhum, a tall, fat, thirty-five-year-old man in orange robes, stood beside the fat and ugly Henry Warringer. "I can't believe this," mumbled Michael. "This goes beyond my wildest dreams."

"Namaste, Gentle Ones. Please greet our new ashram member Partha Henry. Partha Henry, may I present your fellow ashram members?"

"Namaste, Gentle Ones. It's perfectly obvious why I'm here. Everyone knows that food is all and it's ludicrous to believe otherwise." The former Warringer sat at Maria's table and began to eat. Baba Rhum bowed and disappeared.

"Where does Baba Rhum eat?" Maria asked Miranda.

"He eats alone in his rooms. It is necessary for him to be alone so that he can meditate upon the spiritual meaning of each food ingredient."

"What about Henry Warringer? Aren't you surprised he's up here?" whispered Maria.

"I can only give thanks that Partha Henry has accepted

Baba Rhum," replied Miranda.

Within seconds, Michael was at Partha Henry's side. "Mr. Warringer, I'm Michael Weintraub from the *Loma Verde Vindicator*. May I ask you a few questions?"

"Well, young man, I don't usually do this sort of thing, but why not?"

"After breakfast and the discussion groups," interjected Miranda.

"I just can't believe that you have given up all the stuff you believe in, like the exercise of political power!" said Sam Whitt.

"I believe in the power of the god within me. I always have."

"But just last week I saw you on TV, talking about taking a tougher military and political stance against the Russians," said Maria.

"I believe in peace through strength, and I believe in food because it gives me strength. Young man," he said, looking at Michael, "I will talk with you at length after breakfast. We don't need to discuss the issues. It's perfectly obvious to everyone that the croissant is superior to the brioche. Why else would it enjoy such a period of international expansion?"

"Excuse me, Partha Henry," said Miranda, very upset, "we always participate in the discussion groups following breakfast and there are no exceptions."

"We will all have an opportunity for social talk following the discussion groups," said Ann Whitt. "I want to talk to my father."

"Raj Béarnaise," called Partha Henry, "this hollandaise sauce is as good as the Four Seasons'!"

"Yes, I have finally found my true gift after years of searching."

"The only search is for our highest spiritual attainment via input and output," continued the former Carpaccio. "And I might add, my dear Michael, that your eggs Benedict are getting very cold."

"My head is reeling," whispered Michael to Maria after breakfast. "So much is happening so fast. I've got to get to a telephone."

"You can only use the telephone between one and three. It's one of the rules around here. And by the way, as it is because of me that you're here, I think I should get a crack at interviewing Henry Warringer."

"Not on your life, Forsythe. I got to him first and he's promised me the interview. Anyway, it's only fair as I'm senior. You'd better stick to your story. You're trying to interrogate Carpaccio and Miranda, remember? And if they're closemouthed for the time being, take a crack at Bockley or Crockley or what the hell? How about a human interest story? 'Sam Whitt's Search for His Daughter'? There's a dozen stories up here. I can't believe it. I've got to find the telephone."

"Michael, I tried unsuccessfully to use the telephone this morning to call Ted."

"Ted?"

"My friend Ted, the dancer."

"Why would you bother to call him? You ought to be with Miranda or Carpaccio right now, getting your story. What's this shit about calling Ted?"

"Well, who do you want to call?"

"I want to call Ben! He should know what we've got up here. Suck air, Kim Blakely!"

"Michael, I think we'd better go into one of the discussion groups."

"I'm going into Henry Warringer's!"

"Well, that's fine, Michael. But what about the story? You've told me all along that you're here to help me with the Clinic story."

"Forsythe, I'm here to get a phenomenal scoop about Henry Warringer which will further my career, and then to get that little blonde in the red sari into bed."

"You're disgusting. I don't want any part of you."

"You're not getting any part of me!"

"Michael, I think you're a creep. Bug off and leave me alone." Maria began to walk away.

"Hey, Forsythe," called Michael. "You'd look real good in a sari. You move your ass in a most provocative manner."

"Gentle One." Michael looked up to see the former Bockley standing next to him. His arms were folded over his chest. "Gentle One, you seem to have difficulty comprehending that this ashram is a spiritual retreat. I am sure this is the last time I will need to remind you of the fact. Come with me. We will go into the brioche discussion group."

"Listen, Raj. I'm not big on brioche."

"Well, I have a secret for you, Gentle One: neither am I. But Partha Henry, with whom I shared many similar defects in the dark past before my acceptance of Baba Rhum, will be in the brioche group. Perhaps he desires to seek its expansion into the consciousness of Americans. Come, let us join the group. I believe your friend, the young woman with whom you were just speaking, will join the croissant group."

"That's fine, Raj. But I need to use a telephone."

"Not until one o'clock, Gentle One. Come with me."

"If you had read my too-little-known but prescient book *French Power* which I wrote thirty years ago, you would not be surprised today that the croissant is in a superior position to the brioche," said Partha Henry, who was leading the brioche discussion group. "I think that any show of goodwill on the part of Americans will be interpreted as a sign of weakness by the French. Therefore, I propose American bakers refuse to bake either brioches or croissants, and, more important, that we set our political policies in a manner which includes strategic defense of American cuisine. I propose we begin a buildup of bakeries in France."

"But, Partha Henry," gasped the former Bockley, "the homeland of this ashram is Paris."

"We must change this strategy, obviously." The discussion group burst into chaotic protest.

"Partha Henry, Baba Rhum has accepted Paris as our homeland and all of us here have accepted Baba Rhum. Even you," said the former Bockley.

"I am simply stating the obvious, which I stated some thirty years ago. I am sorry that you are no longer aware of what is so readily apparent." Partha Henry walked out of the room and Michael followed him quickly.

"Does your move to Baba Rhum's ashram indicate that you have left the American political arena?"

"I have merely rearranged my priorities. I agree with Schwartz that food is the important issue, but I must convince him that American gastronomical interests must not be ignored. We have ten, possibly fifteen years, to turn this French food invasion around. But of course I wrote all about this thirty years ago. By the way, young man, what are you doing here?"

Michael hesitated. "Well, I'm not a member or anything."

"I can see *that.* You're a journalist, but if you seek to mock my conversion to the higher truth via input and output in print, I warn you, you will attract more people to my new view. Americans take me seriously, as you obviously know by the way you are following me around like a little dog." Michael opened his mouth to protest, but before he could get a word out, the former Warringer had disappeared.

"Dr. Kettle?" asked Maria.

"Tamara Partha Truffle, Gentle One."

"Tamara. You seem so happy here. Are you happier here than at Greenwich?"

"Gentle One, Greenwich is my past."

"Tamara, are you aware that your daughter Susan has given a story to the *Loma Verde Vindicator*, 'My Life With a Swami Mommy'?"

The former Miranda rearranged the folds in her blue sari. "The *Loma Verde Vindicator* has always sought to slight Greenwich University and its residents. But that is part of my past."

"Miranda, before I left for Oregon I had a physical with Joe Kuhl."

"I know Dr. Kuhl. He was my doctor before I came to the ashram. I believe he and his wife are honest and hardworking. They are sincere in their desires to help their patients, but until they discover the gods within themselves they can never help themselves."

"Do you know about Joe Kuhl's TV show on PBS?"

"Searching for ego gratification is a very big problem for many persons in Loma Verde. Perhaps we ought to turn our attention to the discussion. Gupta Gateau will lead the discussion. He is very knowledgeable about croissants. He has taken over many of the bakery duties."

"Were you in love with Dr. Carpaccio before you came to the ashram?" whispered Maria.

Tamara née Miranda smiled. "Gentle One, I love everyone and everything."

"Tamara, were you aware that Dr. Carpaccio was on an investigating committee with Joe and Jean Kuhl and that

Carpaccio knew more about Eele's underhanded activities than either of the Kuhls? Did you know that there is a woman in Loma Verde named Peach Kling who has filed a malpractice suit which contains such strong evidence against Eele that he has been temporarily suspended from the Clinic? Did you know that Dr. Carpaccio risks a legal suit himself because he is withholding information that the court needs?"

"Gentle One," sighed the former Miranda, "this is to be a discussion about croissants, not Clinic scandals."

"There are no croissants in jail, and that's where Carpaccio's going to end up if he doesn't report his whole investigation before the Clinic board of directors."

The former Carpaccio, leading the discussion group in the front of the room, stopped talking. "Gentle One, it seems you persist in discussing the past. Therefore I believe we should open the discussion to include the topic of responsibility. You see, our guest is from the same community in which Tamara Truffle and I once lived. In fact, many of us at the ashram have spent some time at Greenwich. Baba Rhum received his first spiritual callings at Greenwich. So, in fact, though Greenwich University is overrun by massive egos, which are the result of no spiritual tradition and the resulting evil complications, Greenwich has a spiritual significance for all of us at the ashram. Our guest has been speaking of a particularly evil force in the community of Greenwich and of Loma Verde, a doctor who has probably done more to undercut the respectability of the medical profession than any other person. Now, as Tamara Partha Truffle and our guest know, I was, before my spiritual enlightenment, on a committee to investigate this man's—this doctor's—unethical practices. This man has made many, many mistakes. And though this man may be saved from himself by discovering the god within him, we are wise not to grieve over those who do not deserve grief. The wise do not grieve over the dead or the living."

"What are you saying, Dr. Carpaccio?" asked Maria sharply.

"Gentle One, I am saying that this person of whom we speak does not exist."

"Namaste," exclaimed the former Miranda.

"So you are saying that Duke Eele no longer exists? I don't believe this! Why, he's no more than a bungler, a . . . a . . . butcher, a common criminal! The two of you know more about Duke Eele's unethical practices than anyone. I happen to know, Miranda, that you conducted your own personal investigation into Duke Eele's Greenwich practice!"

"Gentle One," replied the former Miranda sharply, "the man of whom you speak does not exist. We will discuss him no further."

"Michael!" shouted Maria. Michael walked into the room and sat next to Maria.

"Calm down," he whispered. "Separate yourself a little."

"Namaste, Gentle One," said the former Miranda to Michael. "And what have you in the brioche discussion group learned today?"

"We learned that Partha Henry wants to change Baba Rhum's strategies. Partha Henry wants a buildup of American bakeries in Paris that will specialize in American cuisine."

"What?" exclaimed Miranda, visibly shaken.

"We must have a talk with Partha Henry," said Carpaccio. "But for now we're discussing the question of responsibility."

"I'm dying to hear your interpretation," said Michael dryly.

"Well," began Carpaccio, but he started to laugh. "No, it will not do to discuss these issues with you, our guests, until you have accepted Baba Rhum into your life."

"Well then, I guess we'll just have to accept Baba Rhum into our lives," said Michael.

"What?" gasped Maria.

"Shhhh," whispered Michael. "Namaste to all of you. Maria and I have many soul-searching questions, and a walk in the good, fresh Oregon air is probably just what we need to clear our minds and . . . open up our spirits."

"Namaste!" exclaimed several of the members of the discussion group.

"Come on, Maria." Michael pulled on her arm.

"What in the hell are you . . .?"

"Shut up, Forsythe, and keep walking. I think this door will get us outside." Michael opened a heavy wood door onto which was taped a poster advertising Baba Rhum's latest book *Overeat: A Personal Documentary of Input.*

"Oh shit," moaned Maria.

"No, that's output."

"God, Michael, what are you talking about?"

"Let's join up! We can be members by tonight! All you have to say is that you're willing to accept Baba Rhum into your life and then work around the ashram. That's it! We can stay here and profile Warringer, Crockley, Bockley. We can get all the information out of Carpaccio and Miranda that we want! They'll trust us if we show that we care enough to join up. God. I can't believe no one else has thought to do this. *This* is what investigative reporting is all about! I can't believe my luck!"

"Michael, what are you talking about? Are you saying that we should suddenly act like we're really serious about this place and that they'll just let us join up by tonight? And then we'll get a bunch of stories, and then we'll just split? Oh, come on! People up here aren't going to buy that one. Besides, I'm no actress!"

"Forsythe, remember when your father told you that Santa Claus brought all your Christmas presents? Remember? How old were you when you finally figured out it was a sham?"

"Well, I have to admit, I was a little naive. I probably didn't catch on till I was eight or nine."

"Well then, think of all those years your dad faked the Santa Claus bit. He could do it because it made him happy to see you happy. And you can fake it for a few days because you're going to be so happy when all your stories are printed and you become a famous journalist. All because you spent a few days at the old ashram! I can just see those UPI by-lines, 'Weintraub and Forsythe'!"

"Why Weintraub and Forsythe? Why not Forsythe and Weintraub? If it wasn't for me you wouldn't be here!"

"And if it wasn't for me you wouldn't stay here for all these great stories. So fair's fair. I even like this place! I like these trees, this nice clean air. It's like a vacation with all of these unbelievable stories thrown in. I'm calling Ben up and telling him the plan. I'll do Warringer and Crockley. You can take a stab at Bockley . . ."

"Michael! Don't forget about Carpaccio and Miranda. It's not going to be easy to get anything out of them with that swami line about Eele no longer existing for them."

"Forsythe, they've only been here a few days themselves. They haven't changed. You'll get your information. It's guaranteed. God, and the food is so good. I loved those eggs Benedict! God, you're even looking pretty good up here, Forsythe. This good country air is doing wonders for your complexion."

"I hadn't realized you were so up on dermatology. Did you learn something from Jean Kuhl?"

"That Jean Kuhl is a juicy tomato. Wahee tomato! Maybe I owe it to myself to learn something from her."

"I want this Eele story, Michael."

"You'll get it, Forsythe. You'll get it. Now here is my plan. We'll go back, act humble, and say we want to join."

"They'll never believe it."

"Oh yes they will. I can be *the* most ingratiating son-of-a-bitch you ever saw."

"I *know*, Michael. Has it ever occurred to you to go to medical school?"

"Forsythe, I was *going* to let you in on my Partha Henry by-line. You'd better follow the program, since I'm the only one who appears to have a program. What time is it? I'm

114

calling Ben as soon as I can."

"I'm only following the program because you seem to know what you're doing. I never dreamed we'd be seeing Warringer up here."

"Let's hope he stays up here for the rest of his life. He's already causing problems at the ashram. Once a Warringer, always a Warringer."

"Gentle Ones." Maria and Michael turned around quickly to see Raj Béarnaise, the former Bockley, walking toward them.

"Oh, hello, Raj. You're just in time. Maria and I have been talking very seriously about Baba Rhum."

"Yes, Gentle One, I believe I understand what you are attempting, in your youthful way, to tell me. I've seen these kinds of turnarounds all of my life. You're young, you're full of spirit, your tendencies are to be iconoclastic, ergo, your comments and attitudes in the kitchen before breakfast. But iconoclasts are simply failed spiritual disciples. And you, Gentle One, are seeking the higher truth through input and output. I saw the way, once you put your mind to it, you relished your eggs Benedict, croissants, and Macedonian fruit salad. But young lady, you are not iconoclastic. And I have not had the opportunity to notice whether your appetite and spiritual convictions are one."

"One what?"

"One bond, Gentle One. I can see that your companion Michael has a true yearning, a true hunger for the Baba Rhum path toward salvation. But you? Are you here only to be with your friend?"

"What?"

"I am saying, Gentle One, are you here simply because you love Michael, or are you here to find the god within yourself?"

"I assure you, Mr. Bockley, that I'm not here because I love Michael."

"Forgive me, Maria, but I was under the impression that

CLINIC

you were only following the man you loved, and that you would be willing to accept Baba Rhum into your life only because Michael desires to accept him."

"Well, I confess to having been a big influence in Maria's life," said Michael.

"You have not!"

"Oh, Maria, come now. You know you want to accept Baba Rhum into your life. Don't you?"

"I do. But not because of you."

"But the both of you seek to find peace and inner knowledge at the ashram. Let me tell you out front, as it were, the work is tough and the hours are the worst in the entire business. Running a three-star restaurant and spiritual retreat requires that Baba Rhum's disciples rise at four o'clock each morning, and work very hard. We can never allow our standards to slip. And of course there is our all-consuming desire to attain self-knowledge via input and output. So you see, you are asking to have your acceptance granted at the toughest ashram in the world. We won't put you through any tests. The mere fact that you have found yourself here is proof enough of your sincere inner searchings. I will take you to Baba Rhum directly."

Maria looked at Michael. He returned her glance with a "leave it to me" expression, and the three walked back to the house.

"I must inform Baba Rhum of your acceptance because we will need to plan the celebration feast immediately."

"The what?" asked Michael.

"The celebration feast. Following the granting of the acceptance of new ashram members, we always have a feast. But you will see for yourselves. Come now. Come on." Raj Béarnaise knocked on a door.

"Please come in," said a muffled voice, over jazz music.

"Baba Rhum must be in headstand position," whispered Bockley. He opened the door slowly and bowed. "Namaste,

Master. I bring you two wise ones who have accepted you into their lives and seek to celebrate the gods within themselves at the ashram."

"Just a minute." Baba Rhum bent his knees and slowly lowered his legs. He turned off his tape cassette.

"So you're a fan of Miles Davis? So am I!" said Michael.

"Gentle One," whispered Bockley. "Baba Rhum is the first to speak."

"Oh, sorry. I didn't mean in any way to offend you, Baba Rhum."

"So. You wish to accept me into your lives? And both of you. Well, let me see . . ." Baba Rhum walked to his desk and picked up a notebook. "Food and restaurant critics for the *Loma Verde Vindicator*? Ha ha ha. Loma Verde. Yes, Loma Verde and I know each other very well. You are both food critics?"

"That's right," replied Michael hastily.

"So the *Loma Verde Vindicator* can afford two restaurant critics?" Baba Rhum eyed Michael suspiciously.

"That's right."

"Well, let's face it. Stomach is big business now. Everyone wants to know how to have a peaceful stomach. Good! Since you're both writers you can help me with the editing of my new book *The Stomach of France*, which will no doubt become the definitive gastronomical history of our ashram's homeland."

"That's a relief because I'm no good in a kitchen!" said Michael.

"You will also work in the kitchen. Both of you. The idea is to create a closer bond between you and the food you eat. You understand the importance of input and output?"

"I have a close relationship with both," replied Michael.

"What about you?" Baba Rhum asked Maria.

"Oh, I too. Everything is input and output."

"Very good! We must prepare the celebration feast. Raj Béarnaise, please instruct the kitchen that we will have the feast following my talk in the dining room this evening."

"Right away, Baba Rhum. Namaste." The former Bockley bowed and left the room.

"Well, my children. Come now. Sit down. This must be a very happy day for you, for you have renounced all superfluous and artificial things for lives of peaceful stomachs and the celebrating of the gods within you. Congratulations and Namaste! Your new names must be decided. You," he said, pointing to Michael, "are like the sun, which in Sanskrit is *ha*. You are like two suns. You are now Partha Ha Ha. And you, my dear," he said, smiling at Maria, "are like a yellow golden-haired monkey."

"No, I'm not!"

"Yes, you are. I shall call you Marika, the yellow golden-haired monkey." Michael turned to Maria and laughed.

"Partha Ha Ha, you are well named! You see, we swamis have our own senses of humor too. I suggest, Marika, that you endeavor to develop a sense of humor about yourself. You have spent the past twenty or so years being a beautiful female, and naturally it has crippled your sense of humor. But as Marika we will help you find it. Namaste, Partha Ha Ha. Namaste, Marika. Please return to the main dining room and announce your glad tidings to the other ashram members!" Baba Rhum clasped Michael, then Maria, and pushed them out of his office. He shut the door and again Maria and Michael heard the Miles Davis tape.

"We're in!" whispered Michael. "I can't believe it! I've got to call Ben. We'll have to do our writing in the evening and our collaborating during the free time after the discussion group. Then I can phone the stories into the *Vindicator*. Oh God! I can't believe our luck!"

"It's not going to be as easy as you think to write, collaborate, *or* phone in stories."

"You're just mad because he's calling you a monkey!"

"I am not! I'm trying to look at it realistically, which is more than you're doing. There's one phone at this place and people all over who could overhear the conversations."

"Well, those are the chances we have to take to get a great story. Right, Maria? I mean Marika?"

"Partha Jack-Ass," she replied.

"Mike! Mike!" Sam Whitt grabbed Michael's arm and whispered, "What's this I hear about you and that girl you're with joining up?"

"I can't explain now," said Michael.

"So you *do* believe in this stuff."

"Sam, goddamn it, I told you I'll explain it to you another time."

"Just tell me one thing. Do you believe in all this crap or not?"

"Sam, for Chrissake, I told you, I'll explain everything later."

"So you're not really a restaurant critic. You're one of those investigative reporters. I'm right, aren't I?"

"Sam, *please*! Knock it off for now. Have you spoken to your daughter?"

"I have. She's more nutty than ever. Warringer's one I can't believe is here. Bockley, well, I always thought he was a fake, and Crockley, very strange guy with that sperm bank deal and all, but Warringer? I can't figure Warringer out. He's really gone off the deep end, hasn't he?"

"Well, he's still the same old Henry Warringer if you ask me. He's already trying to change the ashram's major policies, as he calls them. He wants to feature American food at the ashram and expand it into Europe."

"I thought he was more into politics."

"Just looking at him makes you realize he's always been into food."

"He *is* a real little five-by-five. Just looking at him makes me wonder how we Americans ever took him seriously in the first place." Sam heaved a deep sigh.

"What about Ann?"

"Oh, that girl is so mixed up. And now with people like Warringer up here, how can I ever convince her to come home?"

"You'd think that the mere fact that people like Warringer *are* up here is a reason to leave. I mean, that's what I'd think if I were your daughter."

"So you *are* an investigative reporter. All I ask is that you don't mention my name. But I suppose with all of these famous guys floating around you'd scarcely think about me and my problems."

"Sam, I'd really like to do a story about someone like you who's trying to persuade your daughter to leave. Of course I'd change your name. But I suppose you'll be leaving today, won't you?"

"No, I'm going to stick it one more day. I'm going to try to convince Ann that she doesn't want to be in a place like this with people like Warringer. I have to tell you right now, I was counting on your helping me to convince her that she's in the wrong place, but I guess you don't want to blow your cover."

"Listen, Sam, I'll try to talk to your daughter. Maria and I only plan to be here for a few days. I haven't even talked to my editor yet. He might want me to stay up here as long as I can take it. I mean, Henry Warringer! Now that's quite a story. And Bockley, Crockley, not to mention the Loma Verde doctor who jumped the ship with the Chancellor of Greenwich, just to avoid giving evidence against a sleazy doctor!"

"What's this Baba Rhum look like?"

"Well, let's see. I guess you could say he looks like an overweight Greenwich professor. You know he taught briefly at Harvard before returning to Greenwich to become enlightened or whatever. When I met him he was listening to a

Miles Davis tape and doing a headstand. Come to think of it, he looked just about the way I thought he'd look."

"He sounds like a real snake-oil salesman if you ask me."

"Well, of course he's a real snake-oil salesman!"

"I wouldn't be surprised if he changed directions himself midstream."

"Neither would I. But Baba Rhum is a really bright guy. Ergo, as our friend Raj Béarnaise would say, all the famous people crawling around this joint."

"While you were away, talking to the swami I suppose, I heard a rumor that Dr. Barney Christian, the famous heart surgeon, will be arriving tonight."

"There's an ass for you. And it doesn't surprise me in the least that *he'd* be coming." Michael looked at his watch. "I suppose they make a big deal about lunch in this joint." A woman passed Sam and Michael. "Oh, ma'am?" asked Michael.

"Namaste, Gentle One," replied the woman. "I am Chitra Coriander."

"Chitra, when is lunch served?"

"There will be no lunch today, in preparation for the celebratory feast to welcome you and Marika into the ashram. And we are happy that you, Gentle One," she said, bowing before Sam, "will be able to join us for the festivities." Sam looked away. Chitra Coriander bowed again and disappeared.

"Sam, remember: keep as cool as a cucumber about all of this. I'll try to talk to Ann. I've got to try to use the telephone now." Michael slipped through the hall, avoiding a man in robes who was shouting, "Namaste, Partha Ha Ha!"

Michael began to dial Ben's home number, when the former Bockley slapped his back. "So the festivities are set!" exclaimed Raj Béarnaise.

"Mr. Bockley . . . Raj . . . that's great. I'm really looking forward to the celebration but now I've got to make an important telephone call. You just can't join an ashram without letting at least one of your loved ones know. Didn't you at least call your wife before you decided to join?"

"Bubbles? Well, it's no use calling her. The last I heard of her she was paddling around in a canoe at Lake Tahoe, California, with Gil Glass."

"Well, I'm sorry to hear that, Bill, er, Raj."

"That's why the spiritual life is all-important to me now."

"Raj, after I make my telephone call I'd like to talk with you a bit."

"I'm sorry, Partha Ha Ha, but you must spend the remainder of the afternoon in meditative solitude. You must garner spiritual and physical strength for the festivities early this evening."

"These festivities sound fairly intense."

"To be sure, they are. To begin, all of us wear blindfolds once the feast is on the table. We have a forty-minute period in which we eat joyously. Then we lie on the ground to rest for ten minutes. And then we feast again—the Feast of Highest Input—for twenty minutes."

"All blindfolded?"

"Yes, Partha Ha Ha. When one is blindfolded one becomes childlike, ergo, more spiritual. You will see. I will leave you now to make your telephone call, and then may I suggest you return to your room for quiet reflection until the feast."

"How will I know when the feast begins?"

"Someone will come for you."

"Mr. Bockley . . . Raj . . . I have to admit, I sort of miss that weird accent you used to have."

Raj smiled and bowed. "Until the feast," he replied, and he disappeared.

Michael crept into the women's quarters. "Maria? Maria? Forsythe?"

"I'm in here, Michael!"

Michael slowly opened a door. "Don't worry for now. They're all in the kitchen or somewhere, preparing for this big feast we're having tonight. Did you hear about it? The bit about being blindfolded and all?"

"Yes, I did. This is really a weird place. I agree with your buddy Sam Whitt. This place gives me the creeps. Where is Sam, by the way?"

"I don't know. They've probably pressed him into working. He probably doesn't have to meditate since he's not joining up. Oh, I talked to Ben, his machine that is."

"I talked to my dad and asked him to call Ted."

"Why don't you do yourself a favor and forget Ted?"

"Mind your own business, Michael."

"If Ted is so big in your life, how come I never saw him hanging around the paper waiting for you? If Ted is really your man, how come you were always going out to dinner with Ben?"

"Ted dances in the evening. He's a ballet dancer."

"Forsythe, I cannot believe you. You know, this ashram might really be the place for you. Just think, no sex."

"Michael, why do you always have to be so mean? What have I done to you to make you act like this?"

Michael paused. "Nothing, Forsythe. I think you're a real sweet girl. I just don't think you know what you want out of life and you're just trying the newspaper business on like a new dress."

"Michael, do *you* know what you want out of life?"

"Gee, no, Maria, but now that we're at the ashram maybe we can find out what life's all about!" The two started to laugh, but stopped abruptly when they heard a sound from the hall. "Look out the door, Forsythe. Tell me what you see."

"I don't see anything."

"Then if the coast is clear I'd better get back to my room. They'd probably serve me at the feast if they saw me in the women's quarters."

"What *is* their view on men and women?" asked Maria.

"Eating is like fucking. That's what it looks like to me."

"I just want to go running. Oregon is known for being the perfect running place."

"Forget the running for a few days. Nobody runs up here at the ashram, for God's sake."

"Well, if I just eat like a pig I'll get fat!"

"When everyone has his or her blindfold on tonight, no one will know whether you ate or not. So don't eat if you don't want to."

"But the food's so good here!" whined Maria.

"Food, the new temptation! I'm going to suggest it to Baba Rhum for one of his talks. You know, it used to be sex, but the new temptation is now food."

"You'd better get going. I guess I'll see you at the feast," said Maria.

"First Baba Rhum talks."

"Michael, don't tell Ben about Baba Rhum naming me after a monkey."

"I think it's cute!" said Michael. He looked both ways and crept out of her room.

At six o'clock in the evening, the ashram members and their guest, Sam Whitt, gathered in the main dining room to await Baba Rhum. "He always gives his most spiritually uplifting talk before a celebration feast," whispered Raj Béarnaise to Michael and Sam. "Happy Heart, Partha Henry, and Partha Andy will of course be joining us tonight."

"Who is Partha Andy?" asked Michael.

"Partha Andy was Andy Borall, the former New York avant-garde artist. I salute the god within both him and me that Partha Andy will no longer be functioning in that capacity," said the former Bockley.

"*Andy Borall* is up here? I can't believe it!" exclaimed Michael.

"Miracles do occur, my dear Partha Ha Ha, and let us face it, Partha Andy has always found himself in the highest places of output."

"Andy Borall!" whispered Michael to Maria as they left the room. "I'll just bet he's here to make a documentary film. Who'd ever believe I'd be featured in a deal with a crew like this? Warringer, Borall, Barney Christian, and Michael Weintraub!"

"And Maria Forsythe! I'll bet Andy Borall is faking it too. I'll smoke him out! But Michael, with so many celebrities here, we're losing track of our original mission—getting the goods on Carpaccio and Miranda!"

"Oh God, my head is spinning. Look, there's the famous three now. Look at Borall! He looks like he's about a hundred. So does Barney Christian. I thought Christian was younger looking. Come to think of it, every time I read about one of his big operations in the paper, the patient always died. No wonder Barney Christian looks half dead himself."

"Namaste," exclaimed Baba Rhum as he met his novitiates in a small room adjoining the main dining room. "This is a very happy evening for all of us. Here are your robes, Gentle Ones. And Marika, here is your sari. Please go into the restroom to change into your sari and meet us in here in five minutes. Chitra Coriander will help you with your sari." Chitra Coriander and Maria left the room and the men began to change into their robes. "You will notice that your robes are white," continued Baba Rhum. "I realize it is difficult at first to maintain the celibate state of mind and body which is required at the ashram, and we have found that the color white often promotes a purity of spirit."

"*I* have *always* been pure!" snapped the former Andy Borall, stamping his foot.

"I realize it is also difficult to admit past mistakes. We

need not discuss them, for all of us know only too well how we have abused the god within us. But you have come to the ashram to regain the spirituality with which you were born. Ah Marika, you have returned, and in good time."

"Why doesn't *she* have to wear white?" asked Michael, pointing to Maria's yellow sari.

"Marika is like the yellow golden-haired monkey. And women do not seem to have the same difficulties adjusting to the higher celibate state as men."

"In my limited experience," said the former Borall, "that hasn't been the case."

"Your experience has been very limited indeed," replied Baba Rhum. "Come with me now. It is time to present you to the ashram."

The novitiates fell into single file and walked into the main dining room with Baba Rhum. They stood in front of the room and Baba Rhum announced, "Gentle Ones, namaste. May I present the new brothers and sister of our ashram. Partha Henry, Partha Andy, Partha Ha Ha, Happy Heart, and Marika the yellow golden-haired monkey." Maria gave Baba Rhum an exasperated look which he pretended not to notice. "Please welcome your new brothers and sister." The ashram members rose and applauded. Sam Whitt, sitting in the back of the room, looked more distressed than ever. "Please be seated, Gentle Ones. And make room for our new members. Before I begin my talk I would like to announce the sponsors of each new member. Each sponsor will spend the evening in meditation with each new member. Partha Henry, your sponsor is Partha Paté." The former biochemist Crockley waved to the former Warringer. "Partha Andy, your sponsor will be Raj Béarnaise." Bockley grimaced but managed a smile. "Happy Heart and Partha Ha Ha, you will be sponsored by Gupta Gateau. And Marika, your sponsor is to be Tamara Partha Truffle." Maria exchanged cautious glances with the former Miranda. "So then, down to business.

For, let's face it, stomach is big business now. Nobody wants to have a sad stomach, a restless stomach, a wanting stomach. Now everyone wants to know how to have a peaceful stomach. The stomach is an intrinsic element in self-identity. The more you discover what you want to eat, the more you want to eat. Now we ask ourselves, if the stomach is senseless, am I senseless? No, we are born of this self-appreciation that the stomach exists. The fear of starvation is the original fear. Hunger you may like, but definitely not starvation. And so we say at this ashram, 'Today input, tomorrow output.' Let's face it, nobody wants to be fat. But there are occasions on which we wish we had two stomachs. But we are humans, not cows, and can only eat so much. Hunger is like a time bomb which nobody seems to like. The secret is to make certain that your input is of the highest quality. Today you were in one of two groups discussing the croissant or the brioche. Our new member Partha Henry has pointed to the superiority of the croissant due to its international expansion, but are you aware, Partha Henry, that when the hungry peasants cried out for more bread, what Marie Antoinette really said was not 'Let them eat cake' but 'Let them eat brioche'? We should not forget the glorious history of the tender egg-and-butter-enriched white bread eaten by the court and the upper classes, which is now available to everyone who seeks it."

Michael began to yawn, and Maria kicked him. "I didn't get any sleep last night," whispered Michael.

"But you'll need to be awake tonight to question Carpaccio."

"And now I will stop talking so that we may begin the Feast of Celebration! Namaste, Gentle Ones. Please distribute the blindfolds."

"Speaking of Marie Antoinette, I hope we're not about to be executed," whispered Maria.

"Begin the Feast!" commanded Baba Rhum.

"Snails. These must be snails." Michael groped around the

table. "How can we be expected to eat snails blindfolded? What's this? Paté. Good. I think I can manage this. Find some bread, good. Now find a knife. I can really appreciate what the blind go through when they have to eat." Michael stopped talking and noticed with a start that a verbal silence, punctuated by chewing and swallowing noises, had taken over the room. "O.K.," he whispered. "No talking. Fine. No talking. But I'm not used to not talking when I eat! Maria?"

"Gentle One." Michael felt a hand on his shoulder. It was Gupta Gateau. "We have silence during the feast."

"O.K." Michael continued to eat the paté, which he followed with salmon, then a steak au poivre, then a salad with goat cheese and walnuts, and finally a Grand Marnier souffle.

"Gentle Ones. It is time for our rest period," announced Baba Rhum. The feasters rose from the table to lie on the floor.

"Gentle Ones! The joyous celebration of feasting continues!" More desserts were brought to the table.

"Michael?" whispered Maria. "You ought to try this chocolate cake. I've never had anything like it."

"I can't. I'm stuffed. And all this chewing makes me feel like I'm with a bunch of animals."

"Michael, don't forget what you have to do this evening."

"You neither."

"Gentle Ones! The feast is over. Namaste!" exclaimed Baba Rhum. "You may remove your blindfolds."

At first the light hurt Maria's eyes, and when she turned to Michael she could barely see him. But as he gradually came into her focus and he smiled and winked at her, Maria began stifling giggles.

"Namaste, Gentle Ones. And namaste especially to our new ashram members! Would our new members and their sponsors please retire now for their evening meditation?" The former Carpaccio rose and motioned for Happy Heart née Barney Christian and Michael to come with him. Likewise the former

Crockley gestured to the former Warringer, and Raj, the former Bockley, motioned to the new Partha Andy, the ex-Borall.

"Well, Marika. Shall we adjourn?" asked Miranda. "We will meditate in your guest room. Tonight will be your last night in the guest room. Tomorrow you will be assigned a roommate. Come with me."

"Miranda, are you really used to eating so much?"

"Tamara, Gentle One. You *must* get used to using our names. You must learn to let go of the past which is Greenwich."

"Greenwich wasn't so bad."

"You may say that because you are young and didn't experience the bitter disappointment and loss . . . Well, that is all a part of my past. Never mind." Miranda opened Maria's guest room door and proceeded to sit cross-legged on the floor. Maria joined her. "Did you meditate prior to coming to the ashram?" asked Miranda.

"To be honest, no. But Miranda—Tamara—before I can even begin to entertain the idea of meditation, there are a few things I've got to get off my mind."

"Of course, Gentle One. You may speak freely with me."

"May I really?"

"Of course. You must consider me an older sister."

"Well . . . oh, Miranda—Tamara—I have so much more respect for you now than I did before . . ."

"Before I joined the ashram? I understand."

"No, I mean before I learned about your private investigation of Dr. Eele's practice among Greenwich undergraduates."

Miranda's spine straightened and she frowned. "Gentle One, you are again speaking of the past."

"Mrs. Kettle, I want to discuss a very important aspect of the so-called past with you, because it could affect hundreds of women. You know that Dr. Eele has been temporarily suspended by the Loma Verde Clinic because of Peach Kling's allegations. If you know something about Eele which could speed up his getting kicked out, you've *got* to report your findings to the Clinic's board of directors."

"Marika," said Miranda sharply, "the past is the past."

"It is not! It's the present, and you'd better believe it. And it's the future if responsible people like you, who know the score, go off to ashrams rather than face reality."

"Gentle One, I do not think your commitment to the spiritual life is sincere."

"If it's what Pete did to you which has depressed you so much . . . "

Miranda folded her arms, then unfolded them, appearing undone by what Maria had just said. "What *about* Pete? What are you talking about?"

"You *know* what I'm talking about."

"I do *not* know what you're talking about."

"The abortion. The one Pete arranged through Eele for a Greenwich undergraduate."

Miranda looked away. "You don't know the real story," she said.

"Yes I do."

"No you don't. Not the *real* story. But that is the past. We will talk of it no more."

"Eele is on the loose! For all I know he's practicing illegally at this very moment! How does that make you feel? Just think what he could be doing to a poor woman at this very moment. Maybe Eele doesn't exist for you now, but maybe he's existing all too fully for some woman he's brutalized today by his butchering and his cavalier manner!" Miranda put her head into her hands. "Miranda, I'm sorry to have had to bring this up but you know how important it is that we help to get rid of him, to get him out of Loma Verde, possibly to get him into prison! You've got some really damning evidence against him, haven't you? And Dr. Carpaccio knows plenty too. Both of you *must* report your findings. This goes beyond spirituality, unless of course you don't care about the lives of Loma Verde women!"

"I do!" sobbed Miranda. "It was Vince who talked me into coming up here!"

"Dr. Carpaccio?"

"I wouldn't be here if it weren't for Vince!" Miranda covered her eyes and began to cry.

"How'd you like the feast, Barney?" asked Michael, as Carpaccio led the two new members down the hall.

"I must confess one of my deepest fears has always been a flash of blindness during surgery. And tackling that steak au poivre reminded me of that fear."

"I suppose you also fear the loss of usage of your hands."

"Please!" Barney shuddered. "A fear worse than death."

"Really?" exclaimed Michael.

"I suggest we change the subject," said Carpaccio crossly.

"But it's interesting to hear Barney—Happy Heart's— views."

"Happy Heart's days with the knife are over. And as he discovered tonight he can cut meat blindfolded with no problem," said Carpaccio.

"Always a little animosity between the internist and the surgeon, eh guys?" asked Michael.

"No problem," said Barney quickly. "No problem for me, that is. I've always respected a good diagnostician. There are so few." He looked at Carpaccio and smirked.

"Well, I'll have you know that no one at Greenwich

University was ever the diagnostician that I was!" exclaimed Carpaccio. "Just ask any of the long and luminous list of my patients and colleagues. Why, just last year, who do you think I took care of?"

"Please, my dear Gupta Gateau, let us not drop names," replied Barney.

"Don't let's not drop names on account of me!" said Michael. "I love name droppers."

"I see then that you're in the right company with our luminous Gupta Gateau," said Barney.

"I'll just tell you this, Christian," said Carpaccio. "With any case in which coronary surgery was indicated, I sent the patient to Greenwich University Hospital and my patients lived longer than nineteen days. Most of them are still alive. Of course, the facilities at Greenwich aren't what they are in Johannesburg . . ."

"There's no need to be snide, Gupta Gateau," replied Barney. "Oh, and by the way, you really should drop about thirty-five pounds. It would be terribly good for your heart. I hope at any rate that you're counseling your overweight patients to do the same. That's how I see you internists—well-paid counselors."

"Let us not get into the money question, *please*. I could really blow my stack!" said Carpaccio.

"Don't let's not get into the money question on account of me!" said Michael.

"The boy's right. Are you saying that as a mere health counselor, you're not more than adequately paid for your services?" asked Barney Christian.

"I *resent* that!" shouted Carpaccio. "You know nothing of my work and my reputation!"

"Which proves my point."

"Thank God, anyway, that *you* never chose internal medicine. Who'd want to talk to you? Who, having had a heart attack, would want you at his or her bedside for hours, taking care of them?"

"Minor heart attacks have never interested me."

"And major heart attacks have never been your forte either," said Carpaccio.

"I beg your pardon? Just what do you mean by that last statement?"

"Gentle Ones!" Baba Rhum stood in the hall with his arms folded at his chest, looking like an unshorn Samson. "I knew this would happen, that if I put a former internist together with a former heart surgeon this anti-spiritual claptrap would be spit out! But Partha Ha Ha, I asked you purposely to be with Happy Heart and Gupta Gateau so that this would not happen."

"I've been trying to keep Happy Heart and Gupta Gateau on the spiritual level, but you know how it is when you get a flea and a knife together!"

"Partha Ha Ha, you are levity itself. So, Gupta Gateau and Happy Heart, you will follow the wise and prudent counsel of the spiritually alive and gifted Partha Ha Ha, and cease this meaningless dialogue at once!"

"Forgive me, Baba Rhum. An unspiritual slipup," murmured Carpaccio. He bowed, and the three continued to walk down the hall. "We will meditate in this room." Carpaccio lit a candle and motioned for Michael and Happy Heart to sit on the floor. "We will begin with candle concentration. Look into the light of the candle and concentrate on the flame. Let all thoughts disappear from your mind. Just concentrate on the blue, white, and gold of the candlelight. Let all thoughts drift away. Now think of a particular food, a single ingredient prior to its preparation."

"Eel," said Michael.

"Eel," repeated Carpaccio, seemingly unmoved. "I will tell you how to *limoner* an eel. The *limon* is the slimy substance that covers the body of the eel. To *limoner* means to remove this slime. First, pour boiling water over a live eel. Then scrape the *limon* with your nails. Hold the eel firmly to maintain a full grasp. The word *limoner* is sometimes erroneously used for cleaning brains, but no, it means cleaning eel."

"That sounds simple enough to me," said Barney Christian.

"Then perhaps you'd like to tell us how to skin an eel," replied Carpaccio snidely.

"I'm afraid cuisine is still largely your department," said Barney.

"To peel an eel," began Carpaccio.

"Sounds poetic. I hope you're not simply waxing poetic because of lost opportunities," said Michael.

Carpaccio raised his eyebrow and coughed. "To continue: to peel an eel. First, cut into the skin around the two fins close to the gills. Insert the knife under the skin and loosen it as much as possible. Pull off the skin, working from the head to the tail. Cut off the head, discard the fins, and draw the eel. Finally, cut the eel into pieces."

"I could do it blindfolded and with one hand tied behind my back," sniffed Barney.

"In that case we'll give you the responsibility for cleaning all fish in the future, Happy Heart. Of course, as long as we're concentrating on the eel, we might as well mention how it can be served. Brochette, fricasseed, smoked, and grilled."

"I understand you grilled an eel very thoroughly but didn't report all you learned from the experience to the higher authorities," said Michael, trying to look at Carpaccio in the candlelight.

"You mean there's more than one master at this ashram? Someone other than Baba Rhum?" asked Barney Christian.

"Partha Ha Ha doesn't mean anything. He's just making another one of his little jokes."

"I guarantee that you'll be peeled and cut up if you know something about Eele and don't report it to the Clinic board," said Michael.

"There must be some kind of language gap here. I'm not sure I'm following the conversation," said Barney.

"Partha Ha Ha, you probably know more about what's going on with Eele than I do. I could report he's a slimy no-good fish . . ."

"But you've just reported all of these wonderful ways to cook the eel," stammered Barney. "You said brochette, fricas-seed, grilled . . ."

"But everyone in Loma Verde knows about Eele by now," said Carpaccio.

"I should think the French have been cooking eel for hundreds of years, even when the residents of Loma Verde were doing little more than mashing acorns," said Barney. "I'm referring of course to the true native Californians."

"I'd like to know more about how you're treating the true native South Africans, Christian," said Carpaccio.

"I don't know how we got on to this topic! Oh dear, I think we'd better stick to food," mumbled Barney.

"Oh, not if you don't want to," said Michael quickly. "There are so many things we could talk about and we have all night. I've been wondering about South Africa myself. Who in the hell do you guys think you are anyway?"

"Oh dear," sighed Barney. "I can only say I've come to the ashram to regain my spirituality which I fear I nearly lost in Johannesburg."

"Too late the philanthrope, buster," replied Michael.

"I hate men too." Maria lit a cigarette and leaned back against the wall.

"Better stuff a towel under the door. Cigarette smoking is completely out of the question here. On second thought, I'll have a cigarette too."

Maria lit Miranda's cigarette. "All those goddamned nights I've waited around for Ted to call when he said he would. He's never had the decency to let me know that he was going to be two or three hours late."

"I know what you mean! Pete was always out jogging, and I mean night and day. His running partners were always my female assistants. Especially this one little Sue Santini. I suspect he's hit the sack with her as well."

"But Miranda, are you *really* happy here?"

"I'll tell you—up here I just try to forget the pain. I think it's the same for Vince. When he found out about his wife and his best friend, I think it nearly killed him. I try not to think about the scandal aspect. You know, I wish we had a bottle of something. I could really use a drink."

"I've got a bottle of Chianti. I brought it up with me. I've even got a wine opener," said Maria.

"I was thinking of something else, vodka or gin, but I guess wine will do."

"It'll have to do. Don't you sometimes get disgusted by all this big emphasis on gluttony at the ashram?"

"Oh Maria, of course I do! But I needed an out, and Vince was just *convinced* that this was the place to go. You see, I couldn't have come here alone. I wouldn't have! But Vince is much more into food than I . . ."

"That's certainly obvious."

"But Maria, don't forget. Vince cares much more for the altruistic interpretation of life. I had a party when the Dalai Lama came to Greenwich . . ."

"Yes, I know."

" . . . in which the Dalai Lama invited Vince to become his *personal physician*. Vince could have made a lot of money for a year or two, to think nothing of the prestige of it all, but he turned the offer down. He couldn't leave his patients!"

"But . . ."

"But it wasn't until he learned about his wife's affair with his best friend that he felt the need to look for another kind of life."

"But what about divorce? Why couldn't he divorce his wife? And why couldn't you divorce Pete?"

"Maria, I can't speak for Vince, but I can speak for myself, and no one, *no one* in my family has ever been involved in a divorce." Miranda inhaled the cigarette smoke and began to cough.

"I'll bet no one in your family has ever run off to a swami joint either. God, I can't seem to find a glass. Would you mind just taking a swig out of the bottle?"

"No." Miranda, still coughing, gulped down a fourth of the bottle. "Ahh, that's better. No, no one in my family has ever run off to a swami joint, but lots of my relatives have run away from their husbands. My grandmother Agnes left my grandfather for a Sicilian tenor."

"No kidding!"

"And my Aunt Mary left my Uncle Henry for an Italian circus lion tamer."

"And you've left Pete for an Italian internist. The women in your family must have a thing for Italians!" Maria took a large gulp of wine.

"I didn't leave Pete *for* Vince. I left *with* Vince. There's a big difference." Maria handed the bottle to Miranda and soon the bottle was nearly empty. "Chianti. A wonderful wine. I love Italian things!"

"Maybe if you and Vince left this place you might be able to have a decent relationship. This is what I think you ought to do. I think you ought to both go back to Loma Verde, file for divorces, report everything you know about Eele to the board, and get married."

Miranda looked at the bottle and said, "Shall I kill it?"

"Why not?"

Miranda emptied the bottle and took a deep breath. "Got another cigarette?"

"Sure. Here you go." Maria lit two cigarettes.

"It's not as easy as you think. I don't love Vince. I don't care what anyone thinks. I just don't love him. And I've signed off on sex."

"But Miranda, how *can* you? You've got a lot of good years in you. Just think about your grandmother Agnes and your Aunt Mary. I'm sure *they* didn't sign off on sex when they were your age."

"Sex has been one bitter disappointment for me. Pete, that is."

"Why don't you give it a shot with Vince?"

"Maria, I don't *want* to give it a shot with Vince. And Vince is perfectly happy up here. And I'm happy too, or I was until you came here and began to ask me all of these questions."

"Well, let's change the subject. Do you think Joe and Jean Kuhl know anything about Eele that they're not telling the board?"

"Joe and Jean Kuhl? I highly doubt *that*. Those two are out for themselves."

"But you said . . ."

"Oh sure, I said I thought that Joe and Jean cared about their patients, but it's a kind of ingratiating attitude they have which is so infuriating. You could tell either one of them that they were full of C-R-A-P and they'd say, 'Oh yes, you're so right, I am.' No fighting attitude, just two subservient hand-maidens to the Greenwich egotists. But I'll let you in on a little secret about Joe Kuhl, a little something I culled from my in-vestigative work: ten to one he'll accept the Dalai Lama's offer."

"The Dalai Lama has made him an offer? Are you certain about this?"

"Of course I am. I'm sitting on top of all the medical gos-sip, or I was until I joined the ashram. Just take my word for it. If Joe Kuhl doesn't get the ego gratification he wants from doing his little PBS series, he'll cut out and move his family to wherever the Dalai Lama wants him."

"You're *sure* about this? I mean *really* sure?"

"Just ask Vince. Apparently Kuhl told him all about it. He wanted Vince's opinion on whether or not Vince thought it was a good opportunity."

"But surely Vince told him what he thought!"

"Oh he did. He told Joe it was a real opportunity to make money and see the world. Of course, Vince no longer cares for such unspiritual goals. In some ways, Vince is like me. Do you remember when Greenwich was reported to be the number one undergraduate university in the country, and I told the reporters that beauty contests didn't interest me? I confess, Pete was about ready to belt me when I made that statement."

"Maybe you ought to go back to Greenwich and try to get together again with Pete."

"Not in a million years!" Miranda stared at her outstretched fingers. "They don't have a manicurist at the ashram. I confess I miss my manicure more than anything else."

Barney Christian, Vincent Carpaccio, and Michael were still on the floor, huddled around the candle and egging each other on. "Well, Barney has told his side of the story, the reasons that bring him to the ashram. What's your story, Vince? I can call you Vince, can't I?" asked Michael.

"You certainly cannot. My name is Gupta Gateau and that's what you can call me," snapped Carpaccio.

"Why do you keep playing the heavy?" asked Barney. "I've told my story. Why don't you share with us the reasons why you have chosen to live at the ashram?"

"I still don't buy *your* reasons, Christian, I mean Happy Heart," replied Carpaccio. "Why is it that all of a sudden you feel some kind of consciousness about what's happening in South Africa?"

"Better late than never," said Barney.

"That's what I always say!" agreed Michael enthusiastically.

"What are *your* reasons, young man?" asked Carpaccio, turning directly to Michael.

"Reasons for what?" asked Michael innocently.

"Don't be a smarty-pants. You know damned well what I mean."

"Oh, *I* see. You want to know why *I* joined the ashram!"

"You don't fit the current profile. You're not prominent in your field. You tell us you're a food critic but I've never heard or seen your name in connection with food. And I subscribed to all the major and even the minor food and wine publications prior to coming to the ashram."

"Well, *I* think it's good for the rest of us to *have* young persons among us," interjected Barney.

"I don't care what you think, Christian. I want to know why a kid like this one would join a spiritual and gourmet ashram."

"To further my spiritual relationship with input and output," replied Michael breathlessly.

"I don't like wise guys," said Carpaccio. "And I can spot a wise guy a mile away because I used to be one myself."

"I would never have judged you so harshly," said Barney with mock surprise.

"Do you remember the loo-loo ex-governor of California? The one we all called Governor Starlost?" Carpaccio asked Barney.

"I certainly do and I'm surprised he hasn't paid a visit to the ashram. You know, drop in for a day or two so he can tell the press he's been here."

"Well, I went to elementary school with the illustrious exgovernor of California and I used to give him answers to mathematics test questions when he sat behind me. Consequently, I had carte blanche to visit him after he became governor and give him my views on medicine . . . Anyway, the point of my story is that *I* was a wise guy, or so I thought, so I *know* a wise guy." Carpaccio looked at Michael and smirked.

Michael returned Carpaccio's smirk and replied, "I personally think the former governor wasn't so bad, compared with most politicians. So if you helped him to pass elementary mathematics in order that he could in the future get to be the governor of California, my hat's off to you, doc. Helping him by giving answers is probably the single most worthwhile thing you did when you were young."

"Hey, I didn't say I didn't like the former governor or that I disagreed with him when he was in office. I was giving you an example of wise-guy, smart-ass behavior! It was a mistake to help him pass elementary-school mathematics by giving him my answers. It was unethical . . ."

"Well, if that's the most unethical thing you've ever done, my hat's off to you again, doc. Because, personally, my belief is that you've come to the ashram to escape having to go before the Clinic board with the evidence you've got against Eele."

"What the hell!" sputtered Carpaccio.

"But I thought we'd all agreed that eel was a delicacy!" exclaimed Barney.

"You've got the same kind of mentality you had when you were giving out the answers to math questions. You got no ethics, doc. You neither, Christian. You're both gutless wonders. Dr. Christian, your ego trip with the media was one of the most disgusting phenomena of the twentieth century."

"Now you listen to me, young man!" exclaimed Barney Christian. "I might have made my mistakes in the past but I'm here to rectify them now. And by the way, you still haven't told us your reasons for choosing to come to the ashram."

"He doesn't have to tell us now. I think he's just told us," sneered Carpaccio.

"Input and output. I see it more clearly every minute," said Michael, staring at the candlelight.

"Is that all you have to say, Partha Ha Ha?" asked Carpaccio.

"Yes."

"In that case, I suggest we resume our candle concentration pose."

"I believe I have conclusive evidence that there are radical differences in output," said Partha Paté, the former biochemist Crockley, the following morning during breakfast.

"Really? Do tell," replied Raj Béarnaise, the former Bockley.

"I will report my findings to Baba Rhum first," said Crockley.

"Of course," murmured Bockley. "I do think we ought to review Baba Rhum's philosophy of input and output for the benefit of our new members. Perhaps one of our new members would like to review the philosophy aloud. Partha Henry, would you like to give it a go?"

The former Warringer looked up. "I believe in policymaking, not philosophy. You may call on me for a policy review."

"Of course. Partha Ha Ha, perhaps you have studied the philosophy of input and output and would like to review it for us."

"Sure." Michael stood, at first nearly tripping on the hem of his robe. "Takes a while to get used to this robe. All right. A review of Baba Rhum's philosophy of input and output. First in the order of nature is the ritual of input. Second in the order is the ritual of output. All human activities should be subordinate to input and output. The corollary to this last principle is sexual abstinence. The fundamental rhythm of nature is the rhythm of input and output. The fundamental psychological distinction is that input should be public and output should be private."

"*Very* good, Partha Ha Ha! I assure you, Baba Rhum would be most pleased to hear so concise and eloquent a review of his philosophy. And your subtle psychological interpretation was most sophisticated. You do credit to us all. Has anyone else something to add to Partha Ha Ha's review?"

Maria raised her hand and stood. She smiled at Michael and said, "Input is never output; output is never input."

"Very good. Most eloquent, Marika!" replied Bockley.

"Where is Partha Andy?" Crockley asked Bockley.

"Oh . . . Partha Andy. Well, as you know, Partha Andy and I meditated together last evening. Partha Andy did an admirable job with his meditation, but he fell asleep shortly before dawn, announcing beforehand that he was a night person and to wake him after lunch. I'm afraid Partha Andy has many changes he must make in his lifestyle. Oh, and by the way, Partha Andy revealed to me last night a most ingenious plan for procuring funding for the ashram. Partha Andy proposes to continue his trademark portraiture art, offering to do likenesses of our weekend guests for a modest fee which would of course go into the ashram coffers. Mr. Whitt, does this plan intrigue you? Imagine your likeness as rendered by the hand of the famous Partha Andy! You would be the first, you know, to have your portrait done by Partha Andy since his acceptance of Baba Rhum."

"Well, it doesn't interest me," replied Sam Whitt, glaring at Michael.

"Ah come on, Sam, don't be such a hard sell," said Michael.

"And you don't be such an ass!" replied Sam, and he threw his napkin on the table and walked out of the dining room.

"Poor man," whispered Chitra Coriander. "Oh, where is Tamara Partha Truffle?"

Maria's back straightened. "Oh, Tamara's not feeling well. She, um, said for me to go to breakfast without her." Michael looked at Maria with raised eyebrows.

"I shall go and check on her," said Gupta Gateau, rising quickly.

"Oh no! She said she really just needs to be alone. She doesn't think it's anything serious," said Maria.

"This often happens after one of our celebration feasts. It's one of the hazards we must endure to enjoy the fruits of our labors," sighed Bockley. "Partha Ha Ha, would you please go and see how our weekend guest is managing? He seems a bit disturbed."

"With pleasure!" Michael excused himself and left to look for Sam.

"Sam! Sam! Where are you? Sam! Aw, come on, Sam, I was only kidding in there." Michael, tripping over his robe, caught the older man by the shoulder. "No hard feelings, O.K.?"

"Kid, you look like a genuine asshole," replied Sam, shrugging off Michael's grasp.

"Aw, come on, Sam, I thought you understood what a dog-eat-dog world investigative reporting is. I mean, sometimes we have to sink really low to get a story. How's Ann?"

Sam stared briefly at Michael, then shook his head. "You probably know better than I do how she is."

"Are you kidding? I was up all night with the doctor from Loma Verde and Barney Christian. And if you think we were discussing input and other bullshit, we weren't. This spiritual business is a lot of crap. If I could have a half hour with Ann

I could convince her that this whole ashram is a sham."

"Well, what were you discussing all night with those two doctors?"

"Medical ethics. The ongoing blood feud between surgeons and internists. The fact that a surgeon can make thousands more in one hour than an internist makes all day. Real spiritual, huh?"

"Does that swami still buy that you're serious about all of this?"

"Sure he does. He thinks I have real spirituality!"

"You make me want to vomit."

"It's just all in a day's work, Sam, all in a day's work. Why don't I look for Ann and have a little talk with her? How much longer do you plan to stay?"

"I'm staying till Ann leaves this place. The more I'm here the more convinced I am that this place is about as rotten to the core as it comes. Bockley, Crockley, Warringer, those guys are major disappointments to me. What's happening to this country anyway?"

"As far as I'm concerned, I'm glad they're up here. Maybe in a funny kind of way it's actually a change for the better. Why don't you try to look at it that way? Maybe Crockley, Bockley, and Warringer up here at the ashram signify a change in the country, a swing toward consciousness about nuclear warfare. Why don't you try to see it all more positively?"

"If you could just talk to Ann, I'd appreciate it." Sam began to walk away.

"I will, Sam. I promise you, I will." Michael walked back into the main house and dialed Ben's office number. Ben answered.

"Sounds a lot more exciting at the swami joint than anyone would ever have dreamed. Almost wish I was there."

"What's happening in good old Loma Verde?"

"Oh, not the exciting times you're having! Greenwich plans to sue the paper over the 'Swami Mommy' story. And Joe

Kuhl has just filmed a 'Your Health' segment about herpes in hot tubs. Apparently it's caused quite an uproar among the PBS brass. Listen, Mike. I'd like to get a story from you soon. When do you think you'll have one ready?"

"Tomorrow afternoon. I promise I'll get together with Forsythe and give you the Clinic scoop."

"Oh, have you seen much of Maria up there?"

"Not really. They've kept us fairly active. But I'm sure she'll be calling you soon. I want to stay here until I get stories out of all of them."

"You get those stories, Michael. You're there till you feel satisfied you've got the best exclusives in the country."

"Will do, boss. It's not easy to talk privately. I'll have Forsythe call you. Talk to you later." Michael put the telephone down and turned around to face Baba Rhum.

"So! You have difficulty talking privately? Perhaps you and I could talk privately right now." Baba Rhum took Michael's elbow. "Come with me."

"I haven't been taken away by the elbow like that since I was in the seventh grade," Michael wrote in his journal, following his subsequent confinement to his bedroom. "He's on to me but he's not playing it straight. Maybe he wants the publicity. He claimed he only heard me tell Ben it was hard to talk privately at the ashram. I'm getting a little too blasé about Warringer, Crockley, Bockley, et al. Where does a miner begin when he's sitting on top of the largest gold mine this side of the Rocky Mountains? How deep is the mine anyway? Am I like a Forty-Niner, watching it run through the stream?"

"Hi, Michael," whispered Maria. Michael looked up quickly. "Are you writing your story? Or should I say one of your stories?"

"No, I'm writing to myself." Michael put his pen down. "If someone sees you in here you'll probably get your ass kicked into solitary confinement too."

"So that's what's happened to you! Caused a little uproar and gotten your ass kicked into solitary confinement!"

"It's like goddamned junior high."

"Well, let's see how Michael Weintraub bares his soul in his lonely room to his lonely notebook." Maria picked up Michael's journal.

"Forsythe, give it back!"

"Oh, I like the analogy of the gold miner wondering how deep the mine is. A little naive maybe, but that's what's always made you so charming."

"Forsythe, what the *hell* . . ."

"If you could just get off your macho reporter trip and dry yourself behind your ears, you might catch a few lilting notes."

"What are you talking about?"

"Miranda and I had quite a good little chat last night. She really let down her hair. A bottle of Chianti which I'd brought helped."

"You brought a bottle of Chianti? Why didn't you tell me?"

"Why does it matter? Miranda really let go, and I believe what she says. Her daughter Susan's 'Swami Mommy' story is all wrong. Miranda hadn't been studying up on swamis or anything else. She was disillusioned by her marriage and she was disillusioned by Greenwich. Carpaccio is not the big love of her life. She left with him as an out. And he left because he found out that his wife was having an affair with his best friend. Oh, Miranda says that the Dalai Lama has approached Joe Kuhl to be his personal physician and she believes that Kuhl will take the offer, ten to one."

"Are you joking? What about Jean Kuhl? She's a doctor too. Doesn't she have a say in that kind of decision?"

"A pretty non-macho question for such a macho guy."

"I am *not* a macho guy. Would you just get off my case and keep going with your story?"

"Well, that *is* my story. Joe Kuhl will probably become the Dalai Lama's personal physician. Maybe Jean can set up a practice also. And they can run in the rain! I hear it's wet in Tibet!" Maria and Michael began to laugh uncontrollably. "Like the rain in Spain! The wet in Tibet! Oh—and I just so happened to overhear a conversation at the old public telephone which will interest you."

"You and Baba Rhum ought to form a wire-tapping agency."

"Michael, I think I overheard Sam Whitt talking to someone from the IRS. I think Sam Whitt is an undercover agent for the IRS and he's up at the ashram to investigate the tax-exempt status of the ashram as a religious organization."

"What! What about his daughter Ann?"

"I think she's really his girl friend."

"What about all the stuff he said about her? The Nestlé's Quik and all?"

"Maybe he's a frustrated actor."

"Aren't we all?"

"So the question at this point is where do we go from here? Shall we arrange to have private conversations with War-ringer, Bockley, and the rest of them?"

"I've got a better idea," said Michael.

"Why Michael! What a surprise!" Maria exclaimed as he leaned over to kiss her.

"I think we'd better get dressed," whispered Maria.

"Why? This is the best thing that's happened at the old ashram." There was a knock at Michael's door. "Good God! Who's that!"

The door opened slowly. "Partha Ha Ha, I am disappointed in you," said the former Bockley. "You know what this means, don't you?"

"It was worth it," replied Michael.

The *Vindicator*
Goes International

Michael and Maria returned from the ashram and filed a half dozen exclusives for the *Vindicator*. I was proud of them and happy for the success the stories brought to our newspaper. We sold the stories to newspapers all over the country and Mike and Maria were interviewed by *Time*, *Newsweek*, and the television networks. It wasn't until the week following their return that I figured out the reason for their having been kicked out of the ashram.

I had bought Mike's story about Baba Rhum's learning they were news reporters until one late night when, after stopping by the office to pick up some correspondence, I walked right in on Mike and Maria in a passionate embrace. They seemed embarrassed and tried to make up a story about how they were celebrating Maria's being hired by the *Vindicator*. Unwittingly, I had set the stage for young love. I was a genuine fool to have sent them up to the ashram together, but I was a fool ever to have thought Maria might have wanted me in the first place. Maria now avoided having to look at me, even though the two of us were still working with Peach Kling and her cousin Lester.

We weren't much further on the Eele story now than we were before the ashram visit. Unfortunately, Eele's suspension time had expired and he was back at the Clinic. Lester, it seems, was quite good at digging up raunchy details about Eele, although these details were nothing that could result in Eele's permanent suspension. Prostitutes and booze filled Lester's notebooks on Duke Eele, but the Clinic board knew all about Eele's whores and drinking bouts. As long as Eele would agree to go to a dry-out center twice a year, he was guaranteed a position on the Clinic lineup. We needed something more conclusive, but "that something" was like the elusive butterfly. Duke Eele was a slippery eel. He knew how to wriggle around on thin ice and survive.

Meanwhile, Maria had broken the Joe Kuhl story the day before the Clinic publicly announced his resignation to become personal physician to the Dalai Lama. The Dalai Lama's triumphant return to Tibet was chronicled in every tabloid in the country, and Joe Kuhl, too, had become quite the celebrated figure. It was Mike who had uncovered the reasons behind Joe Kuhl's leaving PBS and the "Your Health" series. The network it seems had become a little nervous about Joe's handling of controversial topics, especially the herpes in hot tubs segment. Joe had insisted on more money from PBS for his part in the series and when PBS threatened to cancel "Your Health," Joe resigned from the series. The Dalai Lama's proposal was in the wind anyway.

So my heart was breaking but the stories were breaking too. I worked like a demon each day and drowned my sorrows in Glenfiddich and the Mills Brothers at night. Maria and Michael were rumored to be nominated for a Pulitzer Prize for their ashram stories. On the basis of this rumor I, like a drunken sailor, sent them both off to Tibet to interview Joe Kuhl.

"Michael . . . Michael . . . I feel really weird."

"It's mountain sickness," replied Paljor, the Tibetan guide.

"Why do we have to *trek*? Why couldn't we just have flown in on a helicopter? I'm serious! I'm going to faint!"

"Don't faint, we're almost here. And you don't actually think that Ben would have sprung for a private helicopter to follow us to Tibet, do you?"

"Michael, if anyone had told me how hard this walk would be, I'd never have come."

"Not you, the big marathoner? Not you, the one who wanted to jog up at the old ashram?"

"I never dreamed this would be so hard."

"Everyone from West gets mountain sickness," said Paljor. "But it will pass."

"Try to concentrate on the mist and the serenity," said Michael.

"I'm trying. I'm *really* trying. But I think I'm going to have to sit down. My God! Who are they?" Maria pointed to two shackled men, sitting by the road.

"Oh, they are habitual thieves," replied Paljor.

"You mean you just keep them by the road in leg irons and handcuffs?" asked Maria.

"They are habitual thieves."

"You mean you haven't got any jails in Tibet?" asked Michael.

"We don't need any jails in Tibet. The method you see works very well."

"Do Tibetans like westerners?" asked Michael.

"I'm serious, I've got to sit." Maria stopped in the road, a few paces from where the shackled men sat.

"Not there! You do not sit with thieves!" exclaimed Paljor.

"I don't care, I'm going to pass out right now if I don't sit." Maria threw her backpack on the road and sat down beside a large stone. Paljor took a tobacco pouch from his pocket and rolled a cigarette.

"Do Tibetans like westerners?" repeated Michael.

"Oh yes," said Paljor, spitting into the road. "We have

our, how do you say, religious groupies?"

"You mean people from the West who follow the Dalai Lama?"

"That's right. We have our western friends. The Dalai Lama was well received in America, wasn't he?"

"I guess he was. But why would he pick an American as his personal physician?"

"The Dalai Lama believes in western doctors. The Divine Doctor Kuhl has helped the Dalai Lama's arthritis, with mysteries of aspirin," said Paljor.

"I guess you have to be a Tibetan to get any good out of western doctors," said Maria, who rose suddenly—too suddenly—and fainted.

"Maria! Are you all right?" asked Michael, running over to her.

"I'm all right. God, what a rush!"

"We're almost at Gyantse. You will see your doctor friend there. I think we should be going now. It's getting late." Paljor threw his cigarette into the road and crushed it with his foot. The three continued up the steep road, which was actually, as Paljor pointed out, a mule track.

"It reminds me of the Alps," said Maria, still listless from her momentary loss of consciousness. "It reminds me of an Alpine climb I made with Daddy and a friend of mine. Except in the Alps, there was always a wooden crucifix wherever two paths crossed."

"And in Tibet we have the *torii*, which you both have seen, the simple structure of wood and stone which is often among the trees," said Paljor. "In many ways it can be compared to the crucifix. Both of them are of religious origin and poetic significance. Of course, we Tibetans are reminded too of all the many human and other beings who pass through the cycle of birth and rebirth down a dark and troubling river toward the state of enlightenment."

"That's quite eloquent," said Michael.

"I memorized it from the Dalai Lama's updated and revised guidebook for western tourists. Come, we will soon be at our destination."

The road began at once to become populated. Michael and Maria saw low hills in the distance and on top of these hills structures with golden gleaming roofs.

"Gyantse!" exclaimed Paljar.

"It's like a fairyland," said Maria. "And where are the tinkling bell sounds coming from?"

"From the yaks," replied Paljor, pointing to an animal with a bell tied around its neck. "Come on. We're almost here. You will be with your western doctor friend soon."

Paljor escorted Michael and Maria to a little bungalow where they would spend the next week. From their room they could see the fortress of Gyantse, rising above the rocks like another hilltop, where Joe Kuhl and his family lived.

"What price would you demand to live and work here?" asked Maria, gazing at the fortress from the window.

"The price I'm being paid—as a journalist for one week. You feeling better?"

"I think so. But an hour ago I thought I was dying."

"Are you planning to smear rancid butter all over your face like some of those women we saw coming into town?"

"It's probably a great moisturizer up here in this rugged climate."

"This makes the old ashram look like a five-star luxury hotel. Yeah, we'll get you all fixed up Tibetan style. Get you one of those lady Tibetan outfits and some old butter for your face. And maybe some fancy jewels."

"Oh sure," said Maria, and she walked away from the window.

"I don't know about you, Forsythe, but I'm glad to get away from Ben for a while. He was beginning to get a bit aggressive. I think he's drinking too much. He's got a haggard look in his eyes. He's different. It's because of you and me, you

157

know. Sometimes I feel like a heel, even though I know I
shouldn't."

"You can't feel like a heel because of *that*. Ben and I never
had any kind of understanding that would make him think you
had no right to be my . . ." Maria hesitated, "my friend."

"Your *friend*?" Michael walked up to her and whispered,
"How's your mountain sickness?"

"Much better. In the morning I thought I would die, but
I feel better now. What time is it?"

"Twelve on the nose. Have you ever heard the palin-
drome 'Sex at noon taxes'?"

"You're so clever! The future Erma Bombeck . . ."

"If Ben doesn't fire me," said Michael, kissing her.

"He's not going to fire you. Not now. Not after our getting a Pulitzer Prize nomination. He's just worried about how
he's going to keep you."

"I've always wanted to have sex in Tibet, haven't you?"
asked Michael.

"Not till I met you."

"I love you, Maria. Do you wish I were a ballet dancer?"

"No."

"Did you tell Ted to drop dead?"

"No."

"Where is Ted anyway?"

"He's in Italy."

"What's he doing in Italy?"

"What do you think he's doing in Italy?"

"Screwing American tourists for money."

"He's dancing, Michael."

"I think Ted's an asshole."

"You haven't even met him."

"I still think he's an asshole."

"Have a little charity."

"Do you think we'll get the Pulitzer Prize?"

"I don't know, Michael. Are we making love or playing

twenty questions?"

"Wanna split the old Loma Verde scene and ask the Dalai Lama for spiritual asylum? Refuse what will surely be our Pulitzer Prize? Work side by side with Joe Kuhl, unselfishly nursing the Dalai Lama in his minutes of need?"

"Michael, if you stopped talking, you'd kiss better . . . *Michael*, have you suffered some kind of new mouth attack? Dateline, Tibet: Michael Weintraub learns new ways to use mouth!"

"I don't believe this." Joe Kuhl jumped from his chair to greet Maria and Michael.

"I have to admit, no one in Loma Verde believes it, Dr. Kuhl," replied Maria.

"Call me Joe."

"Hey, what a way to go, Joe! This is some setup you've got here. I love those rugs," said Michael.

"They're Tibetan rugs, as you can probably imagine. So, what brings you to Tibet, you two?"

"We came to ask you that question," replied Michael.

"The Dalai Lama is great! It's an old wives' tale that the Dalai Lama is an unapproachable deity. He's a very warm and caring person."

"Do you have plans to convert to Buddhism?" asked Maria.

"No . . . not at the present. Converting to Buddhism requires rigorous religious training and quite frankly the Dalai Lama and his family keep me pretty busy."

"How are Jean and the kids? Is Jean practicing up here?" asked Michael.

"Well, I have to admit, the major disappointment is that the Dalai Lama refuses to accept a woman as a doctor. But

Jean's finding temporary fulfillment in redecorating several rooms in the Dalai Lama's quarters. The Dalai Lama was very taken with the 'Loma Verde style' as he calls it, and I have to admit, Jean has quite a touch with making a house a Loma Verde home. So, for now her main duties have been stylistic. We're hoping to convince the Dalai Lama that Jean could make outstanding contributions to health care here. Well, how long are you going to be here?"

"A week."

"Well, I'm sure we'll see a lot of each other. Come have dinner with us tonight. Say about eight. Listen, I know you've come for an interview and that will be fine with me. I only ask that I read what you plan to print before you print it. Hey, and congratulations, you two! I heard about your Pulitzer Prize nominations before I left. That must have been some experience for you. I have to admit, I wasn't crazy about the way you reported my dispute with PBS. It didn't happen the way you reported it at all. The truth is that PBS threatened to cut back on production costs and we couldn't produce a decent series with the budget that was proposed."

"Come on, Joe, everyone knows that the PBS bosses were uptight over your herpes in hot tubs segment," said Michael.

"Mike, I assure you, my leaving the series was due to proposed budget cuts. And if the two of you plan to write more false articles about me, you might as well leave now." Joe sat back down but stood quickly. "Hey, this is no way to treat you after you've come so far. I'm sorry. Listen, let's go and get Jean. We're both actually dying to see people from back home. You're our first visitors."

Joe, Maria, and Michael walked down a corridor, and Michael said, "You know, we went to Baba Rhum's ashram in Oregon to interview Vincent Carpaccio about Duke Eele. We had no idea of who else would be up there."

"Must have been quite a surprise."

"It was a real journalistic field day when we found out

who was there, but I must say it was disappointing not to get anything concrete out of Carpaccio about Eele . . . and now with you and Jean up here, I suppose the Eele investigating committee is completely kaput," said Maria. "Eele is back at the Clinic, you know."

"Yeah, it's too bad about that. There's one guy who shouldn't be practicing," said Joe.

"So why didn't you do something about it?" asked Maria.

"What *could* we do? Oh, there's Jean. Jean! Look who's here!"

"My goodness! I don't believe it! Congratulations, you two, on all those great ashram stories. How on earth did you get here?"

"It wasn't easy," said Michael.

"But you ought to know about these two. They'll go to any length to get a story," said Joe dryly. "They've come here to interview us."

"Well, that's great! Let's have some tea. That's what we drink here. And I'll arrange a sightseeing tour and an evening of Tibetan bell ringing. The most beautiful, the purest bells in the world are made right here in Tibet. And when you hear the bell ringing—it's like a concert— well, you've never heard anything like it in your life. It will make you realize how far away from home you are. Kenrab, please bring us some tea." Jean commanded the young man as though she were Scarlett O'Hara in *Gone With the Wind*. He bowed and disappeared.

"How's the food here?" asked Michael.

"Not like at Carpaccio's ashram, I assure you!" said Joe. "Meat is theoretically not allowed here. Our kids are having hallucinations about Big Macs. But I must say, the Tibetans I've seen are healthy as horses. So, how are things in Loma Verde?"

"Well, it came as a shock to everyone that you both left for Tibet," said Maria.

"That's to be expected," replied Joe hastily.

"People who are afraid to take chances always talk down

those who aren't afraid," continued Jean. "Ah, thank you, Kenrab. Sit down, Mike. Sit down, Maria. These little fried biscuits look strange but they're actually very good. Try one." She passed the plate of confections around.

"The tea's a little intense in flavor, but we like it now," said Joe, as the silent Kenrab poured the steaming liquid into tall bamboo cups.

"Thank you, Kenrab. That will be all," said Jean, and the young man disappeared again.

"I wonder what Kenrab thinks about all of this?" began Michael.

"All of what?" asked Joe defensively.

"You know. You, Jean, and the kids, up here in the middle of nowhere."

"It isn't nowhere for Kenrab. And our relationship with Kenrab and other Tibetans is most cordial. It's a very high honor for Kenrab to be serving the personal physician of the Dalai Lama," said Jean.

"Where are the kids?" asked Maria.

"They're with their tutor. Education here is marvelous. They're continuing with all the subjects they studied back in Loma Verde plus Tibetan language, history, and culture. I'm glad we got them away from that Greenwich scene. It's so . . . so superficial." Jean put her cup on a small table and looked at her husband.

"It's funny how both the two of you and Carpaccio seem to have found the Greenwich scene superficial," said Maria. "I've always suspected doctors were trying to seek mystical answers as explanations when they couldn't understand a situation. Daddy says that's because doctors are illiterate. Oops! I don't mean the two of you. Everyone's opinion of both of you is high. In fact, up at the ashram, Miranda Kettle said that both of you cared about your patients and that the only thing wrong with you was that you lacked spiritual self-knowledge."

"Everyone finds spiritual fulfillment in his or her own

way. Right, Joe?" asked Jean.

"I suppose so," replied Joe, looking distressed.

"So let's get down to brass tacks," said Michael. "What brings the two of you to Tibet? Is it the money? Or is it the prestige associated with working for the Dalai Lama—though of course you both must know that a lot of people think you've flipped out."

"I don't care!" exclaimed Joe indignantly. "Loma Verde stinks. It stinks worse than these goddamn Tibetan cigarettes every man, woman, and child smokes up here. We'll still take Tibet. It's *better* than Loma Verde. Purer. It just is. We have to help the Tibetans change a few of their bad habits, but we like it."

"How can you say it's *better* than Loma Verde?" asked Maria. Joe and Jean settled back in their chairs, smug and silent.

"What are you here for anyway? Money? A change of scene? Or both?" asked Michael.

"Both," said Joe solemnly. "How am I supposed to practice in a clinic with Duke Eele? I'd rather be in Tibet."

"So Duke Eele is the reason you've left the Clinic?" asked Michael.

"Only one of many reasons, some personal. Let's just say that for the time being, Jean and I are very happy. Our kids are happy too. And for the sake of your story, you might just say I have some other irons in the fire," said Joe.

"Care to comment on them?" asked Michael.

"Not at present. The plans haven't completely firmed up."

"You know, it's just so hard to imagine both of you up here in Tibet. You both look just like a Zippi-Cola commercial to me. So clean-cut, all-American . . ." began Maria. Jean and Joe exchanged cautious looks.

"Would you like to see the rooms I've redone?" asked Jean quickly.

"Yes, let's all take a look at the rooms Jean's redone," said Joe.

"Any chance we'll get to meet the Dalai Lama?" asked Michael.

"No. The Dalai Lama is away on a spiritual retreat in his summer villa higher in the mountains," replied Joe.

"I can't imagine being any higher! I suppose the Dalai Lama doesn't get mountain sickness," said Maria.

"Oh, I treated the Dalai Lama for mountain sickness when all of us first came to Tibet."

"I suppose you're both doing a lot of running up here," said Michael.

"I am. Jean finds it difficult."

"This is our living room," said Jean proudly, as she opened the double doors.

"My goodness. This looks just like Loma Verde!" exclaimed Maria.

"A real home away from home," said Michael, in his unctuous interviewer's manner.

"Jean just has that touch," replied Joe proudly.

"Imagine coming as far as Tibet and decorating your house to look like little bourgeois Loma Verde. Calico fabric! Oak wood furniture! Currier and Ives prints! It's all the reasons I would leave Loma Verde behind, and Joe and Jean brought it with them!" said Maria.

"I thought her decorating looked good," said Michael.

"You would."

"Jean's decorating looked O.K. to me."

"It looked trite."

"What do you mean, 'trite'?"

"Like *Good Housekeeping*. Listen. I hear bells." Maria opened the window of their bungalow room.

"What do you think about Joe's 'irons in the fire'?"

"Shhh, Michael! Listen to the bells."

"You were absolutely right," said Michael, shaking his head. "Jean, Joe, and Carpaccio have all fled from Loma Verde to centers of spiritual or pseudo-spiritual significance. All three have denounced Eele. All three have said they have had it with Loma Verde. We ought to do a story with *that* angle. I'd like to talk more with your old man. Doctors seeking mystical explanations for the things they don't understand because they're illiterate!" Michael began to laugh. "My poor dad's just labored on and on for years. Nothing like a mystical thought would ever occur to him . . ."

"Don't sell him short."

"Sell him short! I'm giving him a compliment! Why would a guy like Eele drive his three-doctor investigating committee to such unusual and secluded locations?"

"Michael, keep still and listen to the bells. Is it possible for you to shut up for more than five seconds?"

"Oh, I know. You want me to try my other phenomenal mouth tricks! They *are* phenomenal, aren't they? Aren't they? Well, why don't you answer me?"

Maria turned around and slowly began to undress. "They're phenomenal, Michael."

After making love, Maria fell into a deep sleep in which she had the following dream. She was driving a car and smashed into another car driven by an elderly man and woman. The woman got out of her car and, in the manner of a grand dame, announced that while her husband was uninjured, she, the elderly woman, was slightly injured and Maria needed medical attention. When Maria tried to protest that she wasn't injured in the slightest, the old woman, who called herself Violet, insisted both of them go immediately to the Loma

Verde Clinic for a checkup. When Maria tried again to protest, Violet told her that she had better do as she was told, as the accident had been Maria's fault in the first place. Leaving her husband at the scene of the accident, she drove Maria to the Clinic. Violet exhibited great delight in being with Maria the entire trip, chatting away like a young girl.

At the Clinic, Violet asked Maria who was the best doctor, and Maria said it was Vincent Carpaccio. Violet insisted that Carpaccio see the two immediately, but Carpaccio's nurse replied that Dr. Carpaccio only saw patients after they had undergone extensive laboratory tests. Maria said, "Well, I guess we don't need to see the doctor after all."

"Nonsense," said the old woman. "We will have the tests."

The two went to the laboratory. Violet announced that she wanted the lab technician to draw several vials of Maria's blood. Maria tried to protest, but then resigned herself to having her blood drawn and she lay down on the floor. The old woman looked on with glee as Maria's blood began to fill little vials.

Over a liter of Maria's blood was taken. She felt weak and dizzy. She turned her face around as she lay on the floor and she saw the old woman smiling at her. The lab technician announced that Dr. Carpaccio would be unable to see them that day, and to come back in the morning. "But I thought he was the best doctor!" exclaimed Violet.

"I made a mistake! We'll see Joe Kuhl!" cried Maria.

"You can't," replied the lab technician. "He's on a trek in Tibet with his family. You can see Dr. Carpaccio in the morning."

"Let's go," said Violet, and she and the lab technician helped Maria stand. Violet supported Maria, and the two walked into the lobby of the Clinic, where the old woman's husband awaited them. "Go to him," Violet told Maria. "He needs a young woman. Go to him."

Maria looked at Violet's husband, who was a distinguished-looking man of about eighty. "Go to him or I'll tell the police you were drunk when you hit us!" She pushed Maria into her husband's arms. The old man tenderly helped Maria walk out of the Clinic.

"I need to see Dr. Carpaccio!" cried Maria.

"No, you don't," replied the old man. "Now you will get better. I will take care of you."

"Dr. Carpaccio's let me down! He could have helped me out of this mess."

"I'll help you from now on. You don't need doctors," replied the old man.

"Why do you want me?" sobbed Maria.

"I already have you," replied the man calmly. "And I want you because you are new."

"What?"

"You're new." Maria looked down at herself. She was dressed in street clothes from the turn of the century—a long skirt, a long velvet cape with a hood, a fur muff, and soft, low-heeled boots.

"The old man is Ben, of course," said Michael, yawning and stretching. Maria was sitting up in bed, smoking a Cartier cigarette (she had bought a package in the Tokyo airport.) "And my dad says patients always blame their doctors if they— the patients I mean—get sick or something screws up in their lives. I mean your dream is so typical it's not funny."

"But what about the old woman who pushed me off onto her husband after extracting a liter of my blood?"

"The blood test in your dream symbolized your fear of having your very lifeblood sucked out of you by Ben. Don't look so upset. It's just a dream. O.K.?"

"O.K. But who's the old lady?"

"I don't know. I'm not a psychiatrist," said Michael. He paused. "Although I'd be a damned good one if I were."

"How did you get into the newspaper business, Mike?" asked Joe that evening at dinner.

"I like to write. I like to meet people. Journalism was a natural, I guess."

"What about you, Maria?"

"Oh, the same reasons as Michael. I like to write. And I like to uncover stories. And to be honest with you, I just can't understand why the two of you couldn't get more into the Eele deal. I mean, why didn't you do more to try and get him kicked out of the Clinic?"

Jean looked at Joe and sighed. "How would *you* like to be associated with someone like Eele? Digging up enough evidence to get Eele permanently suspended from the Clinic would have been degrading to us."

"That's right," said Joe. "We leave that kind of stuff to journalists . . . if you'll forgive me."

"Well, you may leave that kind of stuff to journalists," said Michael, "but if you'll forgive *me*, at least journalists don't cover up for other journalists. If a journalist fakes his or her information on a story—and we all know it's been done—they get their asses kicked out the door. I wish we could say that about you doctors."

"Are you trying to intimate that Jean and I covered up for Eele?"

"Yes," replied Michael and Maria in unison.

"Well, we didn't," said Jean. "What is it, Kenrab?"

"Madame Doctor, Paljor is here with a telegram."

"Well, tell him to come in." She turned to Joe and whispered, "I'll bet it's the Zippi-Cola deal!"

"The what?" asked Michael quickly.

"Yes, Paljor, what is it?" asked Joe, rising.

"A telegram, Divine Doctor, for M. Weintraub and M. Forsythe."

"Oh," sighed Joe, and his face fell.

Michael took the envelope and tore it open. "It's from Ben. We got it! Listen. 'You have Prize. Stop. Congratulations. Stop. Ben.'"

"I can't believe it! My first story and it won a Pulitzer Prize!" said Maria, jumping up and down.

"*Our* first story. You always seem to forget *that* angle."

"Well, congratulations, if you go in for prizes, that is," sneered Joe.

"Well, hey, Joe," said Michael quickly, "I hear they're not giving out Nobel Prizes for taking care of the Dalai Lama."

"That's *right!*" snapped Jean, and she left the dining room.

"I hope I didn't start something," said Michael innocently.

"Oh no, of *course* you didn't!" said Joe snidely. "Excuse me for a minute." He followed his wife out of the room.

"Hey, old buddy, thanks for bringing up the message," said Michael to Paljor.

"Is this prize important?"

"In our line of work it is. It would be kind of like if the Dalai Lama asked you to be his personal guide. You know what I mean?"

"Perhaps," said Paljor. "Why is the Divine Doctor so upset?"

"Because maybe he's not so divine," said Michael.

"But he is the Dalai Lama's personal physician!"

"Well, you know how it is, old buddy. Life is tough at the top. Well, the Divine Doctor returns. How's Jean?"

"Jean is just putting the kids to bed. Listen, I'm sorry I popped off like that. I'm really happy for you two. It's really great that you got the Pulitzer Prize. It was a great group of stories that you wrote about the food ashram. My favorite one was the Barney Christian profile. I always figured that old sawbones was a son-of-a-bitch. Kenrab, bring us a bottle of champagne. And tell Jean that we're celebrating our guests' winning the Pulitzer Prize." Kenrab bowed and disappeared. Paljor bowed and waited. "That will be all, Paljor. Unless you two want to send a message back to your newspaper," said Joe.

"No, we'll get a message back later," said Michael.

"No, let's give Paljor a message now. We could write a limerick. You're good at that, Michael. Let's see. What rhymes with 'prize'?"

"Lies," said Joe quickly.

"Hey, Joe, I see you're not so bad at limericks yourself," said Michael.

"I once thought of journalism as a career choice. Briefly."

Paljor quietly left the room. Kenrab returned with a bottle of champagne. Jean followed shortly. "Well, I'm always delighted to open a bottle of champagne," she said. "And to celebrate such a wonderful event!" Upon close examination, Maria noticed that Jean had been crying.

"Yep. We like a good bottle of champagne now and then," said Joe, struggling with the cork, which suddenly popped straight through the ceiling, spilling champagne into the air. "Looks like we lost most of the bottle. It's the altitude."

"Maybe we're in the wrong altitude," said Jean, testily.

"Kenrab, get another bottle. At least the Dalai Lama has fixed Jean and me up with a lot of champagne."

"So what's this Zippi-Cola deal?" asked Michael.

"Sorry," said Joe, "I can't talk about it. Ah, good, Kenrab. Maybe you would open this bottle for us." Kenrab uncorked the champagne and poured it into four glasses. Jean and Joe drank their champagne very quickly and Kenrab poured more for them.

"So what about this Zippi-Cola deal?" repeated Michael.

"I can't talk about it. Let's just say it's a deal which would really set Jean and me up."

"Hey, that sounds like a good deal!" said Michael.

"I've got a good limerick," said Joe. "There was an old doctor named Eele, who liked to cop a feel . . ."

"Joe!" exclaimed Jean.

"Sorry, Jean. The altitude really affects me after one glass."

"So, this Zippi-Cola deal will set you up real good, huh?" asked Michael. Joe nodded. "You *do* mean Zippi-Cola? Not cocaine?"

"Oh, no. I mean Zippi-Cola," said Joe. "Bring another bottle, Kenrab. Nobody gives a shit about cocaine up here. Zippi-Cola's the thing."

"Like they say, it's realer than real," said Michael. "So, the Zippi-Cola Company's going to set you up?"

"We're talking all of Southeast Asia, and possibly the mainland," said Joe. Jean blanched.

"Come on, Jean. Everyone's going to know sooner or later. I mean we're talking big bucks. I'm going to endorse ginseng-enriched Zippi-Cola out here. Say, what do you think of the food tonight?"

"I think it's revolting," said Maria. "What *is* this stuff anyway?"

"Toasted barley flour balls made with butter and yak meat," said Joe. "We've gotten used to it. They say that all Tibetan monks are vegetarians but in reality there's a lot of goat and yak consumed up here."

"Ginseng-enriched Zippi-Cola? Who's idea was that? Yours or Zippi-Cola's?" asked Michael.

"Zippi-Cola's, of course. What kind of doctor do you think I am, anyway?"

"I don't know, Joe. What does ginseng do for you?" asked Maria.

"The Chinese say it's rejuvenating. Since I'll be endorsing it in China and Southeast Asia where they all go for it anyway, you can't say I'm doing anything unethical, can you? I'm just marketing the stuff for the Zippi-Cola Company. We're getting a million dollars for a six-month tour of Southeast Asia. In other words, we're leaving the Dalai Lama. Frankly, I've had it with yak meat and barley balls."

"Me too!" exclaimed Jean.

"You're endorsing ginseng-enriched Zippi-Cola?" asked Maria.

"What's the difference between endorsing Valium and endorsing ginseng-enriched Zippi-Cola? Asians believe in ginseng, Americans believe in Zippi-Cola, and I believe in improving East-West relations. And if I make a little money on the side, why not?"

"Why not what?" asked Maria.

"Why not endorse the product?" Joe looked at Maria and Michael. "I see you don't like the idea. I know. You think it's unethical. Well, it's not! I just explained to you why it's not. Get it?"

"No, Dr. Kuhl, I don't get it. But maybe that's because I don't buy your simplistic little explanations," said Maria.

"Hey, Maria, what do you have against the man's making a million dollars in a one-shot, six-month deal? He's not making it his life's work, obviously," said Michael.

"That's right! Jean and I plan to be back in Loma Verde in six months."

"That's great. We've missed you both!" said Michael. "All the glamour you both added around town." He winked at Maria. "Why, Maria always has said you both looked just like a Zippi-Cola commercial. Anyway, congratulations. Seems like we've all got a lot to celebrate tonight."

Joe opened another bottle of champagne. "I know you're both planning to screw me over in print about my Zippi-Cola deal. I'm just telling you out front that I don't give a shit. I'm making a pioneering effort for all doctors." He left the room.

"You should have seen him before I got him," sighed

Jean. "He drove one of those macho Pontiac Firebirds and ate greasy pizza."

"I'd take greasy pizza right now over this crap," said Michael quickly.

"*I* agree," said Maria. "About Pontiac Firebirds, that is. They are *macho* cars."

"They are *not*. Find an American car on the road with the pickup of a Firebird."

"You know, the Clinic wants us back. If Joe and I return they plan to make Joe the director of the entire staff!"

"You're kidding!" said Michael.

"I certainly am not! Joe's the best doctor there is! The Clinic knows it and they're just happy that we're coming back."

"They'll take you back even if Joe endorses ginseng-enriched Zippi-Cola?" asked Maria.

"Of course they will. With delight and gratitude."

"So you changed Joe, kind of smoothed up his act?" asked Maria.

"That's right. I hate it in Tibet and Joe knows it. He also knows I made him who he is so he's willing to come back to Loma Verde. Yes, I see you're surprised, but I made Joe Kuhl who he is."

"So then, Michael Weintraub, maybe there is hope for you."

Joe returned within minutes and said, "Kenrab says we ought to get going if we want to hear the bell ringing."

"What is this bell ringing anyway?" asked Maria.

"Well, let's put it this way. It isn't Beethoven," replied Jean.

"That's for damned sure," said Joe. "The Asians may have it over us on some things, but even they admit we've cornered the market on music. I think we'd better get going. Oh, and as long as you're up here, you might as well come with me to something even weirder. It's the funeral for the laboratory animals."

"The what?" asked Michael.

"The first Buddhist commandment is: 'Thou shalt not

take life.' Therefore, all doctors and scientists are required to attend a yearly funeral for all laboratory animals that have been killed in experiments. The funeral is tomorrow."

"You're joking!" exclaimed Michael.

"I'm not joking. I will be forced to attend this ceremony dressed in black and I will supposedly pray for the animals slain in the hospital lab up here. That's one of the reasons Jean and I are taking the kids and leaving this place. I don't want my kids growing up thinking this is normal."

"I suppose a lab animal funeral goes with the territory," said Michael.

"That's why we're leaving the territory!" said Jean. "To hell with all of this weirdness!"

"I must say though that to be sitting in your dining room makes me think I'm right back in Loma Verde," said Maria. "Did you move all your furniture up here?"

"That's right," said Jean. "It was a part of the deal. If I couldn't have my furniture up here, I'd never have come."

"It must have cost a fortune to move all your furniture up here!" said Maria.

"The Dalai Lama paid for it," replied Joe.

"What I can't understand is that if you *do* eat meat and you *do* kill animals in lab experiments, how does all of this go down with the Dalai Lama?" asked Michael.

"I don't know. Hypocrisy is all over the place and I can't get involved in some Buddhist conflict. That Eele deal was bad enough. I've had enough conflict for awhile. I've been working hard and taking everyone's shit and I'm sick of it. Besides, the weather is so goddamned lousy up here I don't even feel like running any more. I just want to take Jean and the kids out of this mess I got us in and live high on the hog for a few months. We'll make our headquarters at the Royal Hotel in Hong Kong. We'll only stay in the best hotels in Southeast Asia. If I have to go to some poverty pocket I'll take a company jet and only stay as long as I have to. I'm going to make this lousy Tibet mistake

174

up to my family."

"Joe, you're a living saint," said Jean.

Back in their bungalow, Michael asked Maria, "What did you think of the bell-ringing ceremony?"

"I can't hear you."

"I said 'what did you think of the bell-ringing ceremony?'"

"I can't hear you."

"What are you doing anyway?"

"I'm splashing my face thirty times. I'll be finished in a minute."

"I was also meaning to ask you. What are all those little bottles and shit all over the place?"

"I'm on the Lazlo routine. Now what did you say?" Maria walked out of the bathroom patting her face with some night cream.

"Rancid butter would be cheaper."

"Is that what you were saying when I was splashing my face?"

"How much does all that Lazazo shit cost anyway?"

"*Lazlo.* Hundreds. But it's my skin. What's it to you, Michael?"

"You spend *hundreds* for that shit?"

"What's it to you?"

"You're expensive. I've found that out. Lobster, Lazazo, Laurent Perrier champagne. Who was footing the bill for all of this stuff before you were working? Daddy?"

"No. A very wimpy but appreciated trust fund set up by my mother before she died."

"Maria, you've got a lot of problems."

"Like what? Name them all, Mr. Psychiatrist."

"Oh, your mother dying when you were young, Daddy,

trust funds, expensive tastes. Who's going to be able to afford you?"

"I'm not on the market, Mr. Shrink."

Michael rubbed his eyes. "What did you think of the bell-ringing ceremony?"

"'The bells are ringing for me and my gal'? Are you getting sentimental in your old age, Michael?"

"Joe and Jean seem to have a pretty good thing going. I'm not down on marriage."

"Oh yeah," said Maria. "Joe is just, you know, 'a living saint.' Of course, those kinds of sentiments appeal to you."

"Hey, what's wrong with loving your husband and sticking up for him?"

"She's mawkish, that's all. And I hate her little calico crap all over the place and I especially hate her 'stand by your man' attitude, and all the sentimental nonsense that goes with it. It's like emotional blackmail."

"Hey, take it *easy*, Forsythe. I think you've got a little thing going now about marriage."

"Don't be a sot, Michael."

Michael fell on one knee. "Maria, I love you passionately and I want to love you whether there are stories or there aren't stories. Will you marry me?"

"Are you crazy? I'm putting on my night cream."

"Oh please! My knee is killing me. An old tennis injury, you know."

"Oh, I don't know. Can't we think about it awhile?"

"No, we can't! My brain is about to burst in this altitude. Just think . . . a little Buddhist ceremony up in the Tibetan Himalayas . . ."

"You *want* to get *married* in Tibet?"

"Why not? I'm very attracted to Buddhism. And we can honeymoon in Death Valley. What do you say, Maria? Will you be my bride?"

"No, but I'll be your wife. And no Death Valley."

"Oh joy! Oh joy! Forsythe will have me. Ring out the bells, Tibet! I've got to find Paljor. I've got to get him to get a message to Joe Kuhl. Stay there. I'll be right back. Oh. I forgot." Michael threw his arms around Maria and kissed her. "That cream's a little thick. How much cream do you need on your face anyway?"

"I'm planning to look good when I'm fifty. Do you think you'll still be interested in me when I'm fifty?"

"Of course I will. What do you take me for? 'raucous rogue & vivid voltaire you beautiful anarchist i salute thee!'— e. e. cummings. We will read poetry and win Pulitzers. We will fly across the seas in search of the truth!"

"Settle down, Michael. Why do you need to get a message to Joe?"

"The Divine Doctor could probably set up the marriage for us."

"What makes you think he can do that?"

"Don't question divinity, my dear. Aimez-vous Buddhism? I'll be right back. I think Paljor hangs out across the street with his cronies at night. Maybe some of that shit on your face will have evaporated by the time I return. Did you bring something to get married in?"

"Of course I didn't. Did you?"

"No, but I don't care. I'll be right back. You like the idea, don't you? Marriage in Tibet?"

"I like it, Michael. Hurry up. I want to hear all about your tennis tendon when you get back."

"I have another tendon for you."

I received this telegram from Mike Weintraub in Tibet. "Marriage with Forsythe followed funeral for frogs STOP great stories STOP Pl. wire money STOP."

My God, or should I say My Buddha?

The Royal Hotel
Hong Kong

Dear Daddy,

I know this will come as a shock to you but I got married last week in Tibet to my partner Michael Weintraub. His father, Winston Weintraub, is head of orthopedic surgery at the Medical School and, as you know, has been at Greenwich for twenty-five years. Michael's mother Mimi is from France and Michael says she's a real scream.

Our wedding was a Buddhist ceremony, but the counselor who married us wanted us to feel at home so he played an old Toscanini recording of Beethoven's Sixth. (We said our vows during the Third Movement "Merry Gathering of Country-folk.") Our witnesses were Jean and Joe Kuhl, formerly of the Loma Verde Clinic, and they offered us champagne following the ceremony.

To make a long story short, I'm in love and I'm happy, so I know you'll be happy too. I can't wait for you to meet Michael. You'll love him. He can quote poetry (e. e. cummings—I realize it's not Virgil, Horace, etc., but it's *very* pleasant.) Maybe you could look up Winston and Mimi and just say hello. We'll be in Asia for another week at least.

Take care of yourself, looking forward to having you meet Michael.

Love,
Maria

P.S. How about our Pulitzer? Not bad for the daughter you referred to last year as an "illiterate loafer."

"Zippi-Cola has taken that giant step forward in the name of health by introducing ginseng-enriched Zippi-Cola in Southeast Asia." Joe Kuhl stood in front of an audience of mainly the press in a private room of the Royal Hotel. Jean stood by his side wearing a green silk Chinese dress the hotel tailors had whipped up for her in one morning. "The ginseng is pure Red Panax Extraction from Tianjin and each twelve-ounce bottle or can of Zippi is guaranteed to have in it one gram of Red Panax ginseng. And naturally our consumers will have the convenience of choosing regular enriched Zippi or diet-enriched Zippi or caffeine-free diet-enriched Zippi. I drink caffeine-free diet-enriched Zippi myself. As an American doctor trained in western medicine and clinical methods, I see this new product as a breakthrough for the soft-drink industry which has taken a beating over the years for being calorie-rich and nutrition-poor. Since it's apparent to every sensible person that the entire world loves Zippi-Cola, it's apparent also that an enriched super-Zippi is all that's been missing from most of the world's diets. And so the day has finally come, and I'm proud to be the spokesman for ginseng-enriched Zippi-Cola, a product whose far-reaching manifestations will be undoubtedly profound."

A Chinese representative for Zippi-Cola rose and began to applaud. "Now then, Dr. Kuhl will take your questions. Yes, Miss, you in the blue dress."

"Dr. Kuhl, is it true that ginseng will make you more *potent*?"

"Kim Blakely!" whispered Maria to Michael. "How did *she* get here?"

"Well . . . so the Chinese say. Ginseng is an age-old herb reputed to have rejuvenating elements. It's been used by the

Chinese for at least five thousand years."

"Why do you, as an American doctor, believe in ginseng or in Zippi-Cola?" The burly Chinese man who asked the question stared at Joe for several seconds before sitting.

"Well . . . I think I made myself perfectly clear in my opening statements. Ginseng-enriched Zippi-Cola is the future . . ."

"Does that mean we can anticipate other enriched Zippi-Colas, for instance, vitamin C-enriched Zippi or vitamin E-enriched Zippi?"

"Poor Joe," whispered Maria to Michael.

"Poor Joe, my ass! The guy's making a million dollars off this deal. Don't forget it!"

"Hi, you two," drawled Kim Blakely as she slunk over to where Michael and Maria were sitting. "Congratulations for your Pulitzer *and* for your marriage. A pretty exciting week it's been for you, hasn't it?"

"Hi, Kim. How are you?"

"Fine, Michael. I must say, marriage seems to suit you both. I guess old Ben's really put his faith in you two. He's never spent so much money on two reporters for just hanging around the watering holes of Asia."

"No reporter of his ever got a Pulitzer Prize before," replied Maria, watching Michael walk away.

"How true, how true. I guess what surprises everyone on his staff is that he so willingly lets you traipse all over the place. I mean, didn't he have the hots for you, Maria?"

"I think he likes the quality of our work."

"You know, I taught Michael the ropes. He learned everything from me. I'll bet he won't admit *that* to you. *There's* one man who doesn't need a ginseng pickup, if you know what I mean. Excuse me, Maria, my friend who's *very big* in the San Francisco Chinese community is waiting for me in the lobby. I'm looking for a lavender jade bracelet. See you later I'm sure, because we're staying at the Royal too. Joe Kuhl is quite attractive. I'll bet he doesn't need a ginseng pickup either. Let's have a drink together this evening. Singapore slings. Isn't that what Somerset Maugham drank? Anyway *my* friend doesn't need a ginseng pickup, that's for sure. I'm exhausted! Well, I've got to go. Let's get together tonight."

"See you later, fuckface," said Maria between her teeth.

Michael walked back over to Maria. "Well, did you have a good talk with Blakely?"

"Yeah. She said she taught you everything you wanted to know about sex and that you were *one* man who didn't need a ginseng pickup. She says she's here with her friend who's 'really big in the San Francisco Chinese community.' "

"He's probably the headwaiter at the Empress of China. She's really a screwed-up bitch. I went out with her a few times but I soon realized she was just into fucking people over. Anyway, who cares about her? Listen. Joe and Jean have invited us to have dinner with them tonight on some picturesque shrimp boat on the water."

"Michael, I think it would be a good idea if we didn't get too close to Joe and Jean."

"I think they're really being nice to ask us. After all, they were our witnesses . . ."

"Michael, after we print our stories I don't think I'll be able to see Joe as a friend or as a doctor any more."

"Bullshit, Forsythe! All we're going to do is write the story objectively. Joe Kuhl knows that what he's doing is questionable. He also knows what we're doing. He also understands that he's doing his thing with Zippi to make a million bucks and that we're doing our thing with this story to further our careers. He understands the whole thing. The guy's really smart. *He's only in it for the money.* Get it?"

"What are we in it for?"

"Forsythe, I don't believe you. What are you talking about?"

"I don't know. For one thing, I think you've got lousy

taste in women if you ever went out with Kim Blakely."

"But I married *you*."

"I'll drop the subject of Kim Blakely if you will. I do think it would be better if we didn't go out with Joe and Jean."

"Forsythe, listen to me. If we don't go out with Joe and Jean tonight, I'll lay you ten to one Kim Blakely will. We've *got* to get this story out as quickly as possible. Now do you understand what I'm trying to do?"

"Michael, I feel weird about accepting their hospitality and then writing about them."

"You're accepting Zippi-Cola's hospitality. Remember?"

"All right."

"That's good. It would be such a shame if that bitch Blakely got another story."

"Well hello, you two," said Joe, shaking hands with Maria and Michael. "We're still coming down from that great reception at the Royal. I think the product's going to go over really big, don't you?"

"I'm sure it will. Hi, Jean. Maria and I were just mentioning in the taxi on the way over what a great dress you have— that Chinese one, I mean."

"I just couldn't resist having it made. I think it added a certain authentic touch to the press conference. Who was that blonde woman in the blue dress who asked Joe that obnoxious question?"

"Oh . . ." Michael looked at Maria and she gave him a dirty look. "That's Kim Blakely from KUTK in San Francisco. She used to be on the *Vindicator* staff. She's just a little over-bearing. My advice is to stay away from her and don't talk to her about what you're doing at all costs."

"Oh, I know *that* reporter," said Jean. "She comes across

on TV as a little eager to promote herself. I hate people who are trying so obviously to *promote* themselves."

"Yes, well then," laughed Joe, and he cleared his throat, "I thought we'd begin tonight's dinner with a bottle of champagne. It seems to go well with Chinese food."

"Listen, Joe, this dinner is on the *Vindicator*. You've both been so hospitable to Michael and me. You really helped to make our wedding in Tibet special."

"Oh, by the way, Jean and I would like to see the stories you wrote about us in Tibet. Remember, we agreed that I would have a look at them before they were printed."

"Sure thing, Joe," said Michael. "You'll have them all tomorrow morning. Truth of the matter is that Maria and I have to push off. Back to the old Loma Verde grind."

"Oh! Joe and I thought you might want to come to Tokyo with us. Have you ever been to Japan?"

"No, and we'd like to go, but I don't think it will be possible," said Maria.

"Wait a minute! *I* think we could work something out with Ben."

"Well, I don't, Michael. He's really been generous, but I think we've got to get home. We don't even have a place to live."

"My apartment's good enough for now," said Michael.

"I think we should probably get a new place."

"I know what Maria's saying," said Jean. "Maria wants to make a *home* for you, Mike. And if you need any help finding fabrics or anything, I hope you'll let me know."

"That's great, Jean. I'll remind Maria to call you in case she forgets."

"I won't forget, Michael." Maria shot another dirty look in Michael's direction.

"But I'm serious about one thing. Don't talk to Kim Blakely. She's unable to write or deliver a good objective story and she's not above slander."

"Well, Jean and I have good attorneys if she'd ever try

anything like that. By the way, I really do want to see those stories before you leave. So then, everything sounds so good on this menu . . ."

"Excuse me, sir," said a waiter, "Ginseng-enriched caffeine-free diet Zippi on the house, for the great Dr. Joe Kuhl, his lovely wife, and his friends."

"I think Zippi also goes great with Chinese food," said Joe. He looked at Maria and Michael. "Anyway, aren't you two a little young to develop such champagne tastes?"

Department of Cardiology
Greenwich University

Dear Mr. Boyer:

I have been reading the *Loma Verde Vindicator* for many years. For some time now I have been disillusioned with the medical reporting. Your recent article on vasectomies has aroused in me the need to write; thus I have taken pen in hand. As the ink begins to flow I feel it only a proper discharge of my duty as a medical spokeswoman to bring to your attention the many inaccuracies in your published stories on these important issues.

To begin with, the data are substantial that vasectomies do not decrease male potency—as I know from personal experience from many of my patients. In fact, there is some evidence of a significant positive correlation of penis size following vasectomy.

Dr. Myrtle Menslinger published in a recent issue of *The Olde England Journal of Medicine* showing there was an expected increase of .57 in the number of times intercourse took place on a weekly basis in the year following a vasectomy. Moreover, it was shown in an article published by Dr. Menslinger two years ago in the same journal (Volume 105, page 102) that there is positive evidence that the common form of birth control, coitus interruptus, is a source of male cardiovascular problems. And as you fully understand, such methods are scarcely indicated for those who have had vasectomies.

I have only dealt with one medical subject treated by the *Vindicator*. Similar mistaken notions have been published about the dangers of intercourse for men who have suffered heart attacks. As I believe you know, such cardiological topics as this are close to my heart.

If you desire, I should be happy to give you more details on flagrant medical errors in recent *Vindicator* reporting.

Sincerely yours,
Flora Framingham

Well, I'm no Freud, but I can tell when a lady wants to get laid. I decided I'd better get some more medical advice. We agreed to meet that Friday for lunch at an old Greenwich watering hole on the bay, Dickie's. As I made the reservation, I couldn't help but think of that old Greenwich saying, "Let's dick around at Dickie's."

"Mr. Boyer, may I ask you a personal question?" Flora didn't wait for my response. "Have you had a vasectomy?" I nearly spilled my Scotch over my pants. Flora, sipping a Perrier, watched me closely. "You're under a good deal of stress, Mr. Boyer. That's for certain."

"I certainly am."

"I could show you a few simple anti-stress exercises, some of which you could do right now."

"Well, I'd appreciate that, Dr. Framingham."

"First, put down that drink. You'll only feel more stressed by the time you're finished with it."

"I generally feel less stressed after a drink."

"That's pure fallacy, Mr. Boyer, as you should very well know."

"Do you drink, Dr. Framingham?"

"Only on certain occasions."

"What do you drink?"

"Well, on those certain occasions, it's usually white wine or champagne."

"Dickie! Do you have champagne?"

"Certainly, Mr. Boyer, but only by the bottle."

"What do you have?"

"Domaine Chandon."

"I'll take a bottle of Domaine Chandon."

"Really, Mr. Boyer," whispered Flora, "I have no intention of drinking an entire bottle of champagne."

"Drink as much of it as you want."

"Mr. Boyer, this is really too much."

"Call me Ben."

"Ben, this is really too much."

"I think that your agreeing to meet me for lunch to help set the *Vindicator* straight on our medical coverage deserves a little celebration. You *are* the premiere spokeswoman for cardiovascular matters in this country, are you not, Dr. Framingham?"

"Flora."

"Here's your champagne, Mr. Boyer," said Dickie. "Domaine Chandon. Two glasses?"

"Just one. I'll have another Glenfiddich neat."

"Right away, Mr. Boyer."

"This is really too much, Mr. Boyer . . . I mean Ben."

"Nonsense. How often do I get to take out a beautiful and brilliant woman to lunch?" The cork popped and the bubbly flowed. "Let's see. What were you asking me again?"

"Ahem. Have you had a vasectomy?"

"Not yet, Flora. What do you think? I mean, what's your medical opinion?"

"Well, I believe I've made myself clear on my views. Vasectomies can't be anything but positive for men who no longer wish to have children."

"Well then, Flora, whom do you recommend?"

"For what?"

"For this operation?"

"Oh, there are several doctors at Greenwich who are quite capable. Why? Are you thinking of having a vasectomy?"

I smiled and took a sip of my Glenfiddich. "Quite frankly, Flora, this is the first time I've given any thought at all to the idea." Flora blushed and downed her champagne. I poured her another glass. "And what other medical issues have we incorrectly reported? You mentioned in your letter a story we did about sex being harmful to men who have suffered heart attacks."

"Yes, that story was quite incorrect. Have you ever suffered a heart attack, Ben?"

"Not yet. They tell me at the *Vindicator* that I'm working on it, but I think before I'd ever suffer a heart attack, I'd move back to Miami."

"Miami?"

"Miami." I looked into my glass for waves and palm trees.

"Are you from Miami?"

"That's right. But I've been here in Loma Verde since the late fifties. My two kids went to Greenwich. I suppose I should see Loma Verde as my home but the truth of the matter is that I'll probably end up back in Miami."

"Miami certainly has a pleasant climate. I'm going to Rio next week."

"That sounds exciting, Flora. Business or pleasure?"

"Another medical conference, I'm afraid. But I've never been to Rio and I'm looking forward to it." Flora finished off her second glass of champagne and I poured her a third. "This is marvelous champagne, Ben. What a pleasure!"

"I believe in mixing business with pleasure. Here's to your trip to Rio." I raised my glass and Flora giggled. I heard something drop and soon realized it was her shoe. "You've dropped your shoe."

"I always do that. I feel more comfortable barefoot."

"Really?"

"Oh yes, I always have."

"I guess you know one of my two young superstars, Maria Forsythe. She's just married Michael Weintraub."

"Really! I think they're really and truly wonderful young persons. I *do* think that some of their reporting has been a little . . . slanted."

"Slanted? Not in the least. Their reporting is beautiful, unbiased, objective, investigative work. That's why they won the Pulitzer Prize."

"I read their ashram stories, of course. I enjoyed them. But I know Miranda Kettle and I know Vince Carpaccio and I don't think the stories accurately represented either Miranda or Vince."

"People change, Flora."

"Michael's father was most upset that his son didn't attend medical school. But he must be proud of him now. I know Professor Forsythe is certainly proud of Maria."

"Mike's dad called me after he'd learned his son had won the prize. He thanked me for the help I'd given to Mike and I told him any reason Mike had won the prize was Mike's own doing and that any father had a reason to be proud of a son like Mike."

"Well, there's obviously no stopping those two. In my recent talks with Maria, she seems most intent on getting Duke

Eele kicked out of the Clinic."

"What do you think about Eele?" I poured Flora more champagne.

"No more, please! I really can't drink any more. Well, maybe just this last little bit." Flora's other shoe dropped onto my foot. "Oh, excuse me!"

"No problem, Flora."

"Let's see, where were we? Oh yes. Duke Eele! Oh well, I think he's horrible. You can't imagine how many letters I've written to the board stating my opinions about him. I don't know why he's still practicing. I simply can't imagine! It's really so distressing. So . . . unaccountable. It's doctors like Eele who give patients pause . . . and ammunition."

"What about Joe Kuhl?"

"That's far more understandable. Joe is young, and working with the Dalai Lama will give him a strong name in medicine. Everyone knows that the Dalai Lama has a strong belief in western medicine."

"But as you've probably heard, the Kuhls have left Tibet and Joe has some million dollar deal with the Zippi-Cola Company for endorsing ginseng-enriched Zippi in Southeast Asia."

Flora pursed her lips and looked down. "Joe and Jean have three kids to put through school. I think Joe's mighty lucky to have signed this deal. It's only for six months and it doesn't compromise Joe's medical ethics." I looked down at my fingernails. "Well, do *you* think he's compromising his medical ethics, Ben?"

"I don't know, Flora. Maybe we all ought to get used to doctors in new roles such as product endorsers. Doctors aren't gods, after all."

"Doctors would be the last to think they were gods, I can assure you. It's the media which has put us on this pedestal and then tried to knock us off."

"Come now, Flora, we're not that bad." I patted her hand and noticed she didn't pull away. "Shall we order lunch now?

Why don't you order for me. I'll trust that you'll find something on the menu that's good for my heart. Rio, now *that's* having all the luck . . ."

I decided I needed a vacation. Mike and Maria were on their own track and Dennis O'Brien, my second-in-command man, was anxious to take over editorial duties for a spell. The days were growing shorter in Loma Verde and a chill was icing the evening air. I decided to hit a warm-weather spot, and Rio sounded swell. I packed my old Miami favorites—my white silk suit, ties in shades once known as "Palm Beach pastels," and my deck shoes which my kids had always called "right-off-the-boat stompers." I wore my tan and white two-tone slip-ons and my straw boater to the airport, and a fellow I knew from one of the TV stations saw me and asked me where I'd found my Don Ameche getup. Screw him! I felt grand. I was standing in the economy line waiting to get a seat on the flight to Miami, the first leg of the flight, when Flora Framingham whisked herself up to the front of the first-class line and asked, "Where is the first-class lounge, please?"

That was it. Flora disappeared before I could collect my bags and fall into the first-class line, but I wasn't going to miss any golden opportunities. I choked when they told me the price difference between first class and economy, but I didn't hesitate. I wasn't getting any younger and if a couple thousand dollars is what it took to grab a little bit of pleasure, it didn't matter to me. "Oh, by the way, where is the first-class lounge?" I asked.

"You haven't got time, sir. I'd suggest you go directly to the gate."

I boarded the plane and took a seat. Flora was three rows ahead of me and it looked like the flight wouldn't be full.

Before I had a chance to speak to her, however, we were requested to fasten our safety belts. After an interminable wait for takeoff clearance and we were finally airborne, I casually walked to where Flora sat, writing furiously, and said, "Well, what a coincidence."

Flora looked up at me and smiled, "Why, Ben! What a surprise! I suppose you're going to Miami. Well, *obviously* you're going to Miami since this is where the plane is going."

"No, Flora, as a matter of fact, I'm going on down to Rio to cover the medical conference personally. I've been thinking over the things we discussed at lunch a few days ago and I've decided to assume personal responsibility for any further errors in the *Vindicator*'s medical reporting. I've decided to cover the major conferences myself."

"Well, this is most surprising. I'm sure it will be an interesting conference for the medical writers as well as for the doctors. And of course Rio is such a superb location. I suppose you'll be staying at the Copacabana Palace."

"No, I, uh, prefer Ipanema Beach. I'm staying at one of those little undiscovered places with quiet surroundings." I should have known and planned for the fact that Flora would be put up in a swank joint like the Copacabana Palace, but I was still reeling from the cost of a first-class ticket to Rio.

"I've heard that Ipanema Beach is the rage now. I'm only staying at the Copacabana Palace because the conference is headquartered there. Oh, do you have a program?"

"Well, I received a packet of information from the medical school. I see that you're the keynote speaker."

"Yes, but as you can see, I'm working on my address right now."

"Well then, please don't let me interrupt you," I said, rising.

"Oh, you're not interrupting at all! And as you know, it's going to be a long flight. At this point I'm simply trying to organize some thoughts. The thrust of this conference is preventive medicine. That's why I've been asked to speak."

"You've really made major contributions in the field," I murmured as I eyed the stewardess taking orders for drinks.

"And what will it be for you two?"

"I'll take a Glenfiddich neat and she will take a glass of champagne."

"Ben, really, drinking while flying is absolutely no good for you," said Flora.

"Oh, I'm sorry, sir. We don't have your brand. Will Johnny Walker Red do?"

"I suppose it will have to."

"And you are Mr. and Mrs . . . "

"Mr. Ben Boyer and Dr. Flora Framingham," replied Flora quickly.

"Yes, I'm actually sitting over there," I said, gesturing to my seat.

"Well, if you'd like to change seats there won't be any problem. It looks like we'll be only half full in first all the way to Rio." The stewardess smiled. I looked at Flora.

"Please, Ben, do sit here."

"Well, that will be great, Flora. I shall do just that. I'll just go and pick up my stuff and I'll be right back." I walked to my seat and collected my briefcase, thinking all the while that my last-minute airplane extravagance was actually paying off. Flora seemed delighted to have some company, although I couldn't tell if it was just company she was happy to have or *the* company. I was counting on soon finding out.

"I'm sorry, Ben, but I really don't drink during flights. It's been proved over and over again that alcohol consumed during flight dehydrates you and increases the potential for jet lag. Oh, and by the way, while I normally do not believe in sleeping pills, I always take them during long flights to counteract jet lag. If you'd like, I'll give you one."

"When?" I asked miserably.

"At Miami," replied Flora. "Of course, the quality of sleep

from sleeping pills is poor. Rapid Eye Movement tests have proved this over and over again. But it's just a temporary measure against a temporary problem—jet lag, I mean—which can be so debilitating abroad."

"Have you made your luncheon selections yet, Mr. Boyer and Dr. Framingham?"

"We'll both take the 'lighter selection,'" said Flora. "Let's see, a bountiful bowl of greens with healthy sunflower seeds and crunchy bean sprouts. It sounds delicious."

"Oh yes, delicious," I sighed. My heart had been set on the rack of lamb.

"I confess I was the instigator to get a good wholesome salad as a main course on this airline," said Flora.

"No kidding."

"Well, I mean, look at the food they offer you! Heavy, calorie-laden, fatty menus, chemically preserved peanuts, and all of this alcohol. It's enough to have to deal with jet lag, but after a person has a few drinks and eats this food the airlines offer—well—there's no possible hope that a person will be able to function for the first few days abroad."

Flora was beginning to seem less fun. She talked on and on like a lady preacher about the virtues of a lighter diet, exercise, and anti-stress techniques. I thanked my lucky stars that I wasn't a smoker. Flora viewed smokers as stupid and somewhat retarded. When we hit Miami, Flora insisted we walk up and down the airport corridors as aerobically as possible for the entire hour's layover. We returned to the plane (I was about to collapse at this point) and she handed me a sleeping pill and a blindfold and said, "We'll wake up in Rio in the morning. Boa noite, Ben."

"Boa noite, Flora."

"You'll thank me for insisting we exercise in Miami."

"I'm sure I will, Flora."

"Do you jog, Ben?"

"Why?"

"I'm looking for someone to jog with in Rio."

"Sure I jog, Flora. But I forgot to bring my shoes."

"Well, if you can buy some, let's jog tomorrow morning. That is, the day after our arrival."

"That sounds . . . just . . . great . . . " I whispered. I was going under fast. For a doctor who believed in preventive medicine, Flora had damned strong sleeping pills. At this point I only hoped I wouldn't snore.

I awoke to a stewardess announcing, "Bom Dia, and welcome to Rio de Janeiro. To your left you will see the famous Sugarloaf Mountain."

"My God! How long did we sleep?" I asked.

"You slept the entire flight," said Flora, looking fresh and rested. "That's a very good sign, I might add. It means you probably never take sleeping pills."

"I can't say that I do," I replied, yawning and stretching.

"I've been awake for about an hour. You see, when they are controlled, certain drugs and medications are absolute life-enhancers as well as life-savers. You'll thank me for helping you through your jet lag. Even if you *did* have that one drink."

I paid all that money to fly first class for *this?*

"Meet me tomorrow morning at six a.m. at the Copacabana Palace for our jogging," said Flora.

"But what about dinner tonight?"

"Oh, I'm sorry, Ben. I'm committed to dinner with the conference organizers tonight. But we'll get together tomorrow morning, bright and early. I must say, Ben, you're an individual after my own heart. I appreciate your dedication to your well-being."

"Share a taxi?"

"I'm sorry, but some colleagues are picking me up. See you tomorrow morning."

T all and tan and young and lovely, the girl from
Ipanema goes walking . . .

I was sitting in the Garôta de Ipanema, the bar where "The Girl from Ipanema" was written. Of course the bar wasn't called Garôta de Ipanema when the two guys were writing the song. I asked the fellow behind the counter whatever happened to the girl from Ipanema and he said, "Oh, she grew up, married a rich man, and moved to São Paulo." I had to laugh a little, realizing that two generations of tall, tan, beautiful girls had passed by this bar since the song was written. I was drinking a Johnny Walker Red—I was beginning to think Johnny Walker Red was epidemic—and studying the medical conference program. I couldn't miss Flora's speech of course. I needed something to talk to her about. Any dream of wooing her under the Rio moonlight would no doubt have to include an ode to prevention. And of course I had to find a place where I could buy running shoes. I was a little nervous about my chances of keeping up with Flora during an early morning run. To be perfectly honest, I was worried about my chances of waking up at six in the morning. But I was game. I was actually a strong cross-country runner in high school. I was willing to give it a shot.

"Yes, the original girl from Ipanema is grown up, two or three kids of her own, but there are hundreds of beautiful girls in Ipanema," said the bartender. "Just take a look. You want to go to a first-class samba show? Most beautiful mulatto girls in all of Brazil. I can arrange for you."

How can he tell her he loves her? Yes he would
give his heart gladly . . .

"Samba is in the blood of every Carioca. Forget the elusive girl from Ipanema. I'll fix you up to go to a great samba show. Tonight at eleven-thirty. At the door, ask for João. Say Ricardo sent you." The bartender wrote out an address and gave it to me. "Don't be late. The club fills up early."

Well, why not, I thought.

At eleven-thirty I was at the Oba Oba Samba Club, having spent the larger part of my afternoon in pursuit of running shoes and the early evening deep in sleep in my hotel room. Despite Flora's attempts to aid my jet lag I was exhausted, and it had taken three small but potent cups of Brazilian coffee to get me going. João examined my note from Ricardo and slapped my back. "You like pretty girls? I give you a front row seat." There I was, wedged between a noisy British tour group and a silent party of Japanese businessmen. I was so close to the stage that I knew I'd have to watch the show with my head craned backward. After everyone in the audience had bought a drink, the girls finally came onto the stage, and by God, they *were* pretty. The costumes were as skimpy as could be but it was hot in the club. I couldn't help noticing that no well-marked EXITS existed and one match could light up the entire joint and all of us in it. Anyway, no matter. I was finally here, Rio at night! The guy who owned the club, who doubled as master of ceremonies, began inviting patrons on stage to dance with the girls. It never ceases to amaze me to what lengths people will go to degrade themselves. I sat there, watching a British fellow and a fat German woman making complete asses of themselves. When the master of ceremonies came into the audience to invite other patrons onstage to dance the samba he tapped my shoulder but I shook my head. "Shy guy from U.S.A!" he said into his microphone, and everyone laughed. At least I'd been spared the spotlight. Finally a couple from the audience volunteered to dance onstage. I raised my hand to catch the barman's attention and when I turned to the stage, Flora and a Latin man were gyrating around the dancing samba girls. Of course, Flora's just getting her aerobic exercise was my second thought. My first, I confess, was that she must be stone drunk. I leaned back in my chair and smiled. Flora moved well, so well that when the musicians stopped playing even the samba girls were clapping.

"You're a very good dancer, young lady," said the master of ceremonies. "May I ask your name and where you're from?"

"Oh! I'm Mrs. Smith from the United States," replied Flora quickly. Her companion hit her playfully and laughed. Flora had let me down on that one, especially as her coyness came on the tail, so to speak, of a very steamy fanny-shaking spectacle. Naturally, I couldn't help but wonder who her Latin lover was. I watched them leave the stage and return to their table in the corner. Lover Boy ordered champagne. I was beginning to wonder if Flora would be up at six for our jogging date. I was wondering, too, if I'd come all the way down to Rio in vain. It was beginning to sink in that Flora was probably with this south-of-the-border Lothario at the Copacabana Palace. Well, I'd always heard stories about medical conferences, but Flora had been my unbridled passion fantasy under the schoolmarm facade. What to do?

I mulled over this problem, and came up with a handy rationale: if some Rio Romeo could make himself available to Flora Framingham, so could I. When the two left the club I skulked out behind them and followed them in a taxi to a very posh-looking club in Ipanema called Hippopotamus. After they were inside I followed suit but was stopped by a doorman who informed me that this club was for members only. I showed him my press card and he laughed in my face. I laughed too, and called it a night.

Having predetermined that Flora was probably good for

her word, I asked for a five-thirty wakeup call, and fell into a mildly disgruntled sleep.

At five minutes till six I was in the lobby of the Copacabana Palace, which was quiet save for two or three joggers, probably American, running out the doors. The morning was already warm and the sun was bright. I was looking at a hotel window display of Brazilian gems and wondering what the chances were of Flora's appearing when at six on the dot an elevator door opened and Flora stepped out. "You haven't been waiting long, have you?" she asked breathlessly. She certainly didn't look worse for her late evening wear as her unmadeup face clearly proved. Even with a thick coat of white sunscreen on her nose and forehead, Flora was a damned attractive woman. She was no Maria Forsythe, but at fifty, Flora was a good-looking lady. Her light brown shoulder-length hair was pulled back in a pony tail and her tall, lean body was evenly distributed in a Greenwich tee shirt and a pair of cotton shorts. "I see you found a pair of running shoes," she said.

I was planning to be discreet, but impropriety got the best of me. "Did you have a good night's rest, Mrs. Smith from the United States?" What a cad I was! Flora reeled around and blushed until her sunscreened face looked like the Swiss flag. "You're a marvelous dancer, Flora, seriously."

"Oh, Ben, I don't know what got into me! Eduardo Enrique—he was my companion last night, a Greenwich cardiologist and a good friend—talked me into getting up on the stage. I could never have done it except that Eduardo was so persuasive. He said everyone dances in Brazil and I'd be a ninny to pass up such an opportunity. I simply had no idea that there would be anyone in the audience whom I would know!"

"Flora, the Oba Oba Samba Club is on every tourist map.

But seriously, Flora, you were simply sensational."

"Oh, I feel like such a fool."

"Well, you shouldn't. Your pal Eduardo is right. Everyone seems to dance in Rio. Say, if you're not already booked for tonight, I know about a great little Italian restaurant right here in Copacabana."

"Oh, I . . . well, unfortunately, I'm having dinner with some colleagues."

"Well, that *is* a shame, Flora. Any chance you can meet me for a drink after dinner?"

"Well, perhaps. But I really don't know at this point."

I had the distinctly unpleasant feeling that Eduardo Enrique was warming Flora's bed at the Copacabana Palace this very instant. "Where's Eduardo from?" I asked, trying to sound casual.

"He's a native Ecuadoran but has been a professor of medicine at Greenwich for years. Shall we get going? Why don't we jog for, say, forty minutes?"

Off we ran. My adrenalin was up and I was unaware of any difficulty in keeping up the pace. Instead, I was searching my memory, for the name Eduardo Enrique sounded vaguely familiar. All along the black and white mosaic sidewalks which lined the beach I racked my brain until, racked with sudden pain in my right side, I came to a halt. The pain subsided immediately and Flora smiled at me. "That's only a stitch, Ben. Nothing to worry about. Why, you're in excellent condition. I'm surprised, to be honest." But not as surprised as I was by her samba performance the night before, I'd wager. "Why don't we start running again? That is, if you're feeling up to it. We could run back to the hotel now."

"Sure thing, Flora," I replied, and with a jolt, the name Eduardo Enrique finally registered. This *cavaliere servente* was notorious around Loma Verde for his amorous conquests. I'd actually been to a party at which this Bozo had finagled the rather attractive hostess and wife of one of the big-gun

Greenwich professors into the kitchen, and when Eduardo's wife walked in on the two, Lover Boy was heard to shout, "But I believe in honesty between a man and wife!" From what I remember, Enrique's wife finally left him, and his advances at parties to attractive young women had become a standing joke around Greenwich. So what in God's name was Flora doing with a guy like Enrique?

"Well, Flora, to be honest," I said between huffs and puffs, "I would like very much to interview you after the conference gets under way. I'd like to have your overview."

"Let's do arrange that, Ben. Let's see. I'm speaking this afternoon at four and I'm chairing discussions both tomorrow morning and tomorrow afternoon. Perhaps after tomorrow afternoon's discussion group?"

"Well, I was actually thinking of dinner, Flora."

"Dinner or an interview?"

"Both, actually. Why not take in what Rio has to offer? Will you take me up on my offer to have dinner at that little Italian restaurant? I'd like to attend a bit of the conference myself before we talk. And naturally I'll want to hear your opening address."

"Why yes, that sounds like a good idea. I've no idea at this point how my schedule stands tomorrow night, but why don't we make it a date and if I have a conflict I'll certainly get in touch with you. Well look! We're back at the hotel. Want to jog same time tomorrow morning?"

"I'm not sure, Flora. I think I'd better wait and see how I feel today. I'll leave a message with your hotel."

"I hope you'll want to jog again. And Ben, I'll bring my sunscreen for you tomorrow. Remember, the sun's constant rays are harmful to human skin even this early in the day. So long. Talk to you soon."

"Best of luck on today's speech, Flora." I watched her disappear inside the hotel. I hailed a taxi and slumped into it. It was becoming less clear to me that all of this was worth it.

Flora gave her keynote address to an overflow audience. Lover Boy was hovering around while she spoke, but when Flora began to field questions, Enrique walked out of the room. I headed for the bar after the tedium of the question-and-answer period began to get to me. Enrique was, I noted, ensconced in a cozy corner with a young blonde. It wasn't an absolute that Enrique *was* with Flora, I told myself, as I found my own cozy corner by the bar's view of the pool. A damned good bar it was too, for it was the first place in Brazil at which I'd been able to get Glenfiddich. So there I sat, looking out at the pool and involuntarily listening to Enrique's romantic murmurings when who should stride into the bar but Flora.

"Oh! Hello, Eduardo."

"Flora, my dear," began Eduardo, rising so hastily he spilled his drink onto his companion. "What a marvelous speech. Please join us. Flora, this is Kathy. Kathy is a paramedical practitioner."

"Hello, Kathy," said Flora, looking crushed, or so it seemed. My heart was going out to poor Flora. "I'm afraid I can't because I have a meeting with the conference committee in a few minutes."

Flora began to walk away and I called to her. She turned and raised her head. "Hello, Ben."

"I enjoyed your address. You certainly got a tremendous reception. I have a few concrete items to discuss with you when we do our interview. By the way, how is your schedule shaping up?"

"Well, I think my evening is free after all." Flora cast a look at Eduardo and he raised his eyebrows and laughed. "That is, if yours is."

"I'm at your service, Flora. I'll pick you up at nine-thirty."

"That sounds lovely, Ben. Don't forget to bring your list of questions." Flora smiled at me. "Still feeling tired from our jog this morning?"

"I feel marvelous, Flora." This wasn't true. My knees were aching so badly I couldn't stand for more than a few minutes in the same place.

"Well, see you tonight." Flora turned around and walked past Eduardo and his companion.

"Excuse me, Eduardo, I *must* go to the powder room." Kathy rose and Eduardo looked over at me and laughed. "Women," he said, "who understands them?"

"Oh, I couldn't agree more with you."

"You have a familiar face, Ben. We have met, haven't we? I am Eduardo Enrique from Greenwich University. I'm at the Medical School." He walked to my table with his drink.

"Ben Boyer of the *Loma Verde Vindicator*. I believe we have met a few times."

"Oh yes! Now I remember!" Eduardo began to laugh like a schoolboy. "The Marlowe's party. Quite a memorable night, that one."

"As I recall, you were quite a hit with Mrs. Marlowe that evening. Please join me."

Eduardo sat down and looked around. "Something tells me I've been deserted. C'est la vie! I will never understand women."

"Who does? So, how is the conference, in your estimation?"

"Oh, these things are all the same. Are you covering it for your paper?" I nodded. "But don't you have a science writer?"

"Flora seems to think our science writer isn't up to snuff, so I've undertaken to cover this story and assume responsibility for any errors in the medical reporting."

"I must say, that article warning men who've suffered heart attacks to refrain from having sex—really, Ben! What a lot of baloney, if you'll pardon the expression. Would a heart attack stop you?"

"Flora criticized that article up and down the line. She's one tough lady."

"Yes, I'm afraid she is. She wants honesty and openness and she doesn't."

"Are you speaking medically?" I might as well sound Enrique out here and now.

"My dear Ben," said Eduardo laughing. "I was educated by Jesuits. I am absolutely at ease with examination and re-examination as long as it's not superfluous. Your last question, quite frankly, was superfluous."

I gestured to the barman and my eye caught a familiar face. It took me a few minutes to realize that Lester Kling was in the room. Lester Kling! What in God's name was Lester doing in Rio? "Take the subject of fidelity—or *please* take it, as the vaudevillians might say. Fidelity is a state of mind. This is what I have always said and always believed. The physical and the emotional are completely singular entities, are they not?" It was clear that Eduardo liked to talk and wasn't about to shut up at this point. After ten minutes of his soliloquy, the deserter Kathy reappeared, and insisted Eduardo leave with her immediately. "I hope we will have further dialogue soon, Ben. It's been delightful to see you." Eduardo was whisked away by Kathy, and my eyes fell on Lester.

"What in tarnation are you doing down in Rio, Lester?"

"I'm on a case."

"Join me for a drink?"

"O.K." Lester sat down with me and I ordered a Scotch and a beer. "This is a great bar. The first place I've encountered that serves Glenfiddich. How's Peach?"

"She's fine."

"Well, what in the hell are you doing in Rio, Lester?"

"Like I say, I'm working on a case."

"Is it connected with Eele?"

"Could be. Could very possibly be. I heard from your

reporter Weintraub that you'd be down here covering the conference."

"You've come all the way to see me?"

"No, but I'm glad you're here. How well do you know that fellow Eduardo Enrique?"

"I hardly know him at all. Met him once or twice. That's about it. Why?"

"He burned dozens of pieces of incriminating documents and testimonials against Eele."

"What?"

"And he's cozy down here with Flora Framingham. I've got it all on film. I wonder what role Framingham plays in the Eele coverup?"

"Lester, look. I happen to know Flora rather well and I would be willing to swear up and down that she'd have no part in covering for Eele. Why, I sat with her on the plane coming down to Rio and she told me she'd written to the Clinic board on several occasions to complain about Eele."

"Why is she so cozy with Enrique?"

"I haven't any idea why she is. Surely *that* isn't what brought you down to Rio."

"No. Just a bread-and-butter job." Lester took several rolls of film out of his pocket and smiled.

It dawned on me in an ugly flash. "You've been hired by Flora's husband to tail Flora, haven't you?"

"Sorry, Boyer, but I don't talk about the jobs I'm currently working on."

I sat back in my seat and sighed. "That's a bullshit thing to do, Lester."

"You know what bullshit is, Boyer? It's a lot of chewed-up grass." Lester finished his drink and rose.

"You planning to stick around in Rio for awhile?" I asked.

"Yeah. I like it here."

"Where are you staying, Lester?"

"In the Copacabana neighborhood. We're going to fish

wrap this Eele case in a matter of a couple weeks now."

"Listen, Lester. Why don't we get together for a drink?"

"I'll see you in the bar tomorrow afternoon, same time." Lester put his film back in his pockets and left the bar. I pounded the table with my fist and the barman brought me another Glenfiddich.

I met Flora in the lobby of the Copacabana. She looked regal in a white linen dress, so much so that for a moment I felt I couldn't tell her about Lester. I had to tell her though, because I cared about her. And for all I knew, Lester's little camera was clicking in my direction that very moment. "Flora, you look lovely. Let's get out of here." I maneuvered us into a taxi as fast as I could and then I spilled the beans about Lester.

"But that's absurd! Eduardo and I have never been intimate. We're simply friends, and I can't imagine what those photographs could possibly show. My husband would never stoop to such a demeaning thing, anyway. I've traveled on my own to these conferences for years and Charles has never had reason to suspect me of infidelity. I'm disgusted by what you've just told me. I don't know who this private investigator is or what he hopes to uncover, but I can assure you that Charles didn't hire him to follow me to Brazil and no photograph taken of me in Brazil could possibly show me in a compromising situation. Who is this private investigator, anyway?"

"Flora, he's the cousin of Peach Kling, the woman who's filed the malpractice suit against Eele. His name is Lester Kling and he works out of L.A. Right now he's collecting as much evidence as he can against Eele for Peach's suit, and he told me this afternoon that Eduardo Enrique has burned several incriminating pieces of correspondence against Eele."

"Eduardo? But how could Eduardo possibly have gotten

hold of any such correspondence?"

"I don't know, Flora. Is Eduardo a friend of Eele's?"

"Not that I know of. I don't know that Eduardo has ever had much occasion to talk to Eele. They're in such different fields of medicine."

"I think this is the restaurant. Looks charming, doesn't it? Flora, do you think Enrique and Eele have perhaps some kind of bartering system?" I paid the driver and steered Flora into the restaurant. She looked bewildered but I decided we'd better get to the bottom of all of this as soon as possible.

"What do you mean, bartering system?"

"You know what I mean. Tit for tat. A service paid for a service performed."

"I still can't imagine what you're talking about."

"Think, Flora."

"You mean, destroying evidence for an abortion?"

"I sure wish your pal Miranda Kettle would talk a little more. I understand she knows as much about Eele's undercover abortions as anyone."

"Miranda only investigated Eele's practice with undergraduate Greenwich girls."

"What kind of champagne do you serve?" I asked the waiter.

"Brazilian, sir."

"Is it good?"

"Very good, sir. Made by the same family which produces champagne in France."

I turned to Flora. "Will Brazilian champagne be all right?"

"Of course. Now, as far as this Eduardo and Eele thing goes, I think it's a lot of conjecture."

"Miranda could be subpoenaed if Lester's claim can be proved, you know."

"As I said, Miranda's knowledge of Eele's activities is limited to undergraduates."

"Who's to say Eduardo's activities are not?" Flora sat back

in her seat with her mouth wide open. "Flora, you could be a big help to those of us who would like to see Eele kicked out of the Clinic and de-licensed. Do you think you could see your way to calling Miranda up at the ashram? I don't give a damn whether Eduardo arranged abortions for Greenwich girls with Eele or not. But it might explain Eduardo's destroying evidence for Eele."

"Eduardo wouldn't do that! I mean, certainly I could see him getting into a situation where he'd have to arrange an abortion, but he'd never do something unethical in return for the service performed. It's simply ludicrous to think anything of the sort!"

"Why? Eduardo doesn't strike me as all that ethical. Does he you?"

"Ben, I've known Eduardo for years. He's a bit of a playboy, yes, but he's an ethical man."

"Would he be ethical if he got the wife of a prominent man pregnant, and Eele was available for a service in return?"

Flora sat quietly for a moment. "Ben, you're assuming something which isn't true, or at least which hasn't been proved. If you're going on the word of some two-bit detective from Los Angeles, my respect for you is waning."

"Flora, when Lester says he has information, he always has it, in spades, and dead on the nose."

"Well, he certainly hasn't got any information on me!"

"Then he's down here for other purposes." I recalled Lester's conversation in the bar. He hadn't said he had incriminating photographs of Enrique and Flora. He only said he had taken photographs, and shown me the rolls of film. What in the devil was that sly fox Lester doing down here, anyway? I'd ask him tomorrow afternoon. I was now certain that he wasn't following Flora. I began to unwind and settle into the intimate atmosphere of the restaurant. But Flora, who had appeared so carefree when I picked her up that evening, was now clearly on edge, and the boob of the night was myself.

The following afternoon I met Lester in the bar at the Copacabana Palace as planned. "Lester, I want to talk to you. Let's cut out the crap. I want to know what's going on here."

"Look, I know what you're worried about and I'll be honest with you. I'm not down here to keep an eye on Flora. I'm down here on an Eele deal. We're going to nail that bastard. I happen to know he's in Rio at this moment, and we have some reason to think he's planning to move here permanently. We can't stop that but we sure as hell want to try to keep him from practicing medicine in Brazil. I'm gonna keep an eye on him and I'm also gonna find out what kind of evidence is required to keep him from practicing. Naturally he's been keeping company with Brazilian prostitutes, who are all over the place. I followed him last night till three a.m. That sleazy bastard! I'm going to nail that son-of-a-bitch if it's the last thing I do."

"Well, I'll do whatever I can to help you. I gather you've spoken with Mike and Maria?"

"Their stories are interesting, all right, but they haven't got anything concrete on Eele. I don't have to read Pulitzer Prize stories to figure out that things aren't regular in the Loma Verde Medical Clinic if a guy like Eele is still practicing. What do you think about that doctor who's endorsing Zippi-Cola with some Asian herb in it? What a sham!"

"*That* doctor is highly respected in Loma Verde. Rumor has it that he'll be returning to his practice in a few months."

"I thought these Greenwich types were smarter than that. You think this fellow's patients will still want to see him?"

"I suppose so. Endorsing a product doesn't necessarily take away his effectiveness as a doctor."

Lester grunted. "What about that other doctor up at that guru establishment? I suppose he'll want to come back also.

You think *his* patients would return to him?"

"I don't know."

"Doctors are damned weird. But Eele, that's a fish of a different scale. If people in Loma Verde want weirdos for doctors, that's one thing. But scum . . . no. Eele's going to go."

"Wait a minute, Lester. Joe Kuhl isn't weird. He's an entrepreneur. I admire what he's doing. He's literally saying 'why can't a doctor hype himself?' Well, why can't a doctor sell ginseng-enriched Zippi in Asia? I don't expect my doctor to be a saint."

"The Kuhls and Carpaccio are cleared, by the way. None were covering for Eele." Lester took a sip of beer. "But scum and weirdos—that's what you've got holding down the fort in your Clinic and hospital in Loma Verde."

"Back off a minute, Lester. Did it ever occur to you that maybe Carpaccio and the Kuhls might be reacting to a guy like Eele by leaving Loma Verde for awhile, kind of as a protest? Both Carpaccio and the Kuhls have spoken of a profound distaste for Eele and a distaste for having to work in the same Clinic with him."

"I don't ever buy escapism. You're got to have guts to stay in the ring and fight it out. This Carpaccio and these Kuhls just pulled a disappearing act. They shirked their responsibilities of investigating Eele. They just ran right out of the ring." Lester finished off his beer and wiped his mouth with his hand. "They remind me of those scum weirdos who ran up to Canada or burned their draft cards rather than accept their responsibilities as men of our country. Why, you shock me, Boyer. You actually sound more like one of those college-boy draft dodgers than a man who's been banging around newspaper offices for years."

"Have another beer, Lester." Lester was a funny kind of guy who incorporated a sadistic streak in his flag-flying country-boy act. He liked to watch a guy squirm. His idea of a joke was letting me think he was tailing Flora. I wasn't going to forgive him for that but I had to respect him, for one thing I did know about Lester was that he would make certain he nailed Eele.

"Journalism sold out during Vietnam. All of you journalists went right along with those college-boy card-burners. It really shouldn't surprise me that you'd defend those kook doctors who ran off to those weirdo guru and Dalai Lama joints."

"I'm not defending them, Lester. Look, I'm on your side. Can you tell me what you have on Enrique?"

"No."

"Did Enrique burn evidence against Eele in return for an abortion arrangement?"

"You're pretty clever, Boyer."

"Must have been a pretty important lady for such hush hush treatment. Married, obviously."

"You'd make a good detective, Boyer."

"But how did Enrique *get* to the Eele evidence?"

"He got very friendly with Eele's receptionist."

"I must say, that dame is quite an easy mark. I think she'd get friendly with anyone." I recalled my own early success with her.

"She'll be one of our key witnesses. She's got a lot on Eele and she's willing to sing."

"This doesn't look too good for Enrique. What a story!"

"Yep. We're closing in on that slimy bastard real fast now. He ain't going to wiggle out of my sight."

"Keep it up, Lester."

"Don't worry, Boyer. Oh, and by the way, you go out with Framingham and have a good time. She's cleared."

I cleared my throat. "Have another beer, Lester."

"No, I've got to move on. Maybe tomorrow afternoon."

"That'll be great. I'd like to talk to you a bit more about the media's role during the Vietnam years."

"You fucked things up bad, pal. But we got right on top of those slit-eyed yellow-bellied Chinks and we beat hell out of them."

210

"Lester, you're forgetting. We took it between the eyes in Vietnam."

"No, damn it. We won that war and we showed the world we won't be beat." He stood and stretched his arms. "Trying to get some ass off another man's wife? You ought to be ashamed."

Lester sauntered out of the bar and I ordered another Glenfiddich. It came down to this: victory was a different concept to Lester than it was to me. Getting one gynecologist kicked out of the Loma Verde Clinic and de-licensed was as far as Lester cared to take his battle with the medical profession. I wanted to go one step further. I wanted to make every goddamned doctor in Loma Verde so shook up by this Eele story that they'd think twice before they screwed over a patient. For me, the victory would come in scaring those goddamned doctors to death by our blow-by-blow account of Eele's downfall. Eele was going to pay, and it was going to pay these Loma Verde doctors to remember that someone was finally scrutinizing the medical scene around town.

"Hello, Ben! Aimez-vous Jerry Lewis?" It was Eduardo Enrique, waving a copy of the *Latin America Daily Post*. "Just look at this. 'U. S. comedian Jerry Lewis was named a Commander of Arts and Letters, France's highest cultural honor, in Paris where he is hailed as a profound philosopher.' Can you believe this, Ben? But wait, listen. ' "When Americans ask me why we are honoring Jerry Lewis, I am amazed," said Marc Silvera, head of information and studies at the National Cinema Center. "How can anyone pose such a question? Jerry Lewis is so important, so diverse, so rich in talent that the answer is evident." ' I have never understood the French, have you? A very undisciplined philosophical formation, despite all of their testing and their Grandes Ecoles. And it spills over into their medical system, you may be sure of that. Did you hear that French cardiologist attack poor dear Flora this morning? Just think, in the past thirty years the French haven't made one contribution in cardiology."

"Have a drink, Eduardo."

"I would love to, Ben, but alas I cannot. I'm supposed to speak in an hour. Well, perhaps an aperitif. Cinzano over ice, please. So, you're getting to know Flora. She's concerned about your knees after yesterday morning's run. Lovely lady, that Flora. She has a real drip of a husband, unfortunately. He weighs her down a bit at Greenwich."

"Does Flora see it that way?"

"I'm sure she does, but admitting two failures in marriage is difficult for her. I adore Flora. We've been friends for years. But I don't think she's very happy. But what is happiness, and who would I be to try and define it for her? Of course, she's plunged into all of this preventive medicine spokeswoman thing with a vengeance. It's all sublimating, naturally.

"You talk like a psychologist, Eduardo."

"I'm just stating the obvious facts, my dear Ben."

"Do you read Portuguese?" I handed him the morning Rio paper. A picture of Flora was on the front page.

"A little." Enrique studied the paper and started to laugh. "The Brazilians don't understand Flora's message about cholesterol, caffeine, and smoking. They're reporting it as though Flora were a stranger in a strange land, so to speak. Let me translate. 'Dr. Flora Framingham of Greenwich University delivered the keynote address at the Thirty-seventh Annual International Congress of Cardiology, in which she stated that three of man's great pleasures, good food, strong coffee, and cured tobacco, are also man's great foes. Citing further new evidence to suggest that cholesterol, caffeine, and smoking are positively linked to heart disease, Dr. Framingham strongly suggested on fourteen occasions during her forty-seven-minute speech that the three offenders be dropped from our diets and lifestyles.' "

"Do they cite the evidence in the article?"

"Of course not. Stupid journalists! Oh pardon me, Ben, I

certainly do not refer in any way to the *Vindicator*. Your reporting is excellent. This," he said, slapping the paper, "is Neanderthal. Junk reporting. Good picture of Flora though, I must say. Too bad their reporting isn't as good as their photography. And what angle do you plan to take in reporting this conference?"

"Just the facts, Eduardo. Just the facts."

"Ben," he said, lowering his voice, "there is a man who I seem to be running into everywhere. He's not a part of the conference and I'm beginning to think it's more than mere coincidence. He's just left the bar now. There." I looked up to see Lester exiting from a side door. "Do you know this man, Ben?"

"I don't know, Eduardo. Have you been seeing another man's wife?" I laughed as if to dismiss the issue but Eduardo persisted. "Don't be ridiculous. This guy is some kind of private eye all right, but for what purpose? And why me?"

"I think you probably know the answer better than anyone else."

Eduardo appeared more at ease. "Unfortunately, my time in Rio has been most chaste. It is a state I find depressing but I suppose spiritually purifying. Oh, you can't imagine who I ran into in a small bar in Copacabana last night. Duke Eele, you know, the gynecologist whose escapades your paper has been covering. I know he's not down here for the conference."

"Maybe he's down here for the weather. Maybe it's too hot for him in Loma Verde."

Eduardo laughed. "Very good! Very funny! Your newspaper has a habit of making the climate extremely uncomfortable for certain unfortunate people these days."

"How well do you know Eele?" I asked.

"I don't really know him at all. In my opinion, to know someone, *really know* someone, takes years. I know very few people."

"Eele's been in a lot of hot water recently, hasn't he?"

"I don't follow medical scandals." Eduardo stood and

finished his Cinzano quickly. "So long, Ben. I'm sure we'll meet again soon."

What was I to make of Lester's allegation against Enrique? Lester was so thorough in his investigating that he never left room for doubt. Eduardo was on guard about being tailed and I wondered if Eele had come down here to confer with him. What was Eele doing in Rio anyway? The sands were running out on my time here and thus far I'd only managed to alienate my main object of interest. Frankly, I was beginning to grow weary of this Eele business. I decided that I would have Mike and Maria meet with Lester, and that my part in the nitty gritty fact-finding would be minimal. I would be the patriarch, a role I was finally beginning to relish. Fortunately, male menopause had struck me late and left me quickly. My high-blown dreams of young girls and career glory were fading. Tonight I would concentrate on getting the inside story of Flora's marriage. If wet feet about leaving her husband held Flora back, I knew I could be a very persuasive arguer for divorce. Flora was not only the one doctor whom I felt I could trust, but a lovely woman to boot. If I didn't get to know her better in Rio, I'd never get to know her at all.

"Ben, you can't imagine how bad I felt after I received your message this morning. How are your knees?" asked Flora, floating (or was it in my imagination that she was floating?) into the lobby.

"Oh, they're not too bad." I tried to uncross them quickly in order to stand, but I must have pulled a muscle. I slumped back onto the bench in agony.

"Try to move your leg."

"I can't. That run yesterday morning was deceptive. My knees seem to feel worse today than yesterday."

"You've got to try to move your leg. Can you bend your knee?"

"Maybe in a few days."

"I've got an ace bandage in my room. If you can walk, why don't we go up there now? It will give you some support. Here. Can I give you a hand?"

"I'll be fine. I assure you, this has never happened to me before." Especially as I hadn't jogged in thirty years.

Flora and I walked slowly to her room, where she had me sit while she unpacked the ace bandage.

"Do you always travel with bandages?" I asked.

"I never know when my own knee will go out. Now take off your trousers, Ben, and I'll have you fixed up in no time."

"My trousers?"

"Ben, I'm a doctor. Will you please remove your trousers if you want this bandage?" She gave me a look which made me feel guilty for having asked the question. I took my pants off as quickly as I could and Flora reached for them. "I'll just fold these over the chair." What a nice lady she was. "Now, can you stretch out your leg, Ben? Good. You have very attractive legs, Ben."

"So do you, Flora." She looked up at me as she began to wrap my knee. "In fact, there's not one part of you I don't find attractive." I felt her hands tremble. She began to wrap the bandage more slowly. "You're just about the most beautiful and accomplished woman I've ever known." Flora's hands and eyes rested on my knee. "You know, I only came to Brazil to see you, Flora. And you're even lovelier than I'd imagined. Who'd ever guess that such a beautiful woman was also such a gifted doctor?" I could see Flora was beginning to blush. "Your impact at this conference has been nothing short of phenomenal. And your impact on me, well . . . let me just say that you've given me a new lease on life, even in the few hours in which we've been together."

"Ben . . ."

"Flora . . ."

"I don't know what to say, Ben."

"You don't have to say anything, Flora."

"Let me finish wrapping this bandage. There now. How does it feel?"

"It feels great." I leaned over and kissed Flora. The pain in my knee disappeared.

"I don't even care if some detective is following me," whispered Flora.

"Oh, I was meaning to let you know . . . that detective is not following you, he's following Eele."

"Eele?"

"Yes, Eele is down here, probably trying to establish himself in a practice. But I'm sick of that slimy wriggler."

"So I'm not being followed?"

"No, Flora. I'm so sorry I ever made that inference. I was worried about your reputation."

Flora looked downcast. "I was sort of hoping that perhaps Charles *had* hired a detective to watch me. My marriage is a sham. It's a failure. I don't love my husband. I don't even respect him."

"I've been there, Flora."

"I don't know what to do."

"Get a divorce."

"I can't face divorce again."

"Yes you can, Flora. The best years of your life are still ahead. You're a rose in full bloom."

"Oh Ben!"

"A Chinese peony. Fragile yet strong."

"Ben . . ."

"I adore you, Flora. I'd travel any distance to be with you." Flora began to cry. "Flora, are you all right?"

"Yes. I'm so happy. I've never been able to say these things to anyone before."

"You can tell me anything, Flora. I'm your friend." Flora

looked at me and said nothing. I kissed her again and realized that there was nothing to stop us. The sky was the limit.

We never left the room that night, and Flora missed her morning discussion group. The trip down to Rio had been worth it. I hadn't felt like this since high school. The passion I felt for her made me her slave. She only had to say the word and I'd be ready to drop everything and go anywhere. My only fear was that she might have possibly had this effect on her husband, and I knew I had to watch my tendency to allow her to take over the reins. Flora promised me she'd call as soon as she returned. I left Rio feeling like a million dollars.

How to Catch an Eele

Life at the *Vindicator* seemed to settle down into the usual predictable pattern. Mike and Maria had moved to a small rented house in Loma Verde and though at first I was convinced that Mike and Maria had only married because Maria was pregnant, she showed no signs of pregnancy, only glowing, radiant happiness. Her interest in the Eele story was waning, which I attributed to Mike's lack of enthusiasm for medical scandal. But when I asked Maria if she wanted me to give the story to someone else, she said no. So she plugged away, half-heartedly talking to doctors, patients, and especially to Peach Kling. After Maria told me that Dyke Upjohn had temporarily returned to the Bay Area to work with Peach on a book about Peach's ordeal with Eele, I got tougher. "Get writing," I told her. "Surely you can see that there's more to these medical stories than the mere fragments you've published? Dyke Upjohn has the right idea. Go for the whole story. You've told our readers that Vincent Carpaccio ran away to a swami retreat with Miranda Kettle. You've told our readers that Joe Kuhl went to Tibet to be the personal physician to the Dalai Lama and then chucked the Dalai Lama to plug ginseng-enriched Zippi in Southeast Asia. I've told you that Lester spotted Eele in Rio di Janeiro. Good God, girl. That slimy doctor Eele is going to wriggle right out of Loma Verde before you can say boo."

Maria looked self-absorbed. So do exotic flowers. "Michael wants to do a series on the Harding Institute," she finally said.

The Warren Harding Institute for Normalcy was a conservative outfit on the Greenwich campus which had attracted some bad publicity in recent weeks for its strong pro-nuclear stand. Members of the Harding Institute had been spotted in the San Francisco airport carrying signs reading "Feed Dr. Spock to the baby seals." The Harding Institute appeared to consist of obnoxious, offensive, mediocre individuals, at least from the outside. A series on the Harding Institute would be newsworthy, but I didn't approve of leaving unfinished stories for new ones. Unfortunately, I couldn't get Maria to see that the Clinic story was unfinished, especially as she and Mike now had their Pulitzer Prize for the ashram series. "Ben, I think we *have* uncovered the Clinic scandals. But it isn't our job to indict anyone. What more can we do about Eele? If the Clinic is dumb enough to take him back and people are dumb enough to go to him, what can *I* do about it?"

I was just about to tell her that doing something about Eele was supposed to be her job, at least I had thought it was, when Weintraub came into the office. "Did Maria tell you our new idea for a series?"

"Yes, she did, and I think it's a good idea, except that she hasn't finished her current series."

"Oh, a man and his ideals! The voice of the sadder but wiser generation speaks!"

"Don't *you* have any ideals, Mike?" I asked.

"Nah, I'm just a cynical kid."

"You ought to try being a skeptical kid. It's more flattering to you in every way."

"Did Forsythe tell you the game plan? It actually involves ye olde medical profession."

"When I was young, a husband called his wife by her first name and she took his last name."

"Those were the good old days, Ben. Did Maria tell you what's come our way?"

I looked at Maria. "What's come your way?"

"Well, since you've gotten to know Flora Framingham . . ." began Maria.

"What do you mean, since *I've* 'gotten to know Flora Framingham'?" For God's sake, Flora hadn't even returned from Brazil. Where did these two get their information?

"Come on, Ben," said Mike. "Everyone knows what happened in Rio."

"What happened in Rio?" I asked.

"Congratulations, Ben. She's a first-class lady. But you have the main line to medical scandals now." Mike smiled at me. I looked at Maria and she threw me a little pout, or maybe I was seeing things.

"So what's come your way via the Harding Institute and what does it have to do with medicine?"

"Daddy got invited to a Harding dinner this Friday night. The president of the AMA is speaking. Daddy doesn't want to be associated in any way with the Harding Institute and he was about to decline the invitation when by chance I dropped by to visit him and told him that Michael and I would gladly take his place."

"How does the Harding Institute feel about the two of you taking your father's place?"

"Look, they need all the friends they can get. They have to take their chances that we're friendly. And frankly, I think the Harding Institute can't be as bad as it's portrayed in most news stories. We're just going to see what it's all about."

"Hey, Forsythe, we *know* what the Harding Institute's all about!" said Mike.

"Michael, *I* don't know what they're all about. And that's what will make our series on the Harding good. If they're really terrible people, our stories will reflect our dismay, our shock . . ."

"Our rage!"

"Calm down, Mike. A series on the Harding? Interviews with fellows, members? An in-depth look at their controversial style, their achievements, their failures? A five-part series, Monday through Friday? Who they are, what they do, what they don't do, what they think of Greenwich University, what Greenwich thinks of them? That's a lot of work. You'd have to abandon the Clinic story, Maria."

"I'm ready for a change, at least for the present."

I walked around my office. "You don't seem to be smoking these days, Maria."

"I've given it up, thanks to Michael. Does that mean we can do the series?"

"Mike, you're a good influence on her. I always hated to see her smoke. I also hate to see potential dynamite stories abandoned. I'll need your word that you'll return to the Clinic story, Maria."

"Does that mean we can do a Harding Institute series?" asked Maria.

"Sure, why not?" Maria threw her arms around me, making me feel like the classic indulgent father. Despite my resolution to play the patriarch, I can honestly say I didn't relish the Daddy role. I was looking forward to Flora's return from Brazil.

Michael and Maria drove to the Harding Institute the following Friday. They couldn't find the front door and entered the building by accident from what appeared to be a seldom-used side door. "The party's not in here, that's for sure. This place looks like a bomb shelter. Why aren't there any windows? Hey Maria, come here! Where are you? Come here! I found a plaque. 'May the ideals of Warren A. Harding shine eternally and may his goals for normalcy be carried out by this Institute.' Normalcy? Goals? Ideals? What is this shit?"

"Come here and look at this display of books," called Maria.

"*Normalcy, Now More Than Ever; Warren A. Harding: The Man and His Message; You Only Live Once.*"

"Hey, that sounds like a James Bond ripoff."

"Wait a minute, Michael, I'm not finished. *You Only Live Once, Kremlin.*"

"*You Only Live Once, Kremlin?* Well, good, a little cloak and dagger. I hate Russia, too."

"You've never been there."

"And I'm never going to go there. I suppose you haven't been reading the papers."

"Very funny," said Maria. "Don't get your hopes up though. This isn't the kind of place that supports political prisoners. No one here is pulling to get Sakharov out of Russia. This is just your basic anti-communist kind of institute."

"Well, let's get the hell out of here and find the party. It's dumb to stand here making a priori judgments when we'll be among all the Hardingites in a matter of minutes."

"Excuse me," said a voice. "I believe you'll find the party is on the terrace. Turn down the hall to your left and just go right outside."

"That's Eele," whispered Maria.

"Don't be crazy."

"I'm not crazy. That's Eele. Eele's here!"

"Listen, Maria. The president of the AMA has been invited so I'm sure the Harding Institute has invited all kinds of doctors. So what if Eele's here?"

"After all the work I've done with Peach, I feel like I'm going to be at a party with Enemy Number One."

"Listen, Forsythe. Don't go mixing up your stories. Just forget about Eele. It probably wasn't him. You sure couldn't see who it was. Come on, let's check out the party." Maria and

Michael walked out onto the terrace and Michael recoiled. "The average age here looks about sixty-five. I've never seen so many bald guys in my life. I'll get something for us to drink. They'll probably have champagne."

Michael walked towards the bar and an older woman in a red, white, and blue cocktail dress (Maria presumed it *was* a cocktail dress) approached her. "Hello, dear. What's your name?"

"Maria Forsythe."

"Well, I'll just have to make you a name tag." The woman walked away and Michael returned with two glasses of wine.

"Here you go, Maria. This joint doesn't serve champagne. I'll tell you one thing. If I were running a conservative institute or any institute I'd serve champagne. But at this place they serve the four top Scotches. How's your wine?"

"It's swill."

"Of course, it's swill. It's Armada Vineyards. I overheard someone saying that John Armada is here tonight and he donated the wine."

"Here we go, dear. Put your name tag on so everyone can see it! And who is this handsome young man?"

"This is my husband Michael."

"Michael, I'll just run and get a name tag for you." The woman dashed away and returned quickly. "Here you go, Michael. I'm Doris Dahl. I've got to run now. Nice to meet you both."

Michael looked at his name tag. "Michael Forsythe. Shall I wear it? Mr. and Mrs. Forsythe? Mr. Maria Forsythe, husband of the renowned journalist? Kind of like Flora and what's his name Framingham?"

"Wear it if you want, Michael. It's a common mistake. It could happen to anyone."

"Shall I wear it on my back?"

"No. Wear it on your lapel like a grownup."

"I don't believe we've met." Michael turned around and

found himself face to face with Duke Eele. "At least not formally. I'm Duke Eele. You're Weintraub, aren't you? Going incognito tonight as Michael Forsythe?"

"Yes, I'm Michael Weintraub. They made a mistake on my name tag. This is my wife, Maria Forsythe. Maria, this is Dr. Eele."

"I believe Maria and I met at the Greenwich Golf House. You had a most charming friend with you, a Ms. Dyke Upjohn. I realize Ms. Upjohn is a lesbian, but my years of taking care of women have given me a tolerance to aberrant sexual behavior. You two have made quite a name for yourselves with those Oregon swami stories. My former colleague Vince Carpaccio ought to be ashamed of himself for getting himself wrapped up in a deal like that. He's a blemish on medicine in Loma Verde."

"I don't think he is," said Maria.

"You don't? A doctor, leaving his patients and his family to run off to a swami ranch with the Chancellor of Greenwich? Come now, how much more base can one get?"

"I don't know, Dr. Eele," replied Michael. "How's your malpractice suit coming along?" Duke Eele gaped at Michael, and Maria began to laugh uncomfortably.

"It's not *my* malpractice suit you are referring to, but the bizarre and slanderous suit filed against me by one hysterical and mentally incompetent woman. No one of quality gives it a serious thought. This poor woman needs psychiatric counseling. I can't get involved in that kind of nonsense. I've been a doctor for thirty years and my reputation will not be injured by this pathetic, sick woman."

"Peach Kling is not a sick woman," said Maria quickly.

"Then I feel even sorrier for her, because if she's not sick I'll countersue for slander."

"That's a lot of nerve, Dr. Eele," said Michael.

"Young man, may I remind you that you are a guest of the Harding Institute and guests generally do not insult their hosts."

"So you're a member then?" asked Michael.

"Yes, I am an associate member."

"We should have known," said Maria.

"Young woman, I'd watch my manners if I were you." Duke Eele walked away.

"Son-of-a-dog!" whispered Michael.

"Mr. and Mrs. Forsythe, will you join us in the dining room? I have you seated next to two of our most respected fellows. Have you heard of Elmo Babucoff, the famous Far East expert? You'll be sitting with him and also Frederick Edinbergh, the famous economist. Both of them will be more than happy to fill you in on the history of the Institute. I can't tell you how much I enjoy seeing young people here." Doris Dahl heaved her big bosom and lowered her voice. "This place is full of old conservative bastards. My husband is the biggest one here. But try to have fun. At least the food is good."

"You're all right, Mrs. Dahl."

"You can call me Doris, please! And I'll call you Michael and Maria. And if it's true what I've just heard about you two, I hope you'll write one hell of an exposé about this place."

Doris disappeared and Michael and Maria walked into the dining room to look for their table.

"Here they are! We were wondering who Michael and Maria Forsythe were. You must be the children of Professor Forsythe. What a pretty daughter he's got! We've been trying to get your father to the Harding for years now. He finally sends his children. Edinbergh's my name and money's my game. And as you may deduce by my family plaid tie and my name, I tend to toe a thrifty line."

"So you are a financial consultant?" asked Maria.

"I am, and let me just warn you that if you want my advice I'm very expensive."

"So am I." Maria smiled at Edinbergh and he stared at her in disbelief. He sighted his place and excused himself to sit at the circular table.

"Don't mind old Edinbergh." Maria turned around and a man of perhaps forty or forty-five held out his hand. "I'm Elmo Babucoff. I'm sorry your father keeps making excuses for not coming to Harding functions. I've been a great fan of his since I took his course on Homer twenty years ago. My wife is over there. She looks Indian but I can guarantee she's fifty percent English. She's from a very good family. I'm Russian," he said, whispering, "and my parents were immigrants."

"I suppose you'd probably like to go back to Russia some day to check out your roots and all of that."

"Not on your life! I have vowed never to step foot in a communist country. That's why your dad hasn't seen me around the Classics building in twenty years. Ha ha, get it?"

"No."

"Come on. You know what I mean. The School of Humanities at Greenwich is full of Communists and cranks. I'd think that *you'd* be frightened to be seen here. After all, we're all so evil at the Harding Institute. Just read the newspapers." Maria turned to Michael, but he was talking feverishly to his dinner partner. "Have you read my book *Felling the Sleeping Giant*?" asked Babucoff.

"No."

"Let's just say I have the only reasonable handle on the China issue."

"Do you feel that having a wife from India helps you with your perceptions?"

"I told you, she's half English!" Babucoff slammed his fist on the table.

"What does your wife do?"

"She's my chauffeur. I suppose I'm supposed to ask you what you do?"

"I'm a writer."

"What do you write? Harlequin novels?"

"What are Harlequin novels? You mean those things you get in dimestores?"

"Yes. Those books that set housewives on fire. You can set an American woman on fire but I'd let her go to ash before I'd touch her. I'll tell you something. Indian women are the sexual wonders of the world. Take my word for it."

Maria recoiled from Babucoff and turned away to hear Michael telling his dinner partner, "I think there's a high correlation between super rare beef and conservative rich persons."

Babucoff glared at Maria. "Is that your brother or is that your friend?"

"That's my husband."

"Are you Professor Forsythe's daughter?"

"Yes."

"Since when does a husband take his wife's name?"

"It was a mistake. Someone assumed his name was Forsythe."

"He talks like a socialist."

"Well he's not. He's not political."

"What's he doing here then?"

"We came as guests."

"Then your husband ought to keep his mouth shut. What kind of writing do you do?"

"Newspaper reporting."

"Oh yes. Now it hits me. You're the Forsythe who got the Commie Pulitzer Prize for that story about the ashram. Tell me really, who do you think you're fooling with those lies? You might fool the Commie media of this country, your ABC, CBS, NBCs. But you don't fool me or anyone else sitting here. You wrote trash, lies, slander, sweetheart. You ought to be jailed for what you wrote. But no! The Commie media gave you a prize."

"Mr. Babucoff, let's try to relax and get along."

"Get along with you? I don't want to get along with you." Babucoff folded his arms tightly around his chest and turned away from Maria. Babucoff's wife walked over to her husband and knelt at his side. She whispered to him for about a minute and then Babucoff moved to her place at the table and she sat next to Maria.

"Your husband really seems disturbed about something." Mrs. Babucoff stared at Maria, then turned her back on her.

"I'll tell you why I'm running for president of the AMA," a man was announcing at the table. "The reason I'm running is that I'm wealthy, I'm white, I'm pornographic, and . . ." He raised his arm which was in a sling, "like Ronald Reagan, I've been shot for what I believe in. So I'm even more Republican than I am a doctor."

The lights dimmed and Ian MacGregor walked to the podium.

"I'm, uh, pleased to, uh, have you, uh, here this evening. We, uh, are particularly pleased, uh, to have at the, uh, head table, uh, the first cousin, twice removed, of, uh, Warren uh G. uh Harding. Albert uh Harding is uh a wealthy farmer who uh grows sugar beets near uh Fresno. We are uh also pleased to have uh at our head table uh our three uh distinguished uh speakers, who will speak on the uh coming return of uh normalcy. Let me uh say something uh about each uh of them. First uh is uh Dr. Sam Winger, the distinguished president of the uh well-known pharamaceutical firm, the Oral Thermal House. He will speak on how uh to get rid of uh the F.D.A. The uh second uh distinguished speaker is uh Dr. Fletcher Fletcher who uh is uh current president of the uh American Medical Association and is also uh a fourth cousin uh thrice uh removed of Warren uh G. uh Harding. Dr. Fletcher will uh address the uh important topic of uh how to reduce the enrollments in uh medical schools in order to uh return uh to the Golden Days of uh medicine. Our third uh distinguished speaker uh is uh Nobel uh Laureate uh Dr. Milton uh Bradley, who will speak on uh the good old days or uh before income tax and the S.E.C., that is, the Securities uh Exchange uh Commission.

"In the uh spirit of uh our institute uh we have selected

a uh menu that was served in the uh White House in uh honor of uh the Mayor of Columbus, Ohio, on uh June 19, 1922. Just remember our uh motto uh 'Be free to be normal.'"

Michael turned to Maria and whispered, "Ian MacGregor should take speaking lessons."

"And my dinner partner ought to take lessons in social behavior or maybe he just needs some psychiatric help."

"I was *wondering*. What happened to the guy? He seems to have flipped out."

"I think I need to find the restroom. Michael, will you come with me?" Maria grabbed Michael's shoulder and the two of them slipped out a side door and onto the terrace. "I had to get out of there. If I were Elmo Babucoff, I'd flip out too in an atmosphere like this."

"It's just getting good."

"Well, Michael, I'm leaving. You can stay if you want but I won't."

"What are you afraid of? The truth? Isn't the truth what we want? Did you hear what that guy said about running for president of the AMA? Now *that's* a quote if I ever heard one. I'll bet he'll win. Come on, let's go back inside."

"I can't, Michael. It's too awful."

"Expand your experiences in life."

"I can't, Michael."

"Oh, come on. Pretend it's a funny movie."

"Michael, I just can't."

"Go in, honey. Listen to your boyfriend. It's a real scream in there."

Michael and Maria turned around quickly. Duke Eele was sitting on the terrace with a bottle of Scotch. "Come on, you two. Come on over and have a drink."

"We really don't want to miss the speeches," said Michael.

"Yes, we do," said Maria quickly.

"Oh, who cares about those long-winded speeches made by those pompous old farts? Come on and have a drink and I'll tell you the real story of Peach Kling."

"You're on, Dr. Eele," said Michael. "I'll just pull up a couple of chairs here."

"Here, honey, have some of the Harding's good Scotch."

"No, thank you," said Maria.

"I'll have some, Dr. Eele, thank you. So what's the story on Peach?"

"Oh, that pathetic little woman. I suppose it's one of the hazards of my particular line of work. I mean, dealing with women like I have for so many years, I've come to learn the various signals. If a woman looks like a potential troublemaker, I refer her to someone else. You know what I mean? Makes life easier. You know, in my line of work I have a lot of women who look up to me. Some women just keep it at that level, the doctor on the pedestal. But occasionally I'll have a patient who carries her admiration too far. You know what I mean? And that spells trouble. If you knew the offers I've had over the years, the apartment keys pressed into my hands, the Valentine cards, the presents . . . Well, you'd never believe it. And I've never been involved with a patient. That's one thing I'd swear to up and down. That's the one thing I wouldn't do. But you just take a look around that high-and-mighty Loma Verde Clinic. They *all* do it. They get involved with their patients. I could tell you stories that would make your eyeballs pop out."

"Surely not all doctors get involved with patients. My dad's been a doctor as long as you have and I know he'd never get involved with a patient."

"Your dad's Winston Weintraub, right? No, you're right. The Winston Weintraubs wouldn't get involved with patients. But a lot of them do. Take my word for it. Anyway I took one look at this Kling woman and I knew I saw trouble. She's a horny little bitch, let me tell you. She tried to get to know me better. I mean that woman just didn't know when to quit. I referred her to three other doctors but she never got the message. I finally had to tell her straight out I just wasn't interested. Next week I got some letter from her attorney. Said I'm being sued for malpractice. Now what do you say? What would *you* do in a situation like this?" A shadowy figure jumped suddenly into the bushes and disappeared. Maria, who had looked closely, realized it was Lester Kling. "What in the hell was that?" asked Eele. "You know, one of the problems about spending too much time here at the Harding Institute is the risk you face getting blown up by some terrorist group."

"You've never had an affair with a patient?" asked Maria.

"Your question offends me."

"Must be pretty tempting with all those women you see every day," said Michael.

"I am a professional doctor. My ethics are as high as can be, no matter what anyone else might say. You know, I see more patients than any other ob-gyn in Loma Verde. It's lonely at the top. And people are always trying to beat the winners down."

"I have a headache, Michael. I'd like to leave now." Maria rose.

"It's doctors like Kuhl and Carpaccio who make a bad name for our profession."

"Any other interesting stories, Dr. Eele?" asked Michael.

"No, not for tonight. I'm getting tired. I think I'll just sit here for awhile and have another drink. You have one too." Eele poured Michael more Scotch.

"So, what's it like to be an associate member of the Harding Institute?"

"Michael, I feel sick."

"What's the matter, honey? Let me feel your head."

"I'm not running a temperature, Dr. Eele. I just have a headache."

"You know what the best cure for a headache is? Right here." Eele patted the bottle of Scotch.

"Try it, Maria, it's good," said Michael.

"No, thanks." Maria wandered across the terrace.

"That's what I mean! Women! Always with their little aches and pains."

"These aches and pains have made you a rich man, Dr. E."

"I'm not a rich man. Let's just say I'm not wanting. I have everything a man could possibly want. A great car, a great life, women throwing their panties at me all day long . . ."

"Dr. Eele, you make me sick! Michael, I want to go now. Dr. Eele, I think that thirty years of looking at ladies' diseases have rotted your brain. Michael, I'll be in the car."

Maria walked away and Michael stood and put his drink on the table. "You know what I'd do to a bitch like that if she talked to me that way?"

"No, I don't, Dr. Eele. Excuse me, I think my wife is ill."

"Ah, don't let her pussywhip you. You've got to let that bitch know who's boss in your house."

"Good-bye, Dr. Eele."

"Come back, I've got other good stories! Come back! You didn't even finish your drink! Oh, what the hell." Eele picked up Michael's drink and emptied it.

Michael and Maria, at Maria's bidding, drove straight to the Greenwich Arms Inn, where they were surprised to find Dyke Upjohn, typing furiously in Peach's room. "Peach and Lester are out getting some Kentucky Fried Chicken. So! Long time no see! And so much has happened! I left you novices. I return to find you Pulitzer Prize winners. Congratulations. I just want you to know that I intend to win a Pulitzer Prize on this book I'm writing with or I should say for Peach."

"What are you calling it?" asked Michael.

"*Patient/Victim: One Woman's Ordeal.* It has a bestseller title, that's for sure. It'll be on every woman's magazine book list. I can just see it now."

"So how have you been, Dyke?" asked Michael.

"Oh, you know how it is for us boring garden-variety writers. Just the usual bi-coastal, bi-sexual business. I was just getting used to the New York to California express when I had to hear about the two of you and your adventures. Not only do you get paid for it, you get awarded a prize for it. Does your editor have any more openings?"

"We just lucked out," said Maria.

"Then you both have to do something stupid like get married. Really! I thought you were more sophisticated than that! Well, congratulations all around. Pretty heady stuff. Sit down and help yourself to a drink. I've got to finish off this chapter. You understand. You can turn on the TV if you want. It doesn't bother me." Dyke continued to type and Maria turned on the television.

"Not PBS! Please!" groaned Michael.

"It's 'Wild, Wild World of Animals.' I like the show. It's better than watching murders and stuff like that on the news, or on one of those awful sit-com shows."

Peach and Lester returned with the fried chicken. "I thought you'd deserted us till Lester told me about who you were with tonight," said Peach.

"Who were you two with tonight?" asked Dyke, looking up from the typewriter.

"Eele!" shrieked Peach.

"Thanks for getting him to talk, you two. I've got his sleazy, incriminating words right here on tape." Lester took a tiny tape recorder out of his pocket.

"What did he say?" asked Dyke. Lester played the tape. "Son-of-a-bitch," hissed Dyke.

"'The mate rejects him immediately following ejaculation,'" said the television narrator.

"It's 'Wild, Wild World of Animals,'" said Maria.

"Have some fried chicken," said Peach. "Did Dyke tell you

about our book?"

"Yes. I'm surprised you agreed it would be a good idea, Lester," said Michael.

"Lester worked through it," said Dyke.

"I'm sure it's all for the best, Lester," said Michael. Lester turned away and chewed on a chicken leg.

"'The garden eel simply slithers away when it knows it's threatened,'" said the television narrator.

"Lester! Lester! Eele will try to slither away when he knows how strong our case is!"

"Don't worry, Peach. That's one eel who ain't gonna slither away." Lester licked the bone and threw it into a wastebasket across the room.

"Good shot, Lester," said Michael.

"It ain't my only good shot."

"So what are you two going to do now?" asked Dyke, giving Michael a strangely come-hither look.

"I'm going to have a chat with Pete Kettle," said Maria quickly.

"What can the husband of the runaway Chancellor of Greenwich do?" asked Dyke.

"He can know what kind of place the Harding Institute is. I also think he might be willing to talk to me when I remind him about the time I spent with his wife at the ashram."

"How will you get in to see him?" asked Michael.

"I have my methods. Pass me another piece of chicken."

Michael, having had enough of Dyke, Lester, Peach, and PBS, wound things up fast at the Greenwich Arms Inn. "Gotta get some shuteye. Big day tomorrow. Are you ready to push off, Maria?" He threw Maria's coat over her shoulders and picked up her purse. "We'll keep in touch as ever. Come on,

Maria. You ready? So long, folks, we'll call you tomorrow." Michael quickly pulled Maria out the door.

"Asshole," said Dyke within Michael's earshot.

"What's the big idea?" asked Maria.

"Those people drive me crazy. Lester picking on that bone, that bitch Upjohn picking at the typewriter. And Peach Kling! Forget it! And 'Wild, Wild World of Animals'!"

"One would think you'd actually sympathize with a show like 'Wild, Wild World of Animals.'"

"But not in the same room with that crew. Anyway it offends me that PBS will give three hours a week to coyote mating patterns but 'Masterpiece Theater' only gave Disraeli three segments."

"You're uptight, Michael."

"I've got to get out of journalism. And for sure I can't cover any more medical stories, even if it's Eele."

"What are you trying to say, Michael?"

"I promise you, you're the first to know."

"That's good. Our marriage counts for something."

"I'm going to start applying to medical schools."

"What? Are you out of your mind?"

"I've wanted to become a psychiatrist as long as I can re-member."

"A psychiatrist? Are you crazy? Have you flipped out?"

"You know I have always wanted to be a psychiatrist."

"I've never known that. I mean, you've interpreted a few dreams for me, made your little observations here and there..."

"So you can see why I can't go on with this story. I want to go to Greenwich for all the obvious reasons . . ."

"*What* obvious reasons?"

"It's one of the better medical schools in the country, as you used to know before you got so gung-ho on this ludicrous story. And I'd be blackballed right from the start if I was asso-ciated with all of this crap."

"This *crap*?"

"Yes. This crap. You know what I mean. It's crap. It's just so low I can't stand it any more."

"A psychiatrist?"

"Look at it like I want to become an artist."

"An artist? A nineteenth-century artist, a quaint nineteenth-century artist?"

"Not necessarily quaint and not necessarily nineteenth century. And now you have it. I can't do this story, Maria. I *can* get into Greenwich. You can work at the paper and I'll go to school. I really want to, Maria."

"I suppose that means I'd be supporting us?"

"Not necessarily. Your trust fund can support you and your job can support me. Are you hostile to this idea?"

"No."

"Do you have something against psychiatrists?"

"No."

"Do you understand why I want to do it?"

"Sort of."

"Can I, you know, count on you?"

"Sure."

"Just sure?"

"'Get the guns, Slim.' 'Sure thing, Ric.'"

"I don't get it, Maria."

"I feel like we're Humphrey Bogart and Lauren Bacall in a great moment of truth."

"We are!"

"Do they blackball applicants who have wives associated with writing medical clinic scandals?"

"I don't know."

"Well, if medical schools won't take you, apply to all the law schools. They'll probably appreciate what we've been trying to do with these stories."

"I don't think you're taking me seriously, Maria."

"I don't think you're taking me seriously either, Michael."

"Oh I am, Maria. I think you ought to go right ahead and

get as much information about Eele as you can. But I think you should know what I want to do."

"I do, Michael. I just never dreamed I'd be married to a psychiatrist."

"It'll be great, Maria."

"It takes some time getting used to. I was just starting to accept us as writing partners."

"This'll be better, Maria. You can be the star. Get all those good stories. Of course, I'll always be right by your side with my unassailably accurate analysis of each situation, in the likely event that my expertise will come in handy."

"Don't be an asshole."

"And I don't want you hanging around with Dyke Upjohn. Your language goes to hell in a hand basket when you're with her."

At five forty-five the following morning, Maria, dressed in a white sweatsuit with Greenwich emblazoned across the top, perched on the lawn of Slaughter House, where Pete Kettle currently lived *sans femme*. From her years of living on the campus, the lone figure of Pete Kettle, coming through the neighborhood at dawn in the skimpiest of shorts, was a common sight. As Maria had always jogged early in the morning, Pete Kettle might have provided an ideal jogging partner. At fifty, Pete Kettle was a strong runner, considering he was overweight, and proved he was in reasonable condition by participating in the faculty ten-kilometer race year after year. Pete Kettle preferred to run by himself in the mornings, however. He didn't even greet Maria when their two paths occasionally met. "He obviously has a problem," Maria's father always said when she told him about Pete Kettle's unfriendliness. "That's a medieval historian for you. He was too busy looking at villas when he should have been paying attention to women." Maria's father, too, could speculate on the state of Pete and Miranda Kettle's marriage. "If he can't even say hello to a beautiful young woman while he's jogging, what does he say to Miranda?"

Maria spotted Pete, and gave him a two-hundred-foot lead before she took to the road. Pete and Maria were running a crisp seven-minute mile. After three miles, adequate aerobic exercise for healthy adults during a twenty-four-hour period, Maria raced up to Pete. "Professor Kettle, may I run with you?" Pete Kettle turned around. "I'm Maria Forsythe, Julian Forsythe's daughter." Pete gave Maria a pained smile and continued to run. "I'd really like to talk to you, Professor Kettle. As you may know, I spent a few days with your wife at Baba Rhum's ashram not so long ago." Pete stopped dead in the road. "Keep running, Professor Kettle. You know how bad it is to stop running without cooling down."

Pete turned to face Maria. "Will you join me for breakfast at home?"

"Why, Professor Kettle, your friendliness overwhelms me!"

"Come on, let's do a straight all-out race."

"You're on, Professor Kettle." The two took off, but as they closed in on Slaughter House Maria passed Kettle. "Beauty before age!" she called.

"I respect your running ability, Maria."

"So, what's for breakfast? I suppose you have a bunch of cooks and maids who do everything for you."

"I eat a light breakfast, generally."

"Oh, that's too bad, because I'm starving!"

"You can have whatever you want. I generally take a shower before breakfast."

"Oh, that's O.K., Professor Kettle. I don't mind if you don't take a shower."

"I generally take a shower for myself, Maria."

"But I thought you were interested in what I have to say."

Pete looked at his watch. "Well, I have to be out of the house before eight. All right. Let's have breakfast."

"I could really get into some huevos rancheros. This looks like the kind of setup where you could get all kinds of good food."

"I only eat toast, but if you want eggs I'll tell Raoul."

"Who's Raoul?"

"Who do you think Raoul is?"

"I think he's your cook. Why do you need a cook in the morning if you only eat toast?"

"Why do you ask so many questions?"

"Sorry, it's my reporter's instinct."

"I would have sworn it was your adolescent instinct. Conchita, tell Raoul we have a guest for breakfast. What do you want, Maria?"

"Can Raoul make something good with eggs?"

"She wants huevos rancheros, Conchita. Ask Raoul if he can do that. And we'll take coffee. And the usual toast for me."

"I guess you stay in such good shape because you don't eat too much, Professor Kettle."

"Flattery will get you nowhere with me. My guess is that you got spoiled up at that food ashram and now you think you can get whatever kind of food you want, whenever you want it."

"I must say, I had an unusual experience up at the ashram."

"I'm sure you did." Conchita poured coffee and Pete began to drum on the table with his fingers.

"Oh, that's right! I want to tell you about my conversations with Miranda."

"That *is* why I asked you to breakfast."

"Well, the first thing you should know is that Miranda didn't leave *for* Vince Carpaccio. She left *with* him."

"What in the hell does that mean?"

"Miranda says it is a very important distinction."

"Maybe I'm not subtle enough to understand it."

"Well, let me put it this way. Miranda left you because she found out that you were seeing other women." Pete coughed into his coffee cup. "Undergraduates, in fact. Look, Professor Kettle, I don't care whether you see undergraduates or not. It's no big deal to me. I grew up on this campus and I've seen everything. But I think you should know that Miranda left because she was hurt. And she went to the ashram with Carpaccio because he had told her that he wanted to try a new kind of life. Apparently Carpaccio's wife was having an affair with his best friend. So you see it was like two miserable persons getting together to try a new way of life."

"So you're saying that Miranda claims she doesn't love Carpaccio?"

"That's what Miranda told me. And believe me, if you think there's any sex at that ashram, forget it. My husband and I got kicked out for having sex."

"I'm sure that your both being investigative reporters is what got you kicked out."

"Oh no! Baba Rhum had a very ambivalent attitude toward us when he found out we were journalists. On the one hand he was delighted to be receiving the publicity . . ."

"But back to Miranda! Are you saying that there's a chance she might come back to me?"

"I don't know, Pete. I *can* call you Pete, can't I? Let's just say Miranda was sufficiently hurt to leave you. I think she might even still love you."

"I'd do anything to get her back."

"That's understandable, Pete."

"Tell me what that ashram is like. No! Don't tell me! I don't think I really want to know!"

Conchita brought the breakfast to the table. "Professor Fitzgerald is on the telephone." Pete excused himself and left the room and Maria dove into her huevos rancheros. When

Pete returned to the table, Maria asked him if Professor Fitzgerald was Gerald Fitzgerald, the philosophy professor.

"Yes." Pete buttered his toast.

"Fitzgerald was Baba Rhum's thesis adviser."

"I'm aware of that, Maria. In fact, I'll have to be excusing myself because I'm meeting Gerry Fitzgerald early this morning. Is there anything else you want to talk about?"

"Please tell someone to get the Harding Institute out of Greenwich."

"I'd love to do that, Maria."

"The place is full of mediocre crackpots. I can't believe they're actually at Greenwich."

"The Harding Institute was established long before Miranda ever became Chancellor. The only way you could get rid of them is to bomb the place."

"That's not a bad idea . . ."

"Now don't go getting any strange ideas, Maria."

"The place has got to go. Can't Greenwich make it so uncomfortable for the Harding people that they'd want to go?"

"Maria, Warren Harding's memory is a permanent fixture at Greenwich. I wish they weren't here but they're here. We have to live with it."

"Can I go with you to see Gerry Fitzgerald?"

"No! It's a private matter!"

"If it's about Baba Rhum, what makes it private from me?" Pete Kettle stared at Maria. "After all, who has just been giving you the lowdown on Vince and Miranda?"

"All right. You can come along. I'm meeting Gerry Fitzgerald at his house. It's right down the street."

"I know. It's across the street from where I grew up."

"Of course. You'll excuse me now. Enjoy your breakfast. We'll leave in fifteen minutes."

"Well, hello, Pete, you handsome devil! I've heard a lot about you! I'm Catherine Fitzgerald, the notorious young wife of Gerry. Gerry will be downstairs in a minute. Come inside."

"This is Maria Forsythe, who grew up across the street from you," said Pete to Catherine.

"So *you're* the famous Maria Forsythe!"

"So *you're* the famous Catherine Fitzgerald. I heard that no one sees you without your full-length fur coat and tons of jewelry," said Maria.

"Then don't let me disappoint you." Catherine walked to a closet and threw her fur coat over her flannel nightgown. "Makes a wonderful bathrobe, doesn't it? As for the jewels, you're going to have to imagine them. I don't feel like putting them on."

"How was Gerry's sabbatical?" asked Pete.

"A year's stay at the Paris Ritz, you mean? Darling, it was divine. You know that old saying, 'The Ritz will always be the Ritz'? How true! It was hard to come back to *this* neighborhood. Well, Gerry likes to say that you can't keep 'em in the country once they've seen Paree. Anyway, I learned something in Paris which positively changed my life. A bottle of perfume bought in Paris should last as long as a car trip to Nice. Well, here is Gerry! Good morning, my precious husband!" Catherine showered Gerry with kisses.

"Has she been entertaining you?" asked Gerry. Pete coughed. "Don't let her put you off. She has all kinds of hidden talents." Gerry winked at Pete. "You know what I mean?"

"I'm an excellent masseuse," said Catherine laughing and fluttering her eyelashes.

"Well, you're a beautiful addition to Greenwich, Catherine," stammered Pete.

"Coming from you, I hear that's a compliment. Why don't we all sit by the pool? Have you heard about our new pool? It's indoors. I won't need this coat. It's like Fiji out in the pool area." Catherine threw her coat on the floor.

"Well, I'm glad to see I'm not the only one who wears Lanz flannel nightgowns," said Maria.

"It's that last vestige of virginity that men lust after. Right, Maria? What do you think, Pete?"

"Well, it's quite attractive," said Pete, stammering again.

"Sorry about your wife running off with a crazed internist," Catherine said as she balanced herself along the edge of the pool like a ten-year-old. "What do you think of our pool? You know, Pete, if you weren't dressed I'd suggest you go for a swim. The water is 98.6 F."

"Thanks just the same, but I've had my exercise."

"Pete's come to talk to me about a private matter," said Gerry, pulling up four chairs. "But I always say that a private matter, discussed between two men with a beautiful woman at each man's side, makes discussion all the more private. I call it my conditional law of privacy. Catherine, go wake up Kenrab and ask him to bring us some papaya juice."

"Kenrab?" asked Maria quickly.

"Oh yes, you probably know Kenrab after your little expedition to Tibet." Gerry arranged his silk bathrobe around the knees of his silk pajama trousers. "Catherine and I met up with Jean and Joe Kuhl in Paris. Kenrab was with them. Jean and Joe were taking a little respite from their duties as Southeast Asian spokespersons for ginseng-enriched Zippi-Cola, and Kenrab, who had accompanied them, said he was anxious to come and work in the U.S. So Jean and Joe agreed to let us hire Kenrab, and now he's with us."

"Kenrab was at our wedding!" said Maria.

"He'll be coming with the juice in a minute," said Catherine.

"Kenrab was at Maria's Tibetan wedding ceremony,

Catherine," said Gerry.

"I told Gerry we can stay for a year at the Paris Ritz but it's not the same thing as getting married in Tibet."

"Well, if the little lady wants to renew her vows in Tibet, just say the word," replied Gerry, patting Catherine's hand.

"Well, yes," replied Pete, looking at his watch. "About that matter we were going to discuss, Gerry . . ."

"Ah, here's Kenrab now. Kenrab, an old friend of yours is here."

"Hi, Kenrab," said Maria.

"Ah, Miss Forsythe, good morning to you. I am very happy to be in the U.S.A.!"

"How are Joe and Jean?"

"Fine, fine. Their Zippi-Cola campaign is most successful."

"I'll bet the Dalai Lama was sad to lose Joe."

"Yes, but the Dalai Lama understands the pull of money. He understands that money is a necessary evil. He feels that way about doctors."

"Speaking of doctors," said Pete, "I would like to talk to Gerry about what he knows about Baba Rhum." He drank his papaya juice quickly and handed his empty glass to Kenrab.

"Oh, Baba Rhum is no doctor," said Gerry.

"Yes, I'm aware of that. But Miranda was talked into going up to his retreat by a prominent Loma Verde internist. You probably missed the articles by Maria and her husband Michael Weintraub. They were most informative."

"I hear you got a Pulitzer Prize for your coverage of Baba Rhum's ashram. Congratulations, Maria. If the food is really as good as you say it is, Catherine and I might take in a weekend guest program."

"Baba Rhum was your graduate student, was he not?" asked Pete impatiently.

"He was. Of course his name wasn't Baba Rhum in those days. It was Peter Schwartz. I remember him as a bright little fatso who had trouble keeping his mouth shut."

"Why would Baba Rhum be able to attract so many notable persons to his ashram?" asked Pete.

"Well, I don't know about you, Pete, but I'd be willing to go out of my way for a good meal," said Gerry.

"Why isn't there any sex up at this ashram?" asked Pete.

"Who says there isn't?" asked Gerry.

"I say there isn't," said Maria. "My husband and I got kicked out for having sex."

"Well then, maybe Baba Rhum has a sex problem," said Gerry.

"Being fat has never been known to be a sex enhancer," said Catherine. "I had the most interesting conversation with Kenrab just yesterday. He was helping me organize our overflowing library and he noticed an art book. It was a study of seventeenth-century nudes with gorgeously reprinted plates. Anyway, Kenrab was disgusted. He said it was vulgar pornography. You know, that *is* the Asian view of our flabby, obese nudes. Frankly, if I weren't so conditioned to Rubens, I think I'd find his paintings vulgar in the extreme."

"Yes," said Gerry, "poor Baba Rhum is not very well integrated."

"But think of all the people who aren't very well integrated," said Maria. "I think all of the people at Baba Rhum's ashram have short-circuited. Sorry, Pete, because your wife is up there, but you know, I think she probably won't stay too much longer."

"I hope you're right."

"Let's go for a swim, Maria," said Catherine. "The water's great!" Catherine threw off her nightgown and jumped into the pool.

"She's so natural," said Gerry, beaming.

"I guess maybe I'll join your wife. Then you two can talk more openly." Maria quickly undressed and lowered herself as discreetly as she could into the pool. And although she supposed the issue of Miranda at the ashram was prominent in Pete's mind, every time Maria looked up from the water, Pete was staring at her and Catherine. By the time Catherine and Maria had finished swimming, Pete was gone.

"Next time you come bring your husband and your father," called Catherine to Maria at the front door. Maria walked across the street to her father's house and called Michael.

We printed Mike and Maria's first Harding story the day after their dinner at the Institute. The response to the story was electrifying, to say the least. Our readership was divided into two camps: those sympathizing with Ian MacGregor's ploy to keep the Harding Institute at Greenwich yet free of any Greenwich intervention, and those who agreed with Miranda Kettle that if the Harding Institute wanted to remain at Greenwich, they should maintain the Greenwich standards of academic excellence and be politically nonpartisan. But what stirred the readers, whether pro or anti the Harding Institute, was a statement in the story by the AMA candidate who said he was running for the presidency of the AMA because he was wealthy, white, and pornographic. Once again it was the medical angle that had our readers up in arms. Letters poured into the *Vindicator* from all over the Bay Area. The candidate, a local doctor named Payne, was forced to go on Bay Area television to explain his statement. Payne accused Mike Weintraub of slander; Mike held firm and found a fellow sitting at the same table that evening to testify that Mike's reporting of the statement was accurate. Not surprisingly, the fellow who stood by Mike was thrown out of the Harding Institute immediately. More surprisingly, the AMA disqualified Dr. Payne as a candidate for their presidency, saying in a widely publicized

statement that "the American Medical Association does not recognize Seymour Payne's candidacy nor does it embrace any
part of his recent statements to the press."

Amidst all this hullaballoo, my beloved Flora returned
from Brazil, tanned and radiant. I picked her up at the airport
and as she melted into my arms she whispered, "I cannot go on
living a lie. I cannot go home to Charles." Flora moved in with
me that afternoon. Her fifteen-year-old son Todd, who luckily
for me possessed a gentle temperament, came to visit us that
first evening. "My house is your house," I told him, and although he was at first reluctant to show signs of approval about
my relationship with Flora, he was, before he left, clearly positive about Flora and me.

"I know it's what you want, Mom," he said, and Flora
burst into tears of relief. "It's Dad I'm worried about. What will
he do without you?" I excused myself and left Flora with her
son for a while.

"I never realized how wise Todd is," she told me after he
left. "Apparently Charles has really gone off the deep end since
I left for Rio. Todd says he is reading the literature of Baba
Rhum."

"It's a small world, Flora. What else can I say?" The door-
bell rang and although I was disinclined to answer it, all instinct
told me to do so. Maria and Michael stood at the door with a
bottle of champagne.

"We won't stay," began Michael.

"No, please do," Flora and I replied in unison.

"I guess you know Maria went to visit Gerry Fitzgerald
with Pete Kettle yesterday morning."

"Fitzgerald was Baba Rhum's thesis adviser at Greenwich," I explained to Flora. "What did you find out, Maria?"

"Gerry Fitzgerald and his wife spent a year at the Paris
Ritz during Gerry's sabbatical, and they began the formulation
of a new ideology based on Gerry's philosophy. They've begun
an organization called Pursuit of Happiness, Incorporated, and

their motto, which they took from the writings of Gerry, is 'We've seen the truth and found it wanting.'"

"What does that have to do with Baba Rhum?" asked Flora.

"Oh, Gerry and Catherine plan to vie for the more celebrated of Baba Rhum's converts. They are convinced, for instance, that Henry Warringer finds the truth wanting."

"Well, I'll be damned. What will they think of next?" I said. The only thing that might have surprised me at this point was Mike's announcing that he was applying to medical school.

"I've never been so hyped up on a story in my life," he said. "I thought it was just going to be a straight Harding Institute story, but the medical angle is what people are responding to. I've gotten a dozen or more letters asking what's become of Duke Eele."

"What *has* become of him?" asked Flora.

"Well, I guess you know he's back at the Clinic," said Michael. "He plans to countersue Peach Kling for slander."

"This is where you could come in, Flora," said Maria. "I know that you know the results of Miranda Kettle's investigations into Eele's practice with undergraduate patients." Flora began to wring her hands and pace about the room. "You've got to tell us what Miranda learned. We could get Eele kicked out permanently on the basis of the right kind of documented evidence. If Miranda found out about any arrangement her husband might have made with Eele for an undergraduate to have an abortion, I promise we'd never mention it. But if Eele has fouled up in some way, *we can get him!*"

Flora sighed heavily and fell into a chair. "It's not as easy as you think." She stared at a clock for about a minute, then turned and said in an even, quiet voice, "Eele made one of the most fundamental medical errors in an abortion case and his patient died. He might even have been drunk when he was in surgery."

"How long ago was this?" I asked.

"A year, no more. Her death was covered up by Greenwich because Eele told them she had died of a fatal tubal pregnancy."

"Is this documented?" I asked.

"Yes. Eduardo Enrique was supposed to burn the girl's medical file but his conscience told him he couldn't. Poor Eduardo! I'm so sorry that he had to get involved in this at all."

"How could Greenwich cover up an undergraduate's death at the hand of an abortionist?" asked Michael.

"I've dealt with Greenwich's press office for years," I said. "I can't tell you how many times I've refused payment to keep the name of a Greenwich student out of the newspaper. I guess this one just slipped by us."

"Who's Eduardo Enrique?" asked Maria. I opened the bottle of champagne Maria and Mike had brought and the four of us sat down for a long, hard talk.

There is something enchanting about two wonderfully intelligent and alive kids dropping by with a bottle of champagne to toast a wayward middle-aged romance. And before the evening was over, we had tackled every angle known to us of the Eele story. Flora decided to call Enrique herself the following morning. Enrique agreed to meet with Flora and me at my office.

"It's pretty much out on the table, Eduardo," I said. "Peach Kling's detective cousin Lester has evidence linking you to the removal of some of Eele's records."

"Good God. What will I do?" Eduardo pulled a handkerchief from his pocket and mopped his brow.

"If you still have the evidence, you're going to have to turn it over to the Clinic board," said Flora. "It's the only ethical thing to do."

"Ethics? Aren't we beyond ethics by now?"

"A doctor is never beyond ethics, Eduardo. I'm surprised at you."

Enrique looked at Flora as if she were sentencing him."What do you expect me to do?"

"You must give Eele's records to the board as soon as possible, today if you can."

"My dearest Flora, that will be quite impossible. I will be finished as a doctor if I do that."

"Eduardo, you must hand over those records."

"I'm sorry, Flora, but you don't understand. I will be washed up in Loma Verde if I am involved in this scandal. Kaput."

"You *are* involved, Eduardo," I said.

"What are you going to do, Eduardo?" asked Flora.

"I'm going to return to Ecuador. What else can I do?"

"Eduardo! I would never have guessed that this would be your response. I've known you for years and I'm truly shocked!"

"My dear Flora, you truly do not understand. I have involved myself in a stupid, stupid mistake. There is only one place for me now and that is south of the border."

"You aren't really going to skip town, are you?" I asked.

Eduardo appeared to pull himself together. He put his handkerchief back into his breast pocket and sat up in his chair. "Of course not. I will return the records and assume responsibility for my role in this terrible story."

"That's the Eduardo I've always known!" Flora gave him a hug.

"So, I will be off now. I will do my duty as a responsible doctor of this community." Eduardo rose and shook my hand. "This is a great relief, Ben. You can't imagine how great a relief. But I want you to know that I never saw Eele in Rio nor do I know what he was doing in Brazil."

"He was seeing about setting up a practice in Rio,

Eduardo," I said.

"Well, I think he has the right idea." Eduardo coughed. "I mean, for the situation he's in, it's the right idea."

"Surely you're not thinking of the same idea?" asked Flora.

"Of course not! Medicine south of the border is a total joke. Why they even believe in witchcraft in Brazil! I'll be going now. I must, as I have already stated, do my duty. I will see both of you soon." Eduardo kissed Flora's hand. "And may I say that I am delighted the two of you have found one another. You suit each other so well."

I was a bit concerned about Enrique's resolution and thought Flora or I should go with him to retrieve the records in question. But Flora persuaded me that Eduardo was a man of his word, at least in regard to his profession.

When Lester called me that afternoon from the Greenwich Arms Inn and said he needed to see me and that it was urgent, I thought he probably had more Eele evidence. "Glad you came so quick," said Lester, gnawing on a Big Mac. Peach was wringing her hands, and Dyke, seated at the typewriter, was wearing a frazzled frown.

"Someone screwed up, Ben baby," said Dyke.

"What do you mean?" I asked. Peach started to snivel.

Lester threw his Big Mac carton into the wastebasket and wiped his hands on the sofa. "Enrique has disappeared."

"What? Disappeared?"

"That's what I'm saying, Boyer. He's flown the coop, and that means the Eele evidence he's been hiding has probably been destroyed." The four of us looked at one another. "We had a first-class felony charge that would have sent that son-of-a-bitch to prison. But never mind. We've got evidence I've collected for weeks now that'll put that lout Eele out of business permanently."

"You mean you're ready to prosecute?"

"We've been ready for a month. My only concern now is

that Eele doesn't try to slip away."

"Not after all the work we've done to get this far!" cried Peach.

"And those two little school children," began Lester.

"Mike and Maria, you mean?" I asked.

"Yeah, Mike and Maria. They lost interest in our case, didn't they?"

"Well, I wouldn't say that. They're young and they have all sorts of things they want to do."

"Your bright-eyed boy wants to go to medical school," said Lester.

"Sorry, Lester, but you've got the wrong boy."

"He wants to be a psychiatrist. I'll bet you'll be seeing your two-week notice any day now."

"Lester, I've always respected your ability to get information, but this is one time I can say you've made a mistake. Mike has no more interest in going to medical school than I do. I'd stake my life on that."

"Don't do that, Boyer." Lester turned on his tape machine. Even as I had heard Mike confiding to Maria that he wanted to become a psychiatrist, my first reaction was bitterness to realize that Maria had never told me that *we* were in a "great moment of truth."

"Who are you supposed to be tailing anyway?" I finally managed. "You've invaded the privacy of two kids who have worked their fannies off on this story. What the hell kind of thing is that to do?"

Lester grinned. "Kids today are made of crap. I told you that down in Rio. I'm surprised you're so shocked, Boyer. So your little Boy Wonder wants to follow in the footsteps of the great doctors of Loma Verde. Don't it make you proud?"

"Knock it off, Lester," said Dyke.

"Shut up. I've had just about as much as I can take of you, *Ms.* Upjohn."

"Ditto, Lester. I'm only here because I care what happens

to your cousin."

"You're here because you want to make some greenbacks off Peach."

"Lester, please stop talking like that!" cried Peach. "While all of us are standing around here bickering, Eele could be sneaking off."

"I'm gonna tail that S.O.B. right now." Lester pulled himself up from the sofa and left the room.

"Please forgive my cousin, Mr. Boyer."

"Forget it, Miss Kling. We're all under a little stress right now. I suppose I should be getting back to the office. Please do keep in touch. Remember, all of us are working together. And Ms. Upjohn, I'd like to talk with you about serializing your book."

"Sounds good to me, Ben. I'll be around for at least another week."

I shook Dyke's hand and put my hand on Peach's shoulder. "Call me if I can do anything, Miss Kling."

I drove straight to the office, where I was greeted right off the bat by Maria. "We're doing a story about Gerry Fitzgerald's new organization, Pursuit of Happiness, Incorporated. Because he was Baba Rhum's Greenwich adviser, we can make this story into really something."

I looked at Maria and again her radiant enthusiasm blinded me. I waited for her to tell me about Mike's plans to apply to medical schools, but she simply continued talking about her new story idea in her breathless fashion. "Still running?" I asked, trying not to sound sarcastic.

"Of course I am. Michael runs with me. He's a great runner. Oh, remind me to tell you about my run with Pete Kettle and my swimming naked with Gerry's wife while Gerry was comforting Pete about Miranda's joining Baba Rhum's ashram. Gotta go, Ben. Catch you later." She dashed away.

"Naked swimming?" I walked to my office and shut the door. I poured myself some Scotch. "No calls," I told my secretary.

"It's Dr. Framingham," she said.

I picked up my line. "Oh Ben, something awful has happened!"

"Calm down, Flora. I know about Eduardo."

"Eduardo? What about Eduardo?"

"Eduardo has disappeared. I think he's gone for good."

"Ben!"

"I should have gone with him to get those records. Oh well, win some, lose some. What's so awful?"

"Ben, I feel the whole world around me is falling apart. Your news about Eduardo, and, well, Todd called me at the hospital to tell me that Charles left Loma Verde this morning to join the Baba Rhum ashram."

"I'll be damned."

"And, Ben, he left a note blaming you and me for his having to leave."

"Well, that's a bunch of nonsense. No one just goes to an ashram on account of what two other people are doing."

"I feel so awful, Ben."

"Any second thoughts, Flora?"

"Of course not! I just feel, well . . . what will Todd think?"

"Todd can come and live with us. He's a good kid."

"I knew Charles was weak but I never thought it would come to this."

"You know, if Charles had waited, he could have joined his neighbor Gerry Fitzgerald's new group, Pursuit of Happiness, Incorporated."

"What?"

"Your neighbor Fitzgerald has a new organization and he's hoping to attract Baba Rhum's more celebrated members."

"Good Lord. I'm so disgusted."

"Well, I've had quite a day too. I'll have a lot to tell you tonight. Maybe tonight we can go to your house and pick up some more of your clothes and things."

"With Charles gone . . ." Flora voice trailed, "with him

gone it will be easier to go back."

"That's my girl. Shall I meet you at the hospital?"

"Six-thirty-ish?"

"I'll be there. I love you, Flora."

"Did you ever know this Enrique guy?" Maria asked Michael as the two drove to the Greenwich golf course to look for Eele.

"Only know of him. Supposedly a real womanizer. What a joke! He got in such hot water with so many husbands around here you'd think he would have split for south of the border a long time ago. I'm amazed some irate husband didn't finish the guy off by now. He and Eele make a pair."

"Michael, I think we've got a good idea to go talk to Eele, but if we make him suspicious and he leaves the area before Lester and Peach can present their evidence, I'll feel really guilty."

"Why? We're reporters, out to get the best story. We're not working for Peach and Lester. Lester Kling's got all the evidence he'll ever need to get Eele thrown out of the Clinic, so quit feeling guilty."

"You talk first."

"I will, Maria. That is, if he's here." Michael parked the car. "You want to come in while I ask if he's on the course?"

"Sure. I'm too nervous to be alone."

"Is this the Maria who has donned a sari, climbed mountains in Tibet, and skinny dipped in front of the husband of the Chancellor of Greenwich?"

"No, this is the Maria who doesn't want to tip off Eele that he's in hotter water than he thinks."

"We'll have a great story in tonight's paper, Forsythe. Don't screw up at the last minute. Let's go."

Eele was on the course. Michael and Maria walked the first nine holes before they spotted him. "My God," whispered Michael. "He's with Lester!"

"Come on, Forsythe, hide behind this bush."

"Can you hear anything?"

"No. All right, the coast is clear. See that bush over there? Run as fast as you can, and keep your mouth shut. Do you have the tape recorder?"

"Yes."

"All right. Turn it on now. Is it on? Good. Let's go."

Maria and Michael crouched behind a bush which afforded them easier access to Lester and Eele's conversation. "I don't think I've seen you on this course before," Eele was telling Lester.

"I'm from Los Angle-las. But I love to play on a good course whenever I can."

"What line did you say you were in again, Les?"

"Private communications."

"Private communications? Good shot, Les. What's private communications?"

"Let's just say I work for private individuals."

"You mean you're a private eye?"

"That's right. I don't advertise though. I don't have to! Let's just say I get the job done."

"You know, you might just be the man I want to see. I have something for you."

"Just say the word."

"It's kind of a private matter, if you know what I mean."

Lester looked around. "Ain't no one around here. It's about as private as you're gonna get."

"Well, yes." Eele cleared his throat. "You know, in my line of work—gynecology—you get all kinds of nutty women. Their little minds fantasize about you day and night. A male gynecologist is a prime generator of a woman's fantasies. I mean, what the hell? We listen to them, all their little problems.

We see them undressed, I mean we're central in their lives. And as you can probably imagine, this sometimes can cause a lot of problems. You know what I mean."

"Uh-huh."

"So you see, this one little fruitcake of a dame had the hots for me. As soon as I figured out she wasn't playing with a full deck I gave her three other doctors to see. She got mad at me and she came storming into my office one afternoon a few months ago. She claimed I'd left a surgical instrument inside her body during a routine curettage. The goddamned bitch has sued me, and my attorney says that I ought to hire a private eye to get some hard evidence that this broad is certified crazy."

"You think she's crazy?"

"She's about the craziest bitch who ever walked into my office. And believe me, I've seen all kinds. Good shot, Les, old boy! If your private investigation is as good as your golf game, would you be interested in my case?"

"We'll talk about that later."

"I've really got to get this thing settled. Could you give me your card? Maybe I could call you tonight?"

"I'll call you." Lester and Eele picked up their clubs and walked on.

"I don't think we ought to go out there. Lester would kill us," whispered Maria.

"If we don't go out there, we won't have a story."

"Could we just wait then? Maybe approach Eele after they finish their game?"

"We don't have time for that, Forsythe. You know that."

"Michael, we can't go out there and you know it. Lester would tear your lungs out if we did."

"You're right. We can't."

"What are we going to do now?"

"I don't know. We need a story. I know. Call Gerry Fitzgerald and see if we can interview him about his new

Pursuit of Happiness, Incorporated deal. And if that doesn't work, Dyke Upjohn is always good copy."

Gerry Fitzgerald leaned back in his chair, smoking a Cuban cigar. "My wife Catherine gets these for me. Want one?" he asked Michael.

"Sure. Why not?"

"And how about you, Maria?"

"Thanks, but I'll pass. I quit smoking a while ago and don't want to be tempted."

Gerry lit Michael's cigar and Michael immediately began to cough. "A little strong for you?" asked Gerry.

"Oh no. An excellent cigar, Professor Fitzgerald. So, we're here to ask you about Pursuit of Happiness, Incorporated."

"Well, just let me say the following. I've had it with these baloney eastern ashrams. It's about time someone started a group touting the virtues of western libertarian pursuits of pleasure."

"Why do you need an organization for libertarian hedonism?"

"That's a good question, Michael. We need the organization to advance the ideas in the marketplace. In other words, we need a little baloney P.R. of our own."

"Well, do you expect to make a profit?"

"Of course, that's part of the pleasure."

"I want to ask you something else," said Maria. "What do you know about Duke Eele?"

"Not much firsthand, but the rumors floating around make him out to be a surgical menace and a moral bastard. The trouble is, I don't know any real details. I'd be happy to tell them to you if I did. There is an old Oklahoma saying that is to the point. 'The only good slippery eel is a fried one.'"

Michael and Maria left Fitzgerald's office after a half hour of pleasant conversation but no fact-finding. "Well, at least I got a Cuban cigar out of it," Michael sighed.

Lester called Duke Eele at his house the following night. "I've got some solid evidence for a case against Peach Kling."

"I'm sorry, Les, old boy, but I've got to get out of here fast. That's the advice of my attorney."

"You can't go now. I've got some real dope for you. Eele? Eele? Goddamn it! That slimy bastard's hung up!"

"Go find him, Lester!" screamed Peach.

"For God's sake, don't fuck this one up!" screamed Dyke.

Lester jumped into his car and raced to Eele's house in Forestbridge. Eele had already made his getaway. Lester burned rubber north on the freeway in pursuit of Eele. Lester made a wild guess that Eele would be leaving on Pan Am. Eele was not at the check-in counter, and the only Pan Am flight leaving was for Tokyo, Hong Kong, and Calcutta. He rushed to the departure gate, where he saw Eele talking to his attorney. As he turned on his tape recorder, he heard Eele say, "Maybe Mother Theresa can use another hand, even if it's the hand of a bungler."

"And though it seems incredible that a doctor with such a record of malpractice could have been allowed to remain at the prestigious Loma Verde Clinic as long as Duke Eele had, it is even more incredible that Duke Eele was able to flee the country without ever having been prosecuted. A criminal flew out of the San Francisco Airport tonight on a Calcutta-bound Pan Am flight, leaving in his wake countless devastated lives. This is Kim Blakely at the San Francisco Airport for the KUTK eleven o'clock news."

I turned off the televison and poured myself a drink. Scooped again.

Patient records from the files of Duke Eele, found in the former residence of Eduardo Enrique:

1. The pelvic examination will be done later on the floor.
2. GYN history: patient was taking an oral contraption until recently.
3. Surgical history and physical: Both breasts have been removed with no signs of recurrence.
4. (Probably a typo?) The patient was prepped and raped in preparation for surgery.
5. The patient received "coital" anesthesia.

Mike filed the following story shortly after Eele's disappearance:

Dr. Kingsley Hemlosch, who touched off a furor at the Greenwich University School of Medicine last winter after writing a memo dealing with pregnant workers, will step down as chairman of the School's Gynecology and Obstetrics Department, it was announced Thursday.

Hemlosch, 63, is expected to retire from the Medical School faculty and devote himself full-time to volunteer work at Mother Therasa's hospital in Calcutta.

"There comes a time for any doctor who has immersed himself in a lifetime of clinical care and administrative detail to return to more satisfying humanitarian pursuits," Hemlosch said in a press release Monday. Hemlosch had been department chairman for fifteen years.

His resignation was submitted two days following the disappearance of Duke Eele, the controversial Loma Verde gynecologist who has been served with several malpractice suits. Hemlosch stated at his press conference, "My resignation has nothing to do whatsoever with the criminal disappearance of Duke Eele, and I do not expect to see Duke Eele in Calcutta. It has always been a dream of mine to help Mother Theresa."

And so on and so forth. Since Mike had finally admitted to me that he was indeed applying to medical school, I asked him if he and Maria wanted to do an investigative stint in Calcutta as a good-bye present from me. Naturally Mike said he and Maria would be ready to leave at a moment's notice. "After all," he said, "I've finished the most important thing. I interviewed last Friday at Greenwich."

Maria swore up and down that she planned to stay at the *Vindicator,* and I believe that the hundreds of letters which poured into the *Vindicator* expressing outrage about Duke Eele encouraged her to continue as a reporter. What surprised me as much as anything was how much our readers hated doctors, I mean, really hated them—a deep and uncompromising hatred.

And what of the players who featured in this dark and murky tale? Vincent Carpaccio has remained at the Oregon ashram; he is now Baba Rhum, as Peter Schwartz returned to lecturing in philosophy at Greenwich a few months ago and is also functioning as an organizer in Pursuit of Happiness,

Incorporated. Miranda Kettle is back in Loma Verde but not as Chancellor of Greenwich and not with Pete; she has joined the first California Trappist monastery to admit women. Pete has found true love, in the shapely form of a gorgeous blonde Greenwich graduate student; they run together every morning and shower afterwards. The Harding Institute was blown up by terrorists last month. Fortunately, no one was in the building at the time of the explosion. The Hardingites plan to reorganize on a small private Pacific island in an undisclosed location. Joe and Jean Kuhl are back in Loma Verde after Joe's tour of duty as ginseng-enriched Zippi-Cola's Southeast Asia spokesman. He is now head of the Loma Verde Clinic and running for president of the AMA on a "Two Percent Ticket," meaning a two percent cut in every doctor's charges before the government steps in to do the cutting.

Mike Weintraub has been accepted at Greenwich Medical School. Mike says that his interviewer found it so refreshing when Mike, upon being asked why he wanted to be a psychiatrist, replied that years of watching reruns of the "Bob Newhart Show" had convinced him he, too, could be an analyst. I doubt the Greenwich interviewer realized that Mike wasn't kidding. Maria? She's as beautiful as ever, and she's finally settled down to writing regularly, having realized that Pulitzer Prizes aren't always around the corner. Dyke's book *Patient/Victim: One Woman's Ordeal* has been a smash hit all over the country, and Dyke has begun a nationwide organization for women who feel they have been abused by their doctors. Peach and Lester won a civil suit against Duke Eele and now live together in Eele's Forestbridge spread. Lester drives Eele's Porsche but curiously hasn't changed the HOT EELE license. Flora and I are flourishing; she's one hell of a woman and I'm a lucky man. We were married a week ago and will take off next week for a honeymoon in Rome.

And last but not least, I bid my farewell with an item which recently caught my eye in the *Olde England Journal of*

Medicine. A certain Dr. Russ Red of Jackson Hole, Wyoming, wrote a piece expressing the difficulty some physicians have in accepting the gratitude offered by their patients—those who improved dramatically or had their lives saved by the doctors' actions. The article was entitled "The Stress of Playing God." I've just finished writing an editorial in which I point to the fact that what doctors need to learn now is that the patient is God. Today doctors must adapt to the stress of playing servant to God. In the words of Baba Rhum's disciples, "Namaste, folks!"